MY SISTER'S BIG FAT INDIAN WEDDING

SAJNI PATEL

AMULET BOOKS • NEW YORK

Cataloging-in-Publication Data has been applied for and may be obtained from the Library of Congress.

ISBN 978-1-4197-5453-1

Text © 2022 Sajni Patel
Chapter and folio art credit to: Anna Poguliaeva/Shutterstock.com
Book design by Chelsea Hunter

Printed and bound in U.S.A.
10 9 8 7 6 5 4 3 2 1

Amulet Books are available at special discounts when purchased in quantity for premiums and promotions as well as fundraising or educational use. Special editions can also be created to specification. For details, contact specialsales@abramsbooks.com or the address below.

Amulet Books® is a registered
trademark of Harry N. Abrams, Inc.

ABRAMS The Art of Books
195 Broadway, New York, NY 10007
abramsbooks.com

To Parthkita, who have blessed our families with the amazingness that is unequivocally you. Thank you for the wedding of a lifetime and for the memories that will last lifetimes yet to come.

Thank you for picking up *My Sister's Big Fat Indian Wedding* and taking a chance on this wild, loud, bigger-than-life family. I hope you're ready to embark on all the ups and downs of a fierce girl chasing her musical dreams, the competitive and romantic sides of two young hearts, the bonds of a large and tight-knit family, and—of course—a whirlwind, cinematic wedding week inspired by my sibling's actual wedding events.

Join Zuri and Naveen as they face off against one another, their creative pursuits, and meddling aunties. I sincerely hope you enjoy!

With that being said . . . you are hereby cordially invited to the biggest, fattest, Indian-est wedding of the season!

Many thanks and so much love,
Sajni Patel

In charge of couple's joint social media 'cause ain't nobody else got time?? #AnotherDamPatel

No matter what, DO NOT check Juilliard email!!

Papa **THE FAMILY OF** Mummie

Mr. Akash Damani & Mrs. Anessa Damani

Graciously Request Your Presence &
Blessings on the Auspicious Occasion of
the Wedding Ceremony of Their Daughter

MAITRI ♡

sis

WITH

Jijaji #2

PRANIT

competition 1st level 8 days before wedding. How to sneak out, though??

↙ *Future in-laws* ↘

Son of Mr. Pranav Patel & Mrs. Meena Patel

PLEASE RSVP FOR THE...

Let the festivities begin!

#Haldi

Friday Evening Mehndi & Dinner
Saturday Morning Mangalik Prasango & Lunch

Pack for hotel! "Woohoo!"

Garba dance number →
Saturday Evening Garba & Dinner

Sneak into baraat →
Sunday Morning Wedding & Lunch
Sunday Evening Reception & Dinner

Competition finals. BUT HOW?? WAH!

#TeamBride Games

BIG FAT INDIAN dance number. I ain't ready!

Big violin solo #MicDrop

Umm ... so when, where, HOW without getting caught?!?! SMH

CHAPTER ONE
(Saturday Morning: Eight Days Until the Wedding)

#MySistersBigFatIndianWedding

Being forced down by an auntie armed with nothing but a thread was as scary as being chased through the woods by a clown. Except you actually had a chance of outrunning the clown. You could not, in fact, outrun the auntie.

Getting my eyebrows threaded required aforementioned auntie to hold me down, her elbow pinning my shoulder back, as she deftly plucked hairs. I wasn't a crybaby, but something about threading single hairs from their roots had my nerves on hypersensitive mode, and tears rolled down my cheeks.

"Agh! I can't take it anymore! Stop!" I crawled up the back of my desk chair.

"Stop being a child, Zurika. You *need* this. Look at your eyebrows. When was the last time you maintained them?" She clucked her tongue.

"Never. And now I know why. What sort of torture device *is* this?"

Neha snickered from the doorway. She'd already had her eyebrows threaded this morning, and they were now red and swollen.

But my little sister didn't turn her experience into sympathy. She merely enjoyed my pain, her arms crossed and leaning against the side of the door frame.

"OK! Child. You're done," the auntie announced and grunted as if the amount of facial hair she'd removed had exhausted her. At what point in history had someone decided we girls were supposed to be hairless, anyway? Who'd decided that? Probably not anyone who needed a good threading.

I sighed and melted into my chair.

"What about your top lip?" the auntie suggested.

I immediately shot up. "Oh god, no!"

"You have a hairy face," she exaggerated.

"I don't care." But I hated that I *did* actually care. A little.

"Your cheeks and . . . these sideburns!" She tsked. Leave it to a threading auntie to tell a girl that she was hideously hairy in an untactful and unsolicited manner. No one freaking asked her. Yet I couldn't tell her that because elder respect, etc., etc.

I pushed her arm away before she brought that seemingly innocuous piece of thread back to my face for another round of torture.

She eventually relented with a huff and left as I tried not to rub my tender brows. Pain for beauty? I think not.

Without further entertainment, Neha shrugged and joined the ever-growing ruckus of family downstairs. I bet all twenty-plus in-close-proximity family members were already here.

Mummie walked into my room, startling me with that *look*. The one that said she knew what I was up to and it was time for me to fess up and pay the consequences. Oh my *god*. How did she always know? My hope was that Mummie was actually preempting any potential nonsense rather than having figured out my secret plan.

All the aunties had warned that if anything went wrong (even the teensiest bit) during wedding festivities, kismet dictated it a bad omen that would forever mar the future of the couple. Things like a sick groom, a stained bridal outfit, smeared mehndi, bad food, a dropped cake—even rain or, in the case of humid old Atlanta, heatstroke.

I supposed aunties and their superstitions had left out one minor example: *me*. Aka: younger sisters who ran off to do their own thing instead of tending to wedding duties, starting a domino effect where one missing person led to fumbling and chaos in an absurdly tight schedule laden with a million details.

For a minute, I thought for sure Mummie had discovered something worthy of grounding me for life in this horribly packed room. Not drugs or nude pics or even a note from a boy. But . . . college admission letters. *Dun, dun, dun* . . . The bane of my mortal teenage existence.

Some colleges sent both email and paper notifications. According to my parents, I was to avoid checking electronic responses and wait on the requested paper letters. Something about leaving the unopened letters on the altar so my parents could pray over the results. But there was one college I thoroughly checked on at least once a day.

Juilliard—my dream school—had responded. The email

had popped up in my in-box yesterday morning. But guess who was too chicken to woman up and check the fate of my entire musical career?

Ugh. It was just sitting there, taunting me, telling me to click to behold my future . . . or lack thereof. But see, the thing was that my parents and sisters didn't know about Juilliard. They thought I'd only applied to the best prelaw programs in the country. After all, I had to follow in their very strong law careers. Law was ideal, logical. Not music.

And definitely not *my* music. Mine was, as my parents put it, a disgrace to classical violin. While my sisters enjoyed it for a casual experience (never, ever for a career), my cousins and friends and school thought it was a brilliant mix of violin and hip-hop and rock. To me, it was just the music that moved my soul.

My parents and older sisters kept reinforcing that I was in crunch time now. I had to think of my future . . . something boring and dreadful like law or medicine or whatever else uncles pressed upon Papa as being respectable and prestigious.

They would never understand. Which was why I'd applied to only a handful of colleges that were out of my league and, of course, the one and only Juilliard. All right, hear me out. If I didn't have another college acceptance, then of course my parents would let me attend a music college. Dream big or go home, right? Take my shot. And if by some cruel fate Juilliard said no, then oh well. There was no other college admittance. Therefore, go to Juilliard now or wait until the following semester.

I almost flinched when Mummie chided, "Do *not* ruin your sister's wedding."

"How . . . *what?*"

She placed her hands on her hips, her glass bangles clinking against one another, and tilted her head. She had four bangles on each wrist, red and gold to match the elegant sari draped over her. She only wore saris in Gujarati style, with the end of the long piece of fabric brought over the shoulder from the back so it was pleated and fanned out over her chest and stomach with one corner tucked into the waist of the chaniya underneath. She said it displayed the ornate end better and covered her tummy.

"Who? Me?" I asked innocently.

Nah. She wasn't buying it.

My shoulders slumped in defeat as she gently took the folded-up flyer from beneath my pillow. OK, so there *was* something hidden from Mummie in this mess. How did she always know! But if a printed-out invitation to a musical college contest was the worst thing my mom had ever found in my room, then how bad could it be?

Oh, wait. I *was* Indian. Maybe some folks from my diaspora didn't have this impending doom, but in my family, we did not chase creative dreams. Not to mention my moti bens, Urvi and Maitri—two nearly perfect older sisters. They flourished in law like kick-butt feminists, shattering glass ceilings and taking names. I had a lot to live up to, and I had to be the next role model for Neha, who was only fourteen and incredibly unfocused.

You counted that right. My parents had four daughters and zero sons. So, while my sister's impending wedding was a giant blessing overflowing with joy and excitement, it was also a sorrowful time, because daughters left their parents and joined their husbands' families. Therefore, Mummie was ecstatic at having matched Maitri to an awesome guy but ultimately miserable because she was going to lose another daughter, and now she homed in on every minute, out-of-place detail.

"Do not try to sneak off to do anything this time," she warned, as if she'd long since known about the contest. Maybe she had—she was a *mom*, after all. Did she know that I'd sent an audition tape in to the Atlanta Musical Scouting Competition a few months ago? And that they'd invited me to audition in person *tonight*? And it just happened to fall on spring break, aka during my sister's big fat Indian wedding?

I was thoroughly tempted to go. I mean, not everyone made it this far, and there would be big-name college scouts there, plus the winner would be awarded a full-ride scholarship. It was my duty, actually, to audition. But then Mummie shot her warning look of doom, making my insides sink for fear of getting into massive trouble and bringing negative vibes to my sister's wedding.

Put two and two together, and I had one heck of a wrecking ball of a week coming up. Anxiety was already sprouting across my brain like tiny thistles.

"I would never do anything to jeopardize the carefully scheduled wedding week," I insisted, all innocent-like.

"It is very important to be present and ready for all the traditions. You may not understand them all, but they are crucial for a complete wedding weekend and a harmonious marriage. You are sister to the bride, and everyone will expect to see you there, not to mention the tasks you must carry out. Do you understand?"

"Ha, Mummie. I wouldn't disrupt a single thing."

Papa walked by and touched Mummie's shoulder. His shiny new kurta pajama in orange gold, mustard yellow, and red matched Mummie's new sari. "Come. Let's go. The Brahman is here. And don't worry about my beta, Zuri. She will be perfect for the wedding, huh?"

I nodded, rubbing my tender eyebrows. "Of course."

"I trust my beta."

Mummie leaned toward me, squinting. "Your brows are red and swelling."

"Well, yeah—" I started to explain the threading, but she cut me off and suggested, "Go eat some sweets. They'll make it better."

"Uh . . ." Threading and food had absolutely nothing to do with each other, but my mom swore to the gods that food fixed everything.

Papa nodded in agreement and then looked to Mummie. "One of my acquaintances is in town. Do you remember Mihir Merchant from New York?"

Mummie nodded. "Ha."

"He's here for work. I want to invite him to the wedding."

She laughed, a melodious note in the air. "I say invite whomever you want, but Maitri will have a fit adding an extra person."

Papa put a finger to his lips and winked at me. "Don't tell her, then."

I pretended to zip my lips. I wasn't going to be the one sending my sister over the edge with another unexpected detail.

He said to Mummie, "I'll give him a call. It should be OK, adding one more person. In fact, I'm sure someone here or there will not make it last minute, and then we've wasted money. I'm doing Maitri a service."

I giggled.

"Challo. We need to finish setting up for puja," he ended and gave me a reassuring, proud smile.

"Ha, coming," Mummie said.

Papa clasped his hands behind his back, his chin tilted up as if he were surveying everything, and walked downstairs to add final touches to the preparations for one of many prayer rituals to come. Once he was gone, Mummie turned back to me and whipped out her cell phone.

I eyed it cautiously as she deliberately swiped across her screen with a finger. My parents loved their cell phones. They could jibber-jabber all day long, anywhere, anytime. They had yet to master the text message, sending pictures, and emails. But they had WhatsApp, the most beloved app among my kind, it seemed, to do all that. It was mind-boggling how my mom went from fumbling newbie cell phone user to master of tech with WhatsApp.

She turned the screen to me. "What do you think?"

I glared at a picture of a very attractive dude. Maybe it was the filters. It was almost always the filters.

If my mom was showing me pictures of a boy, that could only mean . . . "He's OK," I replied warily.

"His name is Naveen. He is Jijaji's cousin from South Africa."

I, of course, knew this, thanks to social media. Pranit (aka Jijaji #2, aka the groom) had tagged Naveen in a bunch of his posts, and he always liked or commented on them. I might've even looked through Naveen's social media, too. All right, of course I had! He was about to get tagged in a bunch of wedding posts by me soon enough anyway, since the couple had left me in charge of their joint social media. I had to know who he was.

"He's the boy you're dancing with at the big reception dance, no?"

"Um, yeah . . ." Our dance wasn't, like, some romantic thing, though. We were retelling the couple's story, and Naveen was to play Pranit while I played Maitri. It wasn't some starry-eyed setup. Right?

Mummie went on, "He comes from a good family—good Indian boy. He's starting college next year, majoring in engineering. He's very smart and will make good money. He's a handsome boy, no?"

"Sure."

"You'll meet him this week. You'll like him."

"He's OK."

"No. I'm not asking you. I'm telling you."

"Uh . . ."

Then she took her phone back.

"How serious are you?" I asked her.

"You're too young to think about marriage right now, but maybe start thinking of a boy for down the road. If you like each other now, who knows for later? It's important to know him for a while, huh? See how he truly is."

"Like . . . staking claim now for later?"

"Ha! Exactly." She touched my cheek before sashaying out of the room, leaving me in total bewilderment.

There were no other words to be said.

CHAPTER TWO
(Saturday Morning: Eight Days Until the Wedding)

#DemDamaniGirls

I couldn't help but rub the tender area around my brows when Krish popped her head into my room. I hadn't even noticed who all had arrived, but of course my aunts and uncles and cousins were here somewhat on time. Which was a feat in itself, really.

She beamed as she closed my bedroom door. She only ever smiled that gigantically when she had something juicy to tell me.

I tilted my head as she sat beside me on the bed with a sudden *oomph!* It probably had to do with school . . . or college.

My cousin—and absolute bestie—had her entire life all planned out. Krish had known she wanted to go into medicine since the first day she'd dissected a worm in middle school. Anatomy and physiology classes were her jam. Biology and chemistry—stuff that was way over my head—were her foundation. I couldn't even touch a worm without screaming, much less cut into one.

Sometimes I wondered if Krish and I had been switched at birth, if maybe she was actually the third-oldest sister in our brood, with how she carried herself and followed a solid career path. She, like my older sisters, was functioning and stable. I was chaos in comparison.

"Whatcha got?" I asked, turning toward her and grinning.

"Look!" she squealed and whipped out her cell phone. She scrolled through an email and landed her finger on a big ol' "Congratulations, Krishna Damani! We are pleased to inform you that you've been accepted into Emory College of Arts and Sciences' undergraduate biology program at Emory University."

I threw my arms around Krish's shoulders and tackled her to the bed. We laughed as she pushed me off. "Calm down," she said between giggles.

I took her phone and read the words again. "Yo. Your parents must be ecstatic! Emory is your top med school."

She grinned superhard. "Yep. That's the one. But no, my parents don't know. I was supposed to wait for the official paper letter so they could offer it for prayer or whatever. But I couldn't help it!"

"Ah! So amazing. I knew you'd get in." I handed her the phone.

"So, tell me, tell me! Did you hear from anyone?"

"No. Not even Georgia State."

"What about Emory?"

"Ha!" I cackled. "Yeah, right. Emory was so I could go to school with you if all else failed. But let's be honest, that's wishful thinking."

"Juilliard?" she asked, hopeful.

The adrenaline raging through my veins at her good news stopped dead in its tracks. My heart practically stopped beating for a second. I dramatically threw my head back and groaned. What if I didn't get in? Oh. My. Lord.

I apprehensively scrolled through my emails, my heart turning it up on the beats per second, and glared at the unread message from Juilliard. There it sat—a haunting little ghost whispering into the universe, "Read me . . . *Read* me . . ."

"You haven't even opened it?" she asked, looking at the phone now cradled in my lap.

I shook my head. A foreboding chill scratched down my neck. Like, what if this was it? Either good news or devastating news. What if this was the end of my life? What if they said no, that I was such a joke even applying that they'd laughed all the way to the rejection form letter? I'd never experienced such a weight as the one that was pulling down my shoulders into the depths of possible rejection hell. Curling into a ball and crying didn't seem like an option, though.

I *had* to know.

"I bet it's great news," my cousin encouraged with that genuine smile of hers. No one supported me in pursuing music the way Krish did. She'd made medicine her personal choice, her passion, yet she never thought music was less. "Imagine how much happier it'll make this week!"

I furrowed my brows, glaring at the phone. "And if it's bad news? Imagine how miserable I'll be!"

"You can't change the decision. Either you got in or you didn't. Don't you want to know?"

I bit my lip and nodded. With trembling fingers, I blew out a breath and tapped on the email. The bedroom was suddenly eerily quiet in a haunting sort of way, despite all the noise downstairs rumbling up from the horde of extended family.

I dragged in another long breath and exhaled. Then I read the letter.

Whatever minuscule bit of confidence had floated around inside my soul fled the moment my brain processed the words. My mouth twitched. My heart puttered. My vision turned dizzy, and I saw double.

Dear Zurika Damani,
We regret to inform you . . .

Never had words cut so deep, to-the-bone-marrow kind of deep.

My throat turned raw and achy; tears welled in my eyes. If I blinked even once, they'd cascade down my face and turn me into an emotional wreck right before the kankotri ceremony for the whole family to witness.

My entire meticulously planned future shattered right in front of my eyes.

I'd expected to bounce up and down and scream at the top of my lungs while clutching my phone. I'd expected to celebrate with Krish the way I had over her news. I'd expected to put my foot down with my parents and sisters and be like, ha! My far-fetched dream wasn't that far-fetched after all! I was good enough to get into Juilliard!

I'd expected to learn from the best and wear the Juilliard name and audition for Broadway and show my family and community that pursuing a career in the arts was worthwhile, acceptable, revered, prominent. I'd expected to make my parents proud and make something of this talent that no one else in my family had.

I'd actually thought that I had a chance. I'd actually thought that I was good enough to get into Juilliard. I'd actually thought that if I worked hard enough, my talent would shine like a beacon, that I could be more than what my family thought I should be.

I was wrong. I'd been so stupid.

"Oh," I said, as if this didn't shake me to the core, as if my dreams weren't slipping through my fingers like water. But that one simple syllable hiccuped in my chest, and I lost it. I cried hot, salty tears.

Krish immediately wrapped an arm around my shoulders and hugged me. "Zuri . . ." she whispered, but what else could she say?

"Oh my lord," I mumbled and wiped tears from my cheeks, corralling my emotions and keeping them in check. "I didn't mean to . . ."

"It's OK," she replied. "It's OK to cry."

I pulled away and shuddered, sucking in a breath and wiping my face. "Um. No. I can't even feel sorry for myself, because it's Maitri's wedding. No. No. No. I have to be happy and energetic. Bad omens and stuff."

I hiccupped. Why had I opened this stupid email? I'd known, deep down, that this plain-Jane email was a simple nope. *You're good, Zuri, but not good enough.* And there was no one to really lean on, not this week. I couldn't suck all the joy from Krish's big news. She deserved to celebrate the rewards of her hard work instead of trying to lift me up. I couldn't dampen anyone's wedding mood, especially Maitri's. She was stressed out as it was. My parents and sisters wouldn't even understand why this was so derailing and heartbreaking, so there would be no venting to them.

"Never speak of this to anyone," I told Krish and stood up, dabbing my cheeks dry.

She jumped up after me and said, "It's not over."

"Yeah. It pretty much is." The numbness crawled down my chest like a consuming darkness. It was *so* over.

"Um. Did you forget about the contest?"

I scoffed. "Yeah, right. The one that's happening in less than three hours? That my mom warned me not to run off to?"

She grabbed my shoulders and shook me. Then she grinned, a vow, a reminder. "You are freaking Zurika Damani, girl. Get your crap together. We, my dear cousin, are getting you out of here and to that contest."

Then she tickled me, forcing me to smile. "Stop. No, stop! I can't."

"Put on a happy face. I got you," she promised.

"Whatever that means."

"Trust me. Give me some time."

Except time was one thing we didn't have.

"Zurika!" Mummie called from the bottom of the steps, her voice high from the strain of trying to keep things on time for today's ceremony. Of course, when the Brahman arrived half an hour late, we all got screwed. He was, without a doubt, running on IST—Indian Standard Time—and it was a miracle he'd even shown up this early.

"Beta, we are starting without you!" she added.

"Coming!" I yelled.

Krish flinched and covered her ears.

"Sorry."

She took hold of my arms gently and shook me again. "What do we always say?"

I rolled my eyes and grumbled, "Damani girls don't stay down."

"Say it with some conviction, Zuri. C'mon!"

I piped up and repeated with a little more cheer and determination, "Damani girls don't stay down."

"I don't believe you."

I laughed. "Dem Damani girls do *not* stay down."

She surprise-attacked me with a big bear hug. "Dem right," she teased. "Let's go before your mom comes up here."

"I'll be down in a minute."

Krish left while I took a moment to gather myself. I didn't have time to feel sad. I had to be 100 percent present for this wedding. But also, Krish was right. I had to get to that contest. I might've gotten knocked down by this news, but I hadn't gotten knocked out.

I checked out my reflection one last time in the square, gold-rimmed mirror on the wall beside the door, wiping away any residual tears. I adjusted my tiny diamond nose stud, then fluffed up my wild spirals and smoothed down my frosted green-and-gold salwar kameez. Whoever said tights as leggings were the style had it backward. But at least this top ended at my knees and generously covered my, as Neha called it, bubble butt.

Maitri had approved all my wedding week outfits, and I'd had to indulge her by giving in to current fashion trends. There was nothing worse than having your sister/the bride launch into an emotional cry-fest because you couldn't bring yourself to wear tights.

"Dumb leggings," I mumbled and nonchalantly adjusted the crotch, almost stubbing my toe on the stupid bed frame.

I hated this new bed frame, too. But my parents had insisted on donating my beloved, albeit old and basic, frame to get a new one. One with curled legs and both a footboard and headboard. But *why*? Why did a bed need those things?

My parents upheld the belief that a wedding brought new beginnings and that we had to buy new furniture for those new beginnings. Urvi's wedding three years ago brought in new downstairs furniture. Maitri's wedding required all new bedroom sets.

I glanced around. Wait. Where the heck was my dupatta?

My room, normally a tidy death trap for dust particles, thanks to my mom's belief that cleanliness was of the upmost importance, was a disaster of clashing fabrics, goody bags, ribbons, mesh, bangles, gold, shoes, makeup, and whatever those cone-shaped, metallic, stone-studded things were called that Mummie had to pretend to carry water in. I couldn't even remember the color of my rug, much less where in the heck my matching dupatta had got off to. It had probably crawled away in hopes of hiding out during this production of a week.

Eh. Didn't matter. This was a traditional and important event, *but* it didn't involve a whole lot of people, so it was OK. The camera and video crew weren't going to come by.

For today, only family members were here, and none of them cared if my incomplete outfit brought shame to our house.

My bangles clinked against one another in alternating bands of forest-green glass and textured metallic gold. The dense carpet muffled my steps as I walked across the short hallway and down the stairs, trying to find my calm.

"You sound like an elephant," Neha said, and fluttered into the family room around the pillar in the hallway.

Ah, thank god for the special blessing known as little sisters.

The tiles in the foyer were like ice torches that froze my bare feet to negative degrees the second I stepped on them. They were a marble road leading guests from the open foyer to the winding hallway of oil paintings depicting peacocks and elephants to the family room beyond. My anklets chimed with every step, adding a delicate cadence to the hushed conversations and loud chanting of the Brahman and my parents.

Don't ask me what they were singing about, because my Gujarati and/or religious Hindu game wasn't that strong.

While my elder sisters were doing god knows what yesterday, I had spent all day with our guy cousins moving (heavy!) furniture into the garage. Meanwhile, a wild, squealing conglomerate of Maitri's friends rushed over to surprise-decorate the crap out of our house. The place looked like Diwali and Christmas had barfed up a love child made wholly from lights and DIY decorations under attack by vicious glitter fairies.

String lights were wrapped around the railing leading upstairs, around pillars, across the silk rainbow sari drapes, which doubled as a backdrop for today's ceremony and photo ops for this weekend's events. Blue and silver chiffon saris had been cut apart, twisted in all sorts of artistic ways, and used as curtains and wall coverings to spread all the cheery colors throughout the house. And any intermittent stretches of plain old wall wouldn't do. Nope. Those spots were adorned with hand-stitched murals and glitter cutouts of peacocks and Rangoli-style decorations. It was hard to be depressed when everything was so vibrant.

You did *not* know the meaning of festive until you walked into an Indian wedding week.

CHAPTER THREE
(Saturday Morning: Eight Days Until the Wedding)

Our house was hard to miss, even from the outside. It presided over an Atlanta suburb cul-de-sac as a beacon of lit arches and flashy window frames. Didn't matter if it was ten in the morning—the strobe lights jammed to the rhythm of their own party in alternating beats, casting dancing purple and red dots that moved in and out of patterns across the brick face of the house. A dozen strands of white fairy lights snaked around tree trunks and branches, others in the rosebushes and around the front porch pillars and railing. A large banner that hung over the garage read, THE DAMANI FAMILY WELCOMES YOU.

Just in case anyone doubted if they were in the right place, from the top of the staircase banister hung a giant canvas of the couple's official engagement photo. I mean, the thing could double as a blanket and was the parents' pride and the couple's embarrassment.

Nah. We hadn't gone all out *at all*.

With my brand-new phone and its state-of-the-art camera, I took an artful picture of the monstrous canvas with the background blur filter. Then I posted it straight to the couple's joint social media account for all the world to behold its embarrassingly sweet beauty.

I took my time meandering toward the family room, because . . . c'mon . . . Indian wedding events took *forever*. It was, however, something to take my mind off the awful Juilliard heartbreak and the nausea it'd left. But Krish was right. We Damani girls didn't stay down, no matter how much I wanted to eat a tub of pista ice cream while wallowing in misery.

The puja had begun without me. It was a prayer service that I didn't quite understand and that didn't require any effort on my part. I quietly sat cross-legged on the floor near the hallway, my back supported by the wall, where hanging pink fabric tickled my elbows. The deep, aromatic smell of spiced incense filled the room and my nostrils, fighting for attention against the lit diya and someone's sickening, cheap perfume.

My parents and Maitri sat across from a modest puja setup in front of the altar and kitty-corner to the Brahman. My sister's shiny, loose waves fell down her back. She sat with perfect posture and looked pretty much like a goddess in a floral lavender-and-metallic-gray chaniya choli.

All three sat near the front with that gloriously brilliant sari drape backdrop, adding the right touch of elegance for me to take a few pictures. The colors created a great fuzzy background, highlighting the people and emblems and sparkling flames from the diya.

Over the weekend, my mom had twisted a hundred small pieces of cotton into little Hershey's Kisses shapes to fill up a container. Now, some of them sat in concave diya holders, drenched in ghee and lit like tiny organic candles.

Madhu Masi, my great-aunt on Papa's side, sat the closest to them. She was practically all up in the ceremony, as close as she was to the dais. She'd arrived from India last week to an onslaught of hugs and kisses. She seemed taken aback, as her generation in our family had never been touchy-feely, much less overly excited and lacking the grace of quiet women. Ah, well. That was my fam. Quiet and reserved we surely were not.

We'd wanted to make the most of the time that we had with her: Do tourist things and—although her diet was religiously restricted and her palate limited to Gujarati food—we wanted to share a lot of vegetarian offerings with her, namely drinks.

I'd even made sweet iced tea last week and asked if she'd like some.

"Cold cha?" she'd asked incredulously in Gujarati. "Where is the enjoyment in that?"

She'd loved iced coffee. Whatever floated her palate.

Masi had been a zombie for a good two days until my generation of heathens had bombarded her with a million decorations yesterday. She'd suddenly snapped back to life and was now full of energy. No one could blame her for having been so tired, though. If I were in my eighties and had spent nearly twenty hours on a flight from India to Atlanta, I'd be the walking dead, too.

It meant a lot to Papa to have his only remaining elder attend the wedding. She looked just like her sister, my grandma, which made me miss my grandparents even more. Masi gave me a kind smile from her reverent position beside my parents. Before I grinned back at her, she flicked her wrists to tell me to get back against the wall and stop distracting.

What? I wasn't distracting anybody.

I went back to my spot beside Neha, who stuck her tongue out at me. One of these days, this little girl was going to get popped in the mouth by yours truly.

Urvi and her husband (aka Jijaji #1) sat against the wall near the front, and I wondered how in the world she'd been able to get down to floor level in the first place, as pregnant as she was. More importantly, how was she going to get back up?

All the parents paid attentive care to the ceremonial acts. There was the obvious aarti, with lit diya and partaking of blessings, the flick of rice, dabble of water and milk, delicate drops of honey, and careful placement of the coconut and bright-red sindoor powder. In front of the emblems was a copy of Maitri's kankotri: her wedding invitation on sleek, metallic burnt-orange fancy paper with embossed designs of flowers and paisleys.

Both the bride and groom had handed out their own sets of invitations. Inside the envelopes for Maitri's guests were five detailed cards for her events: fuchsia for her mehndi party, yellow for her pithi, a pista one for garba, red for the wedding, and a blue one for the reception. Each card had all the drawn-out names of parents and aunts and uncles and deceased grandparents and the hosting siblings, plus the actual information about the event. Pranit's invitations included the same cards for garba, wedding, and reception, plus one for his own separate pithi.

Beside Maitri's kankotri was a white cloth scroll with a red-and-gold design and writing completely in Gujarati with the details of names and events. After the ceremony, the guy cousins would deliver the official invitation to the groom and his family, inviting them to the wedding.

Farther away were the cousins, the kids, and—finally—*me*, all the way at the back of the living room and halfway into the hall.

Around the room, the older relatives prayed while my high school– and middle school–aged cousins and I pantomimed banging our heads against the wall while counting down the time. Most of my cousins were female, which was necessary because we needed a strong Team Bride ride-or-die squad to defeat the groom's side in the wedding games. Say what you will about Indian girls supposedly growing up to be quiet and proper—I was surrounded by dynamic women, all loud and opinionated and ready to throw down against the groom's side. We did not come to play; we came to get paid. Quite literally.

One by one, we cracked. Too much quiet, too much idle sitting. Too much time for me to get lost in my bad news if I didn't occupy myself with something soon.

Most of the girls were dressed in nice jeans and blouses, their shoes gathered on the front porch. The best dressed was always my older cousin Priyanka, who was Maitri's bridesmaid and one of her best friends. Like Krish and I, they were the same age and had grown up together.

Priyanka Damani was basically the twenty-five-year-old business financial officer version of Priyanka Chopra, living in upper-middle-class Atlanta. She pulled off stylish rocker-chick bangs, hot-pink nails, and a thin tunic over slim jeans, and I was sure the high-heeled boots on the porch were hers. She was perpetually stuck to her phone, smiling and gushing over something way more important than the ceremony.

A few other cousins, girls around my age, crawled toward me and filled up the space to my left, earning looks from their mothers.

And then we all pulled out our cell phones.

Neha shrugged and tapped away on her device. Much like my other two sisters, she had a long, graceful neck. Her dark hair, wavy and glossy, was draped over one shoulder, exposing a birthmark on her neck. We'd lovingly nicknamed it the shadow-wart.

Krish moved away from her brothers, Meet and Rohan (aka the guy cousins), and scooted next to me. She rested her head on my shoulder and checked her texts.

While I adjusted filters for social media pics, Krish's text popped up.

Krish: Are you ready to break out after this thing is over?
Me: How?
Krish: I told you we're here to help.
Me: Are you sure I won't get caught? I don't want to be the screwup. AGAIN.

Krish sighed, her chest deflating beneath a dark berry top. She tucked her legs beneath her and stared at her phone screen, pondering her next response. Trust me, I was feeling that pain, too, sis. Auditions were happening in just a few hours, and knowing they were possibly my strongest shot at music college was sort of eating away at my brain. Because, sure, the contest was for enough money to cover four years of private university tuition, but anyone winning tuition money granted by a panel of music college scouts was bound to also get offers from those colleges. Juilliard was a sure shot for spring semester with a win like that!

I wanted to go. I needed to go. I had to salvage my musical future or be forever chained to a path toward law. But how could I slip out without being noticed? Kinda hard for the sister of an Indian bride.

Then Krish typed. But not to me.

What were the odds that no one would notice me missing while we mass assembly-line stuffed a million gift bags and snack pouches and chocolate treat boxes? I was pretty sure I was on ribbon-curling duty, anyway.

Several of my cousins read their phones and slowly, one by one, looked up at me.

My eyebrows furrowed together and I side-eyed them. A plan was being hatched, and there was nothing more devious and elaborate than a ploy cooked up by your own meddling cousins.

Krish: Don't worry. We got you covered.

Baffled, I gawked at Krish. Had she just blabbed to everyone? Oh my lord. What were the chances that none of them would accidentally tattle on me?

Me: What's going on?

She simply smiled that impish smile of hers, the one that was a little lopsided and had once been adorable but now promised that mischievous things were afoot. Then she cocked her chin at the ceremony, and I focused on taking more pictures before my legs went completely numb.

I snapped a few pictures and watched Maitri for a second longer, admiring how happy she looked, the shimmer in her eyes, the flush to her cheeks. There was something to be said for having that sort of bliss spinning through the family, despite my little corner of personal college hell. Her happiness had me feeling whole and content, and I totally got what my parents were feeling.

My eye twitched as a tear formed.

She'd lived at home during college because she wanted to be close to us. She had lived closer to campus during law school for convenience and then came back home to make sure Neha and I had her. Her room had always been her room. Soon, it would be empty.

That one tear turned into two pools.

What was happening?

I never cried. Like, ever.

CHAPTER FOUR
(Saturday Afternoon: Eight Days Until the Wedding)
#DamCryBaby

You know who did cry, though? All. The. Time? Maitri Damani. She was the family's biggest crybaby, and everyone knew it. She cried at movies and during songs. She cried when she got emotional about anything. She had cried when Pranit proposed, even though she'd known it was coming (they'd had their official engagement ceremony and wedding venue booked before he did the Western-style proposal). She bawled at her bridal shower. She cried at *every*thing.

This time, her crying saved me from crying. Because before those pools of salty tears rolled down my face, the Brahman had finished and everyone ambushed Maitri for congratulations and hugs and tidbits of advice, and before we knew it, she started crying. I supposed that was a superpower of hers—from normal to bawling in point-two seconds flat.

Mummie ran her hands down Maitri's cheeks. My sister's eyes glistened as tears formed a thick, quivering sheath, ready to unleash a torrent at any moment. Even though Maitri was going to live not more than ten minutes from us after the wedding, the women in our family were acting as if this was the end of everything. I got why all our female ancestors cried at weddings and why the brides of generations past had been so forlorn—they had left their families for their husbands' family. It was not a comfortable transition. But this was not then.

Mummie started to cry.

Which made all my aunts cry.

Which made my dad's eyes water up.

Which made Maitri cry even more. And not gentle tears of happy-sadness that one might expect from such an elegant woman, but a full-on *ugly* cry. That was the only way she knew how to cry. No delicate tear or two patted away with a silk napkin for her.

There went her perfectly applied makeup. Her mascara stayed somewhat in place—thank god for waterproof! But her eyeliner smeared into rivulets down her eyes and extra-rosy cheeks in an unusually artistic way. How did she manage that? How did she manage to ugly-cry her makeup off but still look like a painting?

But now, we were all in the middle of a bawlfest. Big, fat tears with big, fat sobs coming from big, fat heaves.

I tried not to get too emotional, masking my dry throat and glistening eyes with busy camera work, capturing everyone else's tears. A candid shot, one of many, posted to the joint social media account.

The best, rawest one had to be the one of Mummie clinging to Maitri as if this were a final goodbye. As if this were a forever goodbye. Their glimmering cheeks sparkled, and in the background were blurred images of Papa and others. You couldn't see them clearly, but you could tell they were just as emotional.

Thankfully, the camera didn't capture the noise level. All sorts of high and low tones, somber and grateful, proud and joyous erupted in cacophonous ripples.

I'd always been used to the noise. Our house was never, ever quiet, not with a big family filled with loud people who constantly had friends and relatives dropping by.

Noise was not new. But this sort carried an almost ominous foreboding with it. Something that I hadn't fully acknowledged just yet, hadn't actually accepted.

Things were getting real. I was losing a sister. Oh. My. Gods. This time next week, she really *wouldn't* be here to pound on my door to make sure that I was up for school. She wouldn't be here to braid my hair on those days I wanted something a little extra. She wouldn't be here to back me up in solidarity when my parents thought my shorts and skirts were too short or convince them that going sleeveless wasn't a national scandal.

Holy crap.

I drew in a deep, shuddering breath and did what I did best: I avoided the emotional distress handed down from woman to woman in my family and posted the last of today's images . . . the first set of many to come this week.

Our generation gradually split off from the adults, leaving them standing in the furniture-less living room while we huddled in the foyer.

Because I managed not to break down, Maitri hugged me tighter than anyone else and half-jokingly muttered into my curls, "You don't even care."

She had no idea. As soon as the wedding events were over, I'd most likely lock myself in my room and sob into my pillow while all the songs on my saddest of sad days playlist roared around me. I'd get wasted on chocolate and ice cream and curse all men who took away sisters. I would be an inconsolable wreck.

"But you're happy. What *is* this mess?" I mumbled into her rose-scented hair, struggling to keep it together.

"You're going to be so sad when I'm gone."

"I'll have *two* rooms when you're gone."

"Savage." Her amber eyes widened as she pouted glossy pink lips.

She dabbed her eyes in the most sophisticated way. Maitri was the epitome of grace, of poise, and as much as I loved her, I didn't love constantly being compared to her.

Let's face it. My makeup and hair would never be perfect, my posture never straight, my skin never light, my frame never a figure eight, and my style never chic. But she was, hands down, the best.

"You love me," I said, and held her tighter.

Maitri laughed and pulled away. "Always."

She assessed me with the same lingering, hopeful eyes that Mummie had. She could probably pinpoint my notes of sadness, a mixture of her leaving and the awful rejection that lingered like a fresh wound. My heart ached. In more ways than one.

I groaned, playing if off as if nothing was wrong. "Oh my lord. You're becoming Mummie."

"What?"

I could practically see the wheels in her brain start turning the way Mummie's would. "You're thinking about how much I've grown and how much you'll miss me and how we're all stepping into the next chapters of our lives. Urvi is going to have a baby soon, thank the stars and all of Mummie's prayers. You're getting married, also thank the stars and Mummie's prayers. I'm going to graduate high school. Neha will be . . . doing whatever Neha does."

Maitri opened her mouth to protest, but I went on. "Are you twenty-five or fifty-five?"

She gently shoved me. "You're next, you know?"

I smacked my lips. "Oh no, I'm not."

And just like that, because Mummie's hearing was inhuman, she craned her neck, and her head popped up from the crowd of parents across the furniture-less rooms. She waved her phone and mouthed, "Nice boy to meet you!"

Oh gods. This was not happening.

And then, one by one, everyone chimed in to support the theory that I was indeed next.

"No way!" I exclaimed and pointed at each cousin who was in line before me by age. "Priyanka, Sethal, Manisha, Mehur, and Jyoti! Ha! Don't even look at me with that matchmaking nonsense."

"Doesn't mean all the aunties won't be trying to align your future marriage!" Neha cackled.

"You're only a few years younger. Guess they might as well align yours, too!" I shot back.

That didn't slow down an onslaught of taunting. At least now I'd managed to drag in all the cousins of age with me. Amid the teasing, all the aunts and uncles moved around us to get to the kitchen, where lunch simmered and mouthwatering aromas of spices and veggies curled in the air.

"Not anytime soon," Urvi warned and waddled toward us, her hand on her giant seven-months-pregnant belly.

"Oh my god, duckling. You should sit down."

"Eh? Who are you calling a duckling?" She waved off my comment and patted Maitri's cheek.

Raju Fua (my uncle on Papa's side and Krish's dad) approached and asked, "How are you, Zurika, beta?"

I smiled brightly at the way he referred to me as a daughter. "Good. How are you?"

"Hungry!" he bellowed.

My aunt Heena Foi in the back muttered, "Ha, ha . . . we're preparing now. Always saying that you're hungry but never want to help in the kitchen. Zuri, get yourself a boy who can cook!"

He shrugged at his wife's dry humor and asked me, "Have the college acceptance letters come rolling in?"

"Not yet," I said, hoping to hide the pain and the panic in my voice.

"Not yet?" Another uncle, Harsh Fua, inserted himself into the conversation. "Didn't you apply for early admission?"

And just like that, everything went from bridal joy to college misery. "Haven't heard back from the important college, the one

I want to go to." Lord, could they stop probing my open wounds like this?

"Georgia has a few nice universities," Raju Fua said while Harsh Fua added, "No, no, she must go to an Ivy League school."

"Well, you know," I piped up, my voice cracking, "I'm extremely talented with the violin."

"Music!" my uncles roared, deflating my hope and causing me to flinch. Here they went, back and forth. First talking to me, then at me, and then to each other while ignoring me altogether. There were few ways a group of well-intentioned family members could make a person go from at ease to feeling like crap in two seconds flat.

Krish shot me an apologetic glance.

Her dad said, "Music is OK, but it's not a job. Time to put away childish dreams and think of a career."

Harsh Fua added, "True. There's no certainty about income when it comes to music."

"Obtaining a musical job, much less a career, is too hard. Too few jobs out there. Too risky."

"You must be able to make money. *Good money*."

I seethed quietly—aka respectfully. My uncles meant well, they really did, even if they were overstepping. They only wanted all of us kids to make them proud, to be able to do well for ourselves, to be able to hold our heads high.

"Medical school is the way to go," they went on, despite my RBF coming through fast and furious, splintering my sorrow. I felt it dragging down my face as they spoke. But I wouldn't allow them to get to me.

Could we Indian creatives get some support once in a while? Like, dang. Why must we pursue something like medicine or law or engineering to get solace and respect?

"Law school is better. Medical is too competitive these days and there's no guarantee of getting into residency afterward," Harsh Fua went on, having butted me out of the conversation entirely so I couldn't get a word in.

"What about business?"

"Depends! Which area? We have to look at prestige and income. She must be the best."

"Ha," Raju Fua agreed.

"Architects make good money. Look at Sejal from mandir. Then again, we Indians do well at everything. We work hard and take education seriously. We get paid well. We have a lot of pressure to live up to," Harsh Fua added with a finger in the air in declaration.

I groaned. They were slowly killing me with this "Indians are the best at everything" talk.

"It's not pressure! It's just life. We have to aim high. No choice. But you know, dermatologists make excellent money. Less stress than other doctors."

"No medical. Maybe engineering?"

And on and on they went, going through the "big four": medicine, engineering, business, and law. They were picking out my colleges, degrees, and career paths, and then they completely removed me from the conversation by taking it to my dad.

I groaned as Papa said, his hands clasped behind his back, "My Zuri will make me proud, *very* proud! Can you imagine if I have four lawyers for daughters? We can bring change! Maybe one will become a judge!" He looked back at me and smiled that big, proud smile he sported just for me. It splintered my heart even more. I couldn't handle not pursuing music, but I couldn't handle failing him, either.

"Don't worry," Urvi said, and tilted my chin up. "Don't let them get to you."

I nodded mournfully as she frowned.

"Dismiss them, sweets. They'll poke their noses into your life to get their two cents in. We went through this already, being tugged every which way by every uncle who wanted to be heard. It's inevitable, no matter how hard I fought them."

"And you'll never let us forget," Maitri teased.

Urvi cast an impish glance at her before returning to me. "Never, ever forget the women who came before you and paved your path so you wouldn't have to fight as hard, or at all. You make a decision and go with it, no matter what others want."

I put on my best smile. She . . . also meant well. And although her words were completely supportive on the surface, they were meant to remind me how hard she'd worked for us. Just like our parents. They had worked two jobs for decades to make sure we didn't have to. Her words were for law school, not music. "For sure. And that was a great way to stop Maitri from ugly-crying."

"I don't ugly-cry," Maitri protested.

"Come on." I pointed the cell phone camera at the two of us. "Selfie."

Normally, Maitri couldn't resist a selfie. But one look at her reflection, those tearstained cheeks, and she gasped. "Oh no! I look horrible!"

She wrestled the phone away, but I snatched it right back.

"Don't post those!"

I danced away, delighted and laughing. "Too late."

"What!"

"You shouldn't have left me in charge of your joint social."

"Zuri. That wasn't nice!" Neha said with a giggle as she showed Maitri the pictures I'd already posted. Urvi and our cousins joined in the laughter.

"Aw," Maitri said, a hand to her chest. "Those are so pretty. Wait. Did you call me a *crybaby* in this post?"

"It's adorable," Urvi insisted.

"And true!" Neha added.

"I'm going to get you back for that!" Maitri scolded, her lips in a pout but her eyes filled with amusement.

"Ja. Ja." I playfully dismissed her with a flip of my wrist. "It's been a whole three hours since you talked to *Jiju*."

We all made kissy noises with duck lips.

Maitri sighed, and her gaze listed off to the side. "It has been a long time . . ."

"Speaking of the groom-to-be . . ." Rohan interrupted as he unlocked the front door. He held up the ceremonial scroll, signed by the Brahman and tied with a pretty red-and-gold ribbon. "Have to get this to the groom before he thinks the bride backed out of the arrangement."

"I'd never do that." Maitri grinned and glanced at the scroll in his hand. "I couldn't come with you, could I?"

"Nope. You know the rules. You can't step into his house, and he can't step foot in this house until after the official start of the wedding weekend. Those little red foot stamps on the threshold say so." He shrugged, indicating the emblems that were pretty much "thou shalt not pass" signs for the bride and groom.

Maitri sighed. "Fine. Fine. I'll just call him. I have a lot to do today, anyway. So much. Why did we opt for a big wedding?"

I guffawed. "*Big* wedding? Maitri! You guys are having the biggest, fattest, most Indian-est wedding anyone in this family or this town or this state has ever seen."

"It's not that big!" she argued, throwing her hands into the air.

I lifted a hand to all the over-the-top decorations around us. "Oy. It's three entire days, five events, five dress changes, twelve choreographed dances, seven bridesmaids, and a ton of games with guests from literally around the world. Big, fat Bollywood wedding."

"OK. OK. Let's not stress Maitri out any more than she already is," Urvi intervened.

"Sorry," I said, despite knowing that Maitri didn't mind. She had far more important things to worry about.

"Ha," Mummie shouted from the arched hallway. "Get going before the groom thinks we changed our minds. We already waited long enough, sending the kankotri last minute. Zurika and Neha and anyone not going to Pranit's house: Come help in the kitchen. Eat."

While some made their way toward lunch, Priyanka rushed out of the kitchen all tall and elegant with her long, wavy hair. She had a roti in one hand, probably fresh and hot and smothered in ghee, and gave Maitri an air kiss.

"I have to get running. Text me if you need anything, otherwise I'll be over later," Priyanka said to the bride, and waved goodbye to us all.

She opened the front door and, yep, slipped into some super-high-heeled boots. I wondered if I'd ever be able to walk right in something like that, but probably not.

"We want to talk to you really quickly," Urvi said as she and Maitri walked me to the other end of the front room, barely out of earshot of my cousins.

"Your hair came out really nice, Maitri," Urvi said as she fixed a stray wave.

Mummie called it "that good hair." It was funny, really, because I was the only sister who'd inherited curls from my mom's Indo-Trinidadian genes. She had never liked her hair, because all her life she'd been told that straight hair was better.

"Thanks. Took me an hour and nearly burned my forehead," Maitri muttered, then rubbed her arms. "Maybe I should've gotten my arms waxed."

"Did that auntie get to you?" I mused. "None of us are hairy."

"Speak for yourself," Urvi groaned and looked down her top. "I have the biggest boobie hair since pregnancy."

Gross.

"Speaking of waxing, though, Maitri, don't forget to clean up. Ya know? Down there."

Ew.

"Is this what you wanted to tell me?" I mumbled.

They spoke as one. "You *are* planning on being present for every event, aren't you?"

"What?" I asked, shocked that my sisters thought so little of me.

"We overheard Mummie getting on you earlier," Maitri said. "Please don't disrupt a single thing during my wedding weekend. You know how important everything is, and I'm already stressed out over every detail."

"No way. I would never mess anything up. Mummie is over-reacting," I promised. Besides, I knew where there were gaps in the week's many events so I could sneak out. I wasn't planning on messing up a single moment.

They both shot me a dry look. Urvi added, "Do you remember when you snuck out during my festivities to play for a school concert?"

I bit my lip. Oh yeah . . . But it was the *nationals,* and I'd been a *freshman.*

"You missed photo ops, early mehndi, and the groom's welcome," she added. Judging by her current annoyance levels, Urvi was still kinda pissed about it.

She took a deep drink from her water bottle and said, "It's time to put away the violin and focus on your responsibilities.

Do not miss a single tradition this time. It's bad karma, bad fortune for the couple. And as a sister of the bride, you should stop at nothing to make sure every requirement is met and that everything goes perfectly. You're almost done with high school. You're almost an adult. Behave like one."

Maitri nodded.

I gulped, my gut twisting in a depressing way as I realized that my sisters might actually see me as a screwup.

"Which leads to college acceptance letters," Maitri added.

I held my breath. Crap. Did they know my plan?

"I know we've been busy, but we should've been the ones to ask before anyone else did. Lord knows all the uncles and aunties will be prodding you for information." Urvi rolled her eyes and listed her head to the side.

"Isn't that the least of your concerns right now?" I mumbled, trepidation oozing down my insides like tar, my eyes darting to the floor.

Maitri replied, "It should be, but I don't want to be the last to know because I didn't take time to ask. I'm the bride, but I'm also your sister."

"You'll make us proud," Urvi said with a reassuring smile. "We've accumulated many connections to law schools. Your grades are good, but we can give a little extra push."

What she meant was to say was that my grades weren't as sparkling as theirs had been and I needed all the help they could forage. Which . . . was a lot, to be honest.

"I'll let you know when I have news, but it probably won't be till after the wedding," I promised.

Urvi smiled and gave me a side hug. "Thanks. OK. So maybe I came off a little hard. Hormones, you know? I know you'll be perfect this weekend. And there's no doubt that you'll get into every college you applied to."

Their eyes gleamed with hope for me.

Urvi arched a brow. "Your foresisters did not pave the way with our own sweat, blood, and tears and line it with the shredded, futile arguments of all the naysayers and haters for nothing. We did it for us, but more importantly, we did it for you and Neha so your fight for a strong career could be just a bit easier. We're full of resources and help. We'll make this as easy for you as possible as long as you try your hardest, too."

Oh. Well, *dang*. They didn't make it any easier for me to crush their dreams by following my own. That rolling feeling in my stomach? Turned into full-on rocks—jagged ones that shredded my guts.

CHAPTER FIVE
(Saturday Afternoon: Eight Days Until the Wedding)

#LittleBlackDress

Dazed, I turned toward the hallway when Krish and Sethal suddenly grabbed my shoulders and urged me toward the stairs. "Zuri is going, too!" they called back in unison.

"What? Why?" Papa craned his head around the corner, both parents now intently watching us. "This is only for the brothers to send the kankotri. Not girls."

"It's to get pictures, of course!" Krish responded.

He thought about it for a second, whether to break tradition for the sake of pictures, before he nodded once. "Ha. I trust my beta."

Then Mummie crept around the corner and did a head bob thing as if she knew. "Make sure you meet *all* the relatives!"

A bit confused by the entire exchange, I stood immobile. Wait one hot Atlanta minute. Were my busybody cousins trying to hook me up, too? Prearrange my semiarranged marriage?

Mummie smiled triumphantly.

I shuffled up the stairs after Krish, followed by Sethal, Manisha, and Jyoti, while the guys waited at the bottom of the steps. I glanced at them over my shoulders as they watched the hallway for the parents like a pair of bodyguards who meant serious business.

We filed into my room, quiet as mice except for the gentle and rhythmic chimes of our bangles and anklets and the swishes of fabric. If my room had been cramped before, it was claustrophobic now.

"What are you guys up to?" Neha asked, her arms crossed while her petite frame obstructed the doorway to my room.

"Nothing. Don't you have to eat and cut out paper hearts or something?" I asked, gently pushing her back and closing the door on her annoyed huff. Then I locked the door. One could never be too careful in a house full of snooping sisters.

Once I turned to the room, the quiet detonated into giggling, and several conversations broke out all at once.

The cousins plopped down onto my bed, and Krish rummaged through my closet like a freaking tornado. I twitched at the sight of her disturbing my organized layout.

"Um. OK. So what brilliant plan have you guys concocted?" I asked nervously on the heels of my moti bens' warning.

Krish pulled out a few dresses. They were definitely not Indian attire and not meant for the week's wedding events. Not the muted colors or white or black. Not the cut of low collars and high hems.

Sethal nodded to one dress in particular and took it from Krish as she put the others back into their orderly positions inside the walk-in closet, right above the matching shoes.

Sethal pulled me over to the full-length mirror stuck to the outside of the closet door by yours truly, then she stood beside me and held the dress to my body.

The girls clapped and concluded, "Yes! Definitely the one for auditions!"

Krish came over and piled my hair on top of my head, where it sat, fluffy with curls and twice the size of my face. "We'll say you were with the guys."

"Oh lord." I managed to twist away and stared at the crazy mess of girls in my room. "How are we going to pull this off? What if someone asks for pictures, for proof that I was at Pranit's house?" I held up my phone. "Ya know, this thing called social media that I'm supposedly uploading to? And also my parents, who'll want to see everything that's going on at his house."

"My brothers have got you covered," Krish replied. "They'll take some pics for you."

"What if Maitri asks Pranit if I was there?"

"He's going to be way too occupied to notice."

"Why would you guys go through so much trouble for this? If my parents find out, you're all done for."

"Because we've seen you perform. We know you'll go places. We know doing anything else would feel soul-crushing. Would you let me give up on my dreams just because of one setback?" Krish planted her hands on her hips and came at me with a bunch of sass and irrefutable reasoning. "We're Damani girls. Resilient. Hustlers."

I laughed, feeling the edge of the rejection and my sisters' warnings tapering off enough to embrace the Damani determination. It was a squirming sliver of hope, but I grabbed on to whatever I could. "*Yes*."

The girls quietly squealed and jumped up and down in whatever tiny amount of rug space they could find.

Krish handed me the dress while Sethal pulled out matching shoes.

My heart beat faster, swelling and prancing—yep, actual on-cloud-nine prancing—with renewed hope and excitement. This contest was quite possibly my one chance to really wow several college scouts at once, but there would be a Juilliard scout there, too. Maybe they would give me a second chance once they recognized how much I belonged with them. Maybe they would realize that I was good enough for them after all, retract their rejection, and offer me acceptance on the spot.

Wow! Wouldn't that be something!

I felt like Cinderella in that moment with my sparkly shoes instead of glass slippers, my concert dress instead of a ball gown, my gaggle of cousins instead of mice, Krish as my fairy godmother, a violin instead of a pumpkin, and a career-making contest instead of a meeting with a prince.

A girl had to dream. Because without dreams, I was a depressing pile of pointless flesh and bones with no other motivation breathing life into me. Music was my passion and direction.

"No one can see me in this color," I whispered.

My cousins nodded, like it wasn't taboo to wear black during the wedding week. But it was definitely audition worthy, the way the sparkly dress flowed down my waist and showed way too much leg.

"Thank you. I love you guys so much," I told my cousins, even as I shook off the tremors racing through my limbs.

"God. Change already. Before the parents change their minds and decide sending a girl over to the groom's house will bring bad luck," Krish ordered, gently tugging my arm.

"Yeah. Yeah. I'm going." But apparently not fast enough. In a dash, there were fabrics flying all over the place.

Sethal vigilantly texted. "The guys are our eyes. Go. Go. Go!"

"Hurry," Krish said, and practically stripped me down.

"All right! All right!" I lamented. This was definitely giving me wedding shopping flashbacks—so much fabric, so little time, so much speed. At least this time I wasn't stuck inside a dress in a changing room in a little Indian clothing shop.

I somehow managed not to trip over all the hands and feet and clothes as Krish simultaneously yanked on my top and bottom. This wasn't new. There was little privacy in a house with three sisters and an extended family full of women, and even less privacy during a wedding week, when we had to fit into the same room. There wasn't time to cover my slightly robust belly or thighs that perpetually touched.

"Thank god you have on a real bra," Sethal said, and pulled the black dress over my head.

"Thank god you have on a bra, period," Krish said.

"A sports bra is a real bra," I mumbled through the fabric. But also, yes, good thing I was wearing a bra instead of relying on the stitched-in padding that came with Indian outfits for small boobs like mine. I wasn't expecting to get stripped down today.

I stuck my arms through the bell-shaped mid-forearm sleeves, and the smooth, silky fabric kissed my midthighs. I clutched the ruched waist, where little glittery dark threads made subtle patterns like black diamonds and hid my belly.

"And this." Krish handed me my backpack and stuffed it with the outfit I'd worn this morning. "So you can change after the audition, before you get home. Now go!"

"Good idea!" I took the bag and looped it over one shoulder.

We crept through the hallway with my high-heeled shoes in my hands and peered over the railing to see only the guy cousins below. Jyoti carried my violin case. Krish went down first to make sure the coast was clear. She nodded to the guys at the bottom of the steps. She looked at us and nodded, giving the get-out-of-here-fast wave of her hand.

We moved in a line, slightly bent at the waist because . . . I dunno. That's what they did in the movies? Maybe it made us stealthy, quieter.

The guys watched the downstairs hallway. Meet opened the door and awaited the clear signal from Rohan. The second he waved, Jyoti jogged downstairs to hand off my violin to him while Krish practically pushed me down the steps. I ran on tiptoes over plush carpet and slid a few feet when I hit the tiles in my black tights, fighting off a fall.

I fumbled right out the front door. Rohan swung in behind me and closed the door like some sort of smooth dance move, and just like that, we'd escaped the harrowing masses of a big family lunch.

I carefully traipsed toward his black Camry and slipped into the back seat next to my violin, pulling on my shoes.

"You got what you need?" Meet asked, glancing at me in the rearview mirror as he pulled out onto the street. "Violin, directions, admission email . . . um . . . are you guys dropping me off before lunch?"

"No can do. We're already late to the meet-and-greet lunch. We have to give them this very important kankotri, otherwise, how will the groom and fam know that he's getting married this weekend?"

He held up the scroll, the wedding invitation, and a shiny golden box of imported sweets that was the traditional accompanying gift. Right. They were on their own mission.

"You'll have to take the car. We'll be in there for a few hours, getting to know everyone who's flown in from Pranit's side. In other words, we can't just bounce."

I slumped back, leaning my head against the stiff headrest. "OK. Hey, thanks for doing this. Hopefully you don't get caught."

Meet glanced at me in his rearview mirror. "Who? Us? We're innocent. How would we know where you went?"

"Funny," I said. He pulled onto Pranit's street a few minutes later, a street full of nice houses in a ritzy upper-middle-class suburb literally ten minutes away.

His parents' house matched our own as far as over-the-top decorations went. They had a million fairy lights snaked around trees and shrubs that blinked with colorful twinkles in broad daylight. They even had their own giant sign over the garage that read THE PATEL FAMILY WELCOMES YOU.

Subtlety wasn't their flavor, either.

We parked across the street and down a house.

"Knock 'em dead!" the guys said, and hurried out of the car and toward the front door.

"Thanks!" I called back, clutching the back of the passenger seat, suddenly alone in the middle of this wild plan, all the while praying no one noticed my absence.

I crawled out of the back seat and shimmied, as ladylike as possible—which wasn't very, in this short dress—into the driver's seat, adjusting everything to my height. My hands were legit shaking, and I clutched them to my chest.

Don't get caught. Don't mess up the audition.

Someone opened the door for the guys. From the street corner, I caught a glimpse of the gigantic banner of Pranit and Maitri hanging from the second floor to welcome visitors into the foyer, just like the one we had. Ha-ha!

It sounded as if *everyone* had come to the door to greet the guys, to watch Pranit's mom give them blessings with smears of red sindoor on their foreheads and sweets to their mouths before inviting them in.

As soon as they closed the door, I turned the engine back on, took in a few long breaths, checked my mirrors, smacked my red-painted lips in the reflection of the visor mirror, shifted into drive, grabbed the steering wheel, and hit the gas.

A split-second later, something flashed in front of me, and I slammed the brakes. The car skidded to an abrupt stop, the seat belt nearly decapitating me. My heart beat so fast with the sudden surge of adrenaline that I thought it might actually explode.

Oh. My. Lord. I had almost hit someone!

In front of the car, with hands in the air, frozen in place after jumping out of the way of this deadly car with an equally deadly driver, stood the most terrified guy I'd ever seen.

CHAPTER SIX
(Saturday Afternoon: Eight Days Until the Wedding)
#AlmostKilledAGuy

I tripped over my thoughts, my heart hammering, my gut in the worst state of nausea, all while this stranger cautiously came around to my side of the car, tapped on the window, and leaned down. I swallowed hard, willing that *oh crap* moment to ease away and fully expecting him to curse me out. Hitting a person, possibly putting him in the hospital, was not the way a wedding week should start. Talk about bad luck and evil omens!

He tapped the glass again and smiled nervously.

Oh, right!

The automatic window came down with a push of a button, my hand shaking. He gave a short wave. This was *not* some random guy. I'd recognize him anywhere.

Naveen Patel.

Not going to lie that I was staring pretty hard, like maybe I'd forgotten to blink. Because dang, dude. Those attractive Patel genes were strong with this one.

The sun glinted off his smooth, dark brown skin and intense eyes framed with long, dark lashes. His gaze might've penetrated to my soul. He ran a hand over pitch-black hair and said, "Hi. Zurika, right?"

Holy crap. That voice. It was deep, sonorous, and that accent?

"I'm Naveen. Pranit's cousin. From South Africa?"

While girls nearly always went gaga over British, Italian, and Spanish accents (according to friends and movies), I had to say that the South African cadence eclipsed them all. There was something sophisticated and mesmerizing about it. And yet raw.

"Hello?" He gave another short wave.

"Oh! Hi. Nice to meet you," I said, wondering if he thought my slightly Southern American accent sounded dumb and unrefined. Not that I personally thought so, but boy, wasn't that the joke about the South?

He scrunched his face and glanced over the car, at Pranit's house. "Listen, I'm in a bit of a bind. Could you help out?"

I stuttered over my response. Etiquette told me to help, especially considering who he was. But one, he was still a stranger, and two, I had somewhere important to be! Dude! Why ask today, of all days?

"Can't you ask your family?" I found myself saying.

He looked back to me. "That's the thing. I'm sort of hiding it from them."

"Hold on . . ." I said, and checked some social media accounts to verify that this guy was actually Naveen. He sure looked like him. I even went into our giant group chat and messaged his number.

He pulled out his phone and smirked. "Did you just message me to make sure I'm legit?"

"Yes."

He shook his head and replied to the message and then the group message to tell everyone that he couldn't wait to meet the bride's family.

"All right, Naveen, cousin of my soon-to-be Jijaji number two. What's up?"

He bent back down to the window at an awkward angle and tapped the top of the car. "I need a ride."

I checked the time on the dashboard. I was cutting it close and sweating bullets, and this guy was killing me. "I have to be somewhere soon."

"It's not far. It's . . . um . . ." He pulled up something on his phone and showed me the screen.

I read a few key—and very familiar—words. No way. He was going to my school. As in, the music competition held on our campus. Was he for real, or was this some sort of elaborate setup so my parents could catch me in the act?

"Oh. Are you competing in this?" I inquired, trying to sound as chill as possible and hoping he didn't notice that my voice was shaking.

"Yes." He gave a small smile, like maybe he was nervous about my reaction. If it was because of him ditching wedding events and trying to get into a music college by way of a competition, then you and me both, dude.

"Seriously?" I asked incredulously.

"Do you know of it? I sent in my video audition three months ago and received an invitation to try out in person.

Excellent timing, huh?" Then he proceeded to show me the invitation email.

Yep. He was legit my competition. Ugh. Way to exacerbate my barely restrained jitters. I didn't need more musical talent to stand up against, but it felt awfully shady to ditch him. Plus, there was the risk that he'd tattle on me. I groaned and unlocked the doors. "Hop in."

"Yes! I'll owe you for this." He carefully walked around the hood of the car, keeping an eye on me as if I might run him over, and climbed into the passenger seat. His heady but soft cologne smelled like a bouquet of cinnamon and nutmeg, which had me wondering if I'd even put on deodorant this morning.

This time I triple-checked all areas around the car before slowly moving onto the street and getting on the highway. My fists were gripping the steering wheel so hard that my knuckles ached. My gut was doing ridiculous flips as my gaze flitted between the road and the dashboard clock. I'd never in my entire life wanted to get to school so badly.

Naveen cleared his throat, as if reminding me that he was here and we hadn't said a word for the last five minutes. "Thanks for taking me. It should be fun." He smiled a megawatt smile.

"Oh no!" I rasped with realization.

"What?" he asked, surprised, now full-on watching me.

"Did you tell anyone where you were going?"

"No one knows. Why?"

I exited the highway and checked over my shoulder as I merged onto a main street. "No one? Your parents and the family won't wonder where you disappeared to? In a whole different country?"

He scratched the back of his head.

"Oh. Spill it!" Because we didn't have time to waste, and if he was going to blow my cover or hold this over my head in any way, I was prepared to drop him off anywhere except the school.

His cheeks flushed a little, and a devilish grin hiked up his lips. He had dimples, too. Can you believe that? Dimples so deep a person could drink water out of them.

"Well?" I pressed, waiting at a red light and tapping the steering wheel with an impatient finger.

"My parents think I'm on some date."

"Really?" I wasn't sure why that surprised me. Not every Indian was bound by the dating laws of my family. Plus, he was a guy, and although it wasn't fair, there were definite double standards that might allow him to date and run around alone in a foreign country. My parents would've had a tracker on me if I were in his shoes.

He quickly explained, "I mean, not *my* date. See, my brother, Neelish—he's a few years older than me—met this girl on one of those date-to-marry apps, and he went out to meet her. But my parents insisted that he could only go if I went, just to be safe. Of course he didn't want me tagging along. Pretty sure he's not seeing her to ask about marriage, you know what I mean?" He cleared his throat, as if just now realizing that discussing his brother's hookup habits was too spicy for this first encounter with me. "As far as the rest of the family knows, I'm chaperoning a date set up by some biodata site approved by my parents."

I stifled my laugh. Gotta love the biodata, though. The most direct set of personal info to inform others of their stats. I hadn't seen many of them, and I thought they must be seriously outdated, but Mummie had mentioned them to Urvi back in the day, so we'd checked. Name, age, gender, location, education, likes, dislikes, etc. Swipe left or right on potential marriage match. Bam! Set for life. Urvi had laughed Mummie right out of the room on that one.

Naveen side-eyed me and grinned even harder. "Sounds absurd, huh?"

I laughed. "C'mon. Americans have *Tinder*." Albeit for totally different purposes, but apparently Neelish was Tinderizing whatever app he was on.

Naveen shrugged. "She seems like a nice girl . . . online. I just hope she isn't a stalker."

The light turned green, and I drove ahead. Just another few minutes. Hopefully the parking lot wasn't packed. "And she knows he doesn't live around here?"

"Yeah. But you know? He's willing to move here."

"For a stranger?" I croaked.

"Not for her, no. He wants to live in the States and work here."

"That's so far from family," I said, unable to comprehend living an entire an ocean away from my family.

"I want to move here, too. I'm hoping something works out for my brother so I can move to the States with him."

"Oh. So this music contest? You're trying to get noticed by college scouts?" I asked, trying to gather intel on how determined my competition was.

"Yeah. My parents, and maybe even my brother, would kill me if they knew I wanted to go into music."

I swallowed, hoping that he wasn't good enough to be direct competition. Was it awful of me to hope he sucked so I didn't have worry every time I had to see him throughout this entire week?

"What instrument do you play?" I asked casually, all the while praying it wasn't in the strings family.

"Vocals."

A sigh left my lips. Competition, but at least not for the same thing. "Oh! You're a singer? That's cool."

"Thanks. I'm singing during the reception, too."

I almost slammed my brakes when I slowed down for a stop. He lurched forward but didn't say anything.

I glared at him for the briefest of seconds at the stop sign before passing through. "You are?" I asked, a bit harsher than I meant. I was supposed to be the only one performing a musical talent. There were lots of dancers. Everyone and their auntie was going to dance. But I was going to play a song.

That was *my* thing. I was sister to the bride. Naveen was just a cousin, never to be seen again. How had I missed this in the schedule? Was it even in the schedule?

Annoyance lingered in the back of my mind like the onset of a pimple you knew was coming. All right. Just calm down. He wasn't going to steal the spotlight or make my gift to my sister less special.

Nope. No matter how hard I tried to put those negative triggers in the background, they came careening to the forefront.

My grip on the steering wheel tightened. I had to compete against him during the contest *and* at the reception? Oh, bhel no. Much like my mom's favorite crunchy, tangy dish, this wouldn't last long.

Naveen went on, totally unaware of the tension filling up the car, "My family thinks singing is nice, but they'd never consider me pursuing it as a career. I'm set to go into engineering. But if I can get college scouts to notice me, then maybe my parents will relax and be OK with it."

"I didn't know the competition was open internationally . . ." I mumbled through gritted teeth.

"If they pick someone from overseas, they have to be able to make it here. It's not cheap. I don't think many people try it from overseas, but I happened to have a wedding to go to anyway. Perfect timing." He shrugged as if his kismet was no big deal.

"You're willing to move all the way here to pursue singing?"

"Yeah. This is my only chance, really."

So he was determined, then.

Naveen got quiet. And so did I. I guessed we both had a lot riding on this. How was a girl supposed to act around her competition? Maybe we weren't going after the same college or competing with the same instrument, but we were both trying to get noticed, and scouts offered limited seats and only one full-ride scholarship. Had he applied the traditional way but hadn't gotten into a music college, like me? Was he as cornered as I was?

It didn't have to be said that he was good enough to get this far. Getting past video auditions wasn't something to shrug off.

The competition got hundreds of them. We both had a lot to prove, a lot to gain, and a lot to lose. And here I was, giving him a freaking ride.

After a few minutes, he inquired, "Where were you headed off to?"

"Same. The auditions." I glanced at him.

He asked pointedly, "Are you competing, too? Is that why you're so dressed up?"

"Yes." I side-eyed Naveen to find him checking out my dress. My very-short-while-sitting dress in all its sparkling glory. Heat swept across my body. I'd worn this dress a dozen times for recitals and shows, but I'd never clocked a boy noticing it.

"What do you play?" he asked.

"Violin. I play in my school orchestra."

"That's very cool."

Most people said that to be polite. In fact, I'd heard so many people respond with an indifferent "cool" that hearing the word made me want to crawl out of my skin and punch them. They might as well not say anything at all. But Naveen had genuine enthusiasm in his tone as he asked all sorts of questions about me being in orchestra. Little did he know that "cool" wasn't a big enough word to encapsulate my awesomeness.

"I like classical music," he added. "Can't name a lot of the older composers, but it blows my mind how much soul can come out of that little instrument. There are so many mainstream violinists now, too. Is that what you want to do? Go to university on a music scholarship and play for an orchestra?"

"Yeah. And then some." My words trailed off. I'd only ever admitted that to Krish and a few teachers.

"Do your parents know?" he prodded. He had his hands in his lap, a silver ring on his left pointer finger, which he fidgeted with his thumb, moving it back and forth.

I shrugged at his questions, not wanting him to know me or my story or give him entry into the headspace of his competitor. He hadn't earned any right to know about my dreams or how to use any of this against me.

So, no. Obvs my parents didn't know. But yes, I had some huge musical aspirations and a lot of inspiration to follow in the footsteps of leading ladies before me.

There was the original hip-hop violinist, Miri Ben-Ari, who broke through in a major way in rap and hip-hop songs. Not to mention that her hair—a wild, curly mane—reminded me of my own hair. No one thought hers was untamed or ugly or unprofessional. She'd performed abroad and for presidents. She'd performed for the richest, most powerful people in the world with grace and class. She'd worked with the most hard-core rappers. She'd sold out countless solo concerts. She was my idol. Oh, and she was Israeli. More power to the WOC making their dreams come true.

Then there was Lindsey Stirling—soul-moving epicness. She had such a theatrical presence. She danced, for goodness' sake, while she played.

I liked to think that I was a combination of those two women— my musical, glass ceiling–breaking, genre-defying role models.

Cool, Naveen Patel? He had no idea. He wouldn't expect all this when I walked across the stage. But it wasn't something that I could explain to someone, playing violin to hip-hop beats or pop or rock and roll vibes. Sounded a bit silly, even to me. People had to hear it to understand. I wanted to make others feel what I felt with music thrumming across my skin—whole and otherworldly and utterly free.

To change the subject, I asked, "Are you staying at Pranit's house?"

"For a few days. We managed to get a room at the hotel the wedding is at. I was trying to give Pranit and his family space without a bunch of people using the house and stressing them out. But my parents and other family ended up staying anyway."

His house, much like ours, had four bedrooms and three bathrooms, but nicer. Still too small for a bunch of visitors, though. I clucked my tongue. "Indians always want that free room, but I bet Pranit's parents insisted . . ."

He laughed. "Yeah. I get it. We're family and haven't seen each other for a while. Free means crowded, though. I hope the groom gets his rest. He's stressed as it is."

Ahead, just past one more red light, the spread-out campus on the corner of two major streets appeared beyond the trees. Time was ticking, oh my lord! I would've bitten my nails if not for the fact that the bride would kill me if I messed up this enforced manicure. "No kidding. Maitri is on the verge of freaking out."

"Did you see the four-page schedule?"

The document hit my thoughts like war flashbacks. How many drafts had we pored over? "See it? I helped create it! Can you believe that? I'm scheduled for a dozen things, too."

He looked down at his phone and scrolled. "I think we're walking down the aisle together."

"Are we?" My competition was really going to be in my face all weekend, huh?

"Yep."

CHAPTER SEVEN
(Saturday Afternoon: Eight Days Until the Wedding)

#HolyCrap

Finally! I swerved into the parking lot of my high school. The competition was already set up and underway, the parking lot packed with cars and eager performers.

As soon as I turned off the ignition, my thoughts became cluttered with a hundred little things to do between now and my performance. Naveen climbed out of the car and walked around to my door, opening it for me. Baffled, I looked up at him and paused. His polite smile dragged down into confusion, but he offered a hand anyway and pulled me out.

He was incredibly tall, or maybe I was on the shorter side at five foot four. Naveen was about Pranit's height—around six feet, I guessed. Although Maitri was a few inches taller than me, she loved the height difference between her and her groom. She found something incredibly romantic in being able to press her cheek against her man's chest when he hugged her.

I could see why she liked that. There was something mesmerizing and kinda sexy about a tall guy. Like, protective, or cozy—I couldn't quite put my finger on it. I kind of really liked it, but I also hated the fact that I liked it. Annoying AF.

What was wrong with me?

He was my opponent, my adversary, my self-proclaimed nemesis. I didn't come to make friends or lower my guard, so I put on my game face (aka RBF) and focused.

I had stuff to get done. I was going to make it in music, and no pretty-faced, cinnamon-scented, South African–accented boy was going to knock me off my game. I stepped back and muttered, "Thanks."

"Of course." He scratched the back of his neck.

I pulled my violin case from the back seat and locked the car, leaving my backpack behind. The double beep of the locks engaging were muffled by other cars and chattering crowds. The sun shone bright over us, and brick buildings loomed ahead, beckoning kids with pillars painted in school colors.

We walked toward the inviting banners bearing the school's initials beneath the electronic notice board that flashed in bright colors, ENJOY SPRING BREAK MARCH 7–11!

"I can carry that for you," Naveen suggested, reaching for my case.

I pulled back. Nah, man. Trying to touch my instrument was like going for my hair: Don't even try. "No thanks. I don't like anyone touching my stuff." Oh my *word*. Who was this polite? I mean, was he really this nice, or was he trying to sabotage me?

Ahead, a news reporter covered the event amid a ton of excited chatter and all sorts of people taking selfies.

Trekking toward thicker crowds meant attracting more

attention. Naveen's good looks didn't go unnoticed. All sorts of girls were eyeing him like some fine guy candy from across the seas.

The place was more packed than I had expected as we walked toward the side entrance of the school, following giant signs directing hundreds of people to the newly renovated auditorium. There would be about fifty of us auditioning, all nervous, all hopeful, some cutthroat.

It was easy to tell who was here to watch and who was here to conquer. The latter crowd had definite levels of shade, sizing up the others, and/or nervous energy. I was about to join that nervous energy any second now. My case handle slipped in my clammy palm.

Although I'd walked around these grounds for nearly four years, today my school felt like a concert hall. The air shivered with excitement and possibilities as some really important college scouts filled up the front center seats inside the auditorium.

My brain was already on hyperdrive, telling me to hurry up and sign in and get into full competition mode. But there was that tiny, fickle spark that kept bursting in the back of my thoughts, telling me to make an effort with my sister's future family. It probably had to do with Mummie pounding it into my head that nice begat nice and kind deeds brought good karma. Or whatever. But she was right. I couldn't step onto that stage with negative energy.

"Is this the first time you've seen an American school?" I asked Naveen.

"No. I've visited before and saw Pranit's school. It's a little different from mine. We go to a private school in Durban, and it looks like a giant mansion with lots of landscaped grounds. The architecture is more ornate. This is so compact."

Dang. Was he rich? He didn't need this scholarship money the way I needed it. "Welcome to the city."

As we walked, I searched the crowds for familiar faces, wondering if anyone from the many competitions and concerts I'd participated in would be here. Some of them had to be. My senior year was filled with virtuosity, and this competition was perfect for them.

Everyone started to blur together. It was hard to make out individuals when my vision pulsated with each heartbeat. Oh boy. If I ever passed out because of a performance, today could *not* be it.

We continued past the parade of talent to the check-in desk. A lot of the faculty were present today. The music teachers were all here, including my orchestra director, Mrs. Dyson. She grinned at me and handed me a stylus from her spot behind the check-in table. I grinned back as I signed in on the tablet. She always made me feel like I could accomplish anything.

"I was so excited when I saw your name," she told me. "Don't worry. You'll do amazing!"

Easy for her to say. Doing great wasn't the issue. I'd done great on my Juilliard audition video. She'd said so herself, having helped me film it. Standing out enough to make the Juilliard scout want me and change their mind about my admission was the issue.

Mr. Wallace, the band teacher, handed me a number. Fifteen.

"You'll get in line in order of number. Your name and information are already in our database, so the host, judges, and audience will know who you are as they call you onstage. There will be an attendant at the bottom of the stairs to check your information. If numbers and names get mixed up or out of order, they'll correct it. After you finish performing and exit stage left, you can stand in the wings and watch others perform. The committee will notify you via email either way and let you know if you're advancing to the next level, where the top twenty competitors will audition for the final round."

"The final round is still Saturday afternoon?" I asked carefully, mentally going over the logistics of how much time I had in between Saturday wedding events.

"It had to be moved back to this Saturday at eight P.M."

Oh crap. *Of course* it had gotten moved! My chest sort of imploded. Why was I even here? Worst-case scenario, they'd reiterate that I sucked by rejecting me twice. Best-case scenario, they'd think I was good enough to advance, and then I'd have to decide between my entire musical future or my sister's wedding garba.

Mr. Wallace went on, "When you receive a response, please confirm the committee's email, whether you're moving forward or not."

"Tha-thank you," I said, my shoulders trembling as I stuck the number to my chest.

"Don't be nervous, Zurika. You'll do great." He offered a reassuring smile.

I tried to return the smile, but it faltered. Sneaking out today was one thing, but sneaking out during Maitri's garba? Talk about a mission impossible.

Naveen checked in after me, and we shimmied into line. He leaned a shoulder against the wall, and I regarded him carefully. He seemed so mellow and calm, and here I was about to have a panic attack. Anxiety reared its head like a monster waiting in the dark.

"What?" he asked just as the line started moving.

"Did you know I'd be auditioning today, even before I told you?"

"How could I have known?" he asked, even as he started pushing around his ring again.

I arched a brow. His face turned all sorts of pink.

He sighed and said, "I had a strong feeling you would be."

"What is that supposed to mean?"

"When Pranit got engaged, we looked at all of his social media pics. He had posts of Maitri's family, of you. And then I sort of looked at your posts, too. And your videos. You stand out."

"So . . . earlier when you asked me what I played, were you pretending not to know or making conversation?" I asked pointedly.

"Both?" He scratched the back of his head. "You make interesting music."

Interesting? What the *crap* did that mean?

"Huh . . ." I turned back to the front of the line as a teacher called for our attention.

The line shuffled forward, and my grip on my violin case stiffened.

I focused on the front of the line as we listened to some of the best teen musical artists around. Most were local, but some came from all over the country, and a select few from around the world. A serious trumpet player really jammed up there, not to mention the vocals of the singer who came on next. I couldn't see her, but her Adele rendition with a Mariah Carey vocal range filled the auditorium. Her resonant voice left goose bumps on my skin. Then came a pianist with a haunting composition, a cello player, a guitarist, a drummer, a flutist . . .

Oh lord. Did I even stand a chance? They were all so amazing and mind-blowing. My entire body was shaking now. What if this didn't work out, either? What would I do then? I couldn't put off college forever trying to get into music schools.

"You're not freaking out, are you?" Naveen asked a little too innocently behind me, but there was a sharp, telling edge to his tone.

I narrowed my eyes and replied, "No." Nope. He was *not* going to get in my head. Not today!

"Because you're great. You'll knock 'em dead."

I tamped down my annoyance and asked over my shoulder, "Are you trying to psych me out? Because don't bother."

"Why would I do that?"

"Because we're both competing for the same thing."

He shook his head. "Have you seen yourself? On playback? Because you're amazing."

"What?" I spun around to face him.

He glanced away. "Maybe that sounded wrong. Promise I'm not a creeper. I've just never seen someone do what you do with a violin. It's extraordinary. The music, it's a whole other level."

"Oh . . ." I breathed. Then I rolled my eyes. Ha! He'd almost gotten me. I could not with this back-and-forth, trying to figure out his intentions. I had to focus on my performance, not on him.

Naveen looked past me and cocked his chin toward the shortening line. We were moving fast. Too fast. Nerves, pressure like this? It was no joke. Especially when it felt like your entire future depended on one single performance. Because mine sorta did.

I fully turned from Naveen and tried to find my inner calm. It was rolling around with a bunch of what-ifs. What if I failed at my last chance to get noticed by Juilliard scouts for next year? What if I couldn't make it to the final level? What if I did, but I couldn't leave Saturday's garba to compete? What if I got caught?

All right.

All right.

Let it all go, like a pent-up breath, before my head exploded.

Now that the negativity was swarming inside my head, it was time to weaponize it, taking all that energy and pouring it into competition mode. Energy was energy. It was all about how I used it.

I puffed out a breath. Easier said than done.

As we rounded the corner, the auditorium I'd practically lived in for the last few years turned larger than life. Suddenly, the ceilings were sky-high and the seating vast, the audience more numerous than I could count.

From here, the front row of seats was in full view. There were ten scouts in those chairs, armed with tablets and cell phones and the keys to my future. What sorts of notes were they jotting down? Were they supercritical, just one missed note enough to reject someone? Would they send videos back to their colleges?

Most importantly, which one was the scout from Juilliard? According to the audition website, she was a tall, blond, stern-looking woman named Lillian Ronald. I spotted her now as she pushed up her round-rimmed glasses and gave the slightest smirk at the performer. Beside her, an Indian scout nodded in thoughtful meditation. I didn't know of a lot of Indians in the music biz, so he stood out. According to the website, his name was Mihir Merchant, and he was a scout from the Manhattan School of Music.

Maybe it was just me, but it seemed like it was hardest for Indians to impress other Indians. Like, he probably thought I was out of my league here and would be better off in a lab. Woefully, I could pretty much cross him off the list of scouts who might be interested in me.

All the scouts looked hyperfocused as they studied each competitor, all dressed nice and elegantly in slacks and blouses and skirts.

Behind them, excitement and anxiety shimmied through the crowd as the current performer ended on a final exhilarating note.

I usually loved this kind of stuff, this feeling, the nervous high. I normally thrived on it, something both devasting and necessary. The what-ifs and terrible worries sort of eased away as my body remembered the love of playing. It was the only thing that had a chance of keeping my anxiety in the corner. Yet today anxiety gnawed on the edges of my thoughts, just waiting to take over.

My body was a battleground right now, and I couldn't tell which side was winning.

I gulped as we stepped forward, the stairs and the stage looming closer and closer.

The audience was probably filled with friends and family of those who were auditioning. Even though Krish wasn't out there, sitting in the front row cheering me on, I felt her presence, her force. *Dem Damani girls . . .*

Any moment now, I'd reach the bottom of the stairs, and there would be no more curtain to hide behind.

"Wow . . ." Naveen mumbled behind me. Yeah, he wasn't helping.

Anyone who had been nervous before was probably shaking in their shoes now. And anyone who didn't have the jitters before absolutely had them now. I definitely had them. They racked my body, had my hands shaking, my lips trembling, my heart spasming.

"Oh lord . . ." I muttered, and clutched my stomach with one hand while the other sweated around the violin case handle.

"Are you nervous?" he asked teasingly.

I was about five seconds from telling him to shut it. "Obviously."

"Why?" He smiled like this was no big deal. "You've done this a hundred times. It's no different. Just relax."

Yeah. Because that advice was, like, something I'd never thought of on my own. *Just chill. Stop making this a big deal.* Easy.

Also, he'd sounded quite condescending.

Naveen, a little too cocky, asked, "What's the problem, any-way? They're just people, those judges."

"They stand between you and your dreams," I reminded him. Except he knew that.

He shrugged. "If you think too long about it, you'll mess up," he whispered.

I narrowed my eyes and turned toward the front. Yep. Naveen Patel was definitely trying to throw me off my game. How dare he. We didn't even know one another, but he sure was making an enemy of himself. Some people seemed nice on the surface but were savage underneath that pretty exterior.

CHAPTER EIGHT
(Saturday Afternoon: Eight Days Until the Wedding)

#LoseControl

Maybe Naveen had given me a final gesture of encouragement/sabotage. Maybe I had accidentally tripped on my way up the steps. Maybe the auditorium had gotten dead quiet as I placed my purse on the table. Maybe the host had mispronounced my name. Maybe the contestants who'd already performed, who were watching from the other side of the stage, snickered and threw shade to tip me off my game.

I didn't really know. The seconds before a performance were always a blur, a haunting silence where only the *tip-tap* of my high heels against the steps and then the floor of the stage reverberated in the auditorium.

I moved to the front of the stage and took a moment to squint out at the several hundred people crowding the room. From the steps, the crowd had been an intimidating behemoth. But thank goodness for stage lights. A halo of light nearly blotted out the audience so performers like me could focus on their work instead of glaring eyes and distracting movement. It was about the only thing that made this moment slightly calmer.

Ever heard that saying that you could hear a pin drop, it was so quiet? Quiet wasn't a typical thing for me, not with a bunch of sisters and a big family and lots of friends and all the noise in my head. *This* was quiet—unnerving, haunting, eerie. One could drop a pin on the floor, and we'd all hear it as loudly as the person coughing in the back of the crowd.

All the nagging doubt I'd had waiting in line melted away . . . and puddled at my feet. Out of my head, but still here.

But I'd been here a hundred times in a hundred places, performing a hundred songs. Muscle memory kicked in, which was great, because it kept me from having to think.

This is my domain. I'd earned it, and I would own it.

Everything and nothing rode on this performance, because music had always been an extension of me. A part of me. It didn't stress me out or mess with my head. It completed me, made me whole, and brought me utter peace the second the violin touched my shoulder, the moment I settled against the chin rest and my bow flushed against the strings.

I swallowed hard and stared out at the halo of light and then at the blurred scouts who waited for me to actually do something. I had to close my eyes to forget them, to forget where I was, to forget how intense a moment like this could be. Instead, I let the music thrum through my veins, connect to my fingers, and escape through my perfectly chosen instrument.

There was a piece perpetually missing from my soul until my wrist and arm moved with emotion over the violin, and sweet music fluttered into the air like butterflies of a million colors dancing through the skies and touching the hearts of every person who could hear.

The music started with a mellow, classical rhythm to ease the audience into my melodious realm, to show the scouts that I was technically skilled. And then . . . I dropped the beats. Sudden cuts across the strings, slants and drags as I played the chords to a well-known hip-hop song, a chart-topper meant for clubs and parties.

I just had to do it. Missy Elliott's "Lose Control."

At first, the audience was quiet, and in the back of my barely perceptive mind, I wondered if they didn't get it. But then, because I knew Atlanta, my school, and what jams made my friends want to dance, the crowd erupted into cheers and *ooh*s and *ahh*s and *oh, damn*s.

I smiled to myself, lost in the music, until I opened my eyes and saw some of the people closest to the stage, those in line to my left, and those who had already performed to the right, all bobbing their heads and shrugging their shoulders and rolling out a little dance. The crowd was getting into it, and so was I. Because not only did I play the violin, I swayed to my own music. It flowed through my body, and I couldn't stop the beat. *No* one could stop the beat.

I played as long as I could, adding stretches just to keep the hype going, just to make sure the scouts remembered me: Zurika Damani . . . the girl who played hip-hop violin.

With a final swish across the strings, I ended with a sudden stop and lowered my arms to my sides, the bow in one hand, the violin in the other, and gave a short bow. A deafening applause mixed with whistles rumbled through the room. It vibrated up from the floor and showered down through the air.

Exhilarated—and relieved, more than anything—I retrieved my purse and walked offstage. Everyone near the wall excitedly congratulated me. I couldn't manage any words. All I could register was some of the scouts grinning hard and several taking fervent notes.

But Ms. Ronald of Juilliard? She didn't seem as impressed, and that had my head fighting to stay high.

My smile faltered as I looked at her. The greatness of success was quickly drowned out by my fear of failure. Was I truly not good enough?

Naveen took the stage next. It didn't take long for the crowd to fixate on him and forget all about me, not when he possessed such a commanding presence. I didn't really expect anything too astounding from him. I wasn't sure why.

The neck of my violin was slick with sweat from my hand. I laid it carefully on a table in the wings as I watched Naveen. He walked up to the microphone, glanced across the audience, found me on the sideline . . . and winked.

Was he taunting me? The freaking audacity!

Even if I *had* expected something incredible from Naveen, nothing would've prepared me for what happened next. Nothing would've made me believe that this Patel dude could croon like Ed Sheeran and Nelly smashed together. That didn't even make sense!

Naveen made vocal love to that microphone, barely touching it as his body swayed like some boy band member. His accent played soulfully through the mix of . . . what was that? My ears definitely picked up on the hip-hop vibes, and maybe some jazz? But there was something more.

We'd already heard some pro-level talent, but Naveen blew them out of the water. That voice, those lyrics reached deep into my being and actually made my heart palpitate. Before I could stop myself, my head was bobbing along with others and my hips were swaying to the seductive beat of his song.

Ugh. He was the one to beat. He was definitely the one to worry about. I couldn't believe he was a strong enough candidate to make me nervous, but would he show me up at the reception, too? He could not. I was sister to the bride! And just like that, like never before, a niggling jealousy clawed its way to the front of my thoughts.

While everyone was busy applauding and cheering and losing their minds, I bit my lower lip and frowned.

Naveen bowed and walked offstage with a wave to his admiring throng. He strolled down the steps right toward me as if what he had done was no big deal. He stopped a mere few inches from me and looked down from that ridiculous height of his, the elation glimmering in his eyes and dabbed across his rosy cheeks, the heaving of his chest making me feel like he had only two things on his mind at this very second: his amazing performance . . . and having succeeded at getting into my head.

Before I could congratulate him, he said, "And that's how it's done." Then he had the nerve to mime a mic drop and mouthed, "Bam."

What. The. Crap? *This* was the guy my mom liked for me? *This* guy? Oh, hell no. There was no way I wanted to get to know him, much less entertain the idiotic notion of dating him one day.

My mouth dropped open. I had no words. Part of my brain called out *good sportsmanship,* but the other part was screaming *take him down!*

He walked past me to thank everyone who had congratulated him along the wall.

All right. So he had done a phenomenal job. And what? So had a bunch of others. He had something to be proud of, but could he stop grinning so hard, like he'd already won this thing?

I searched the scouts for Ms. Ronald, but she was concentrating on the stage. I couldn't watch the rest of the performers, and I didn't want to talk to Naveen, who was chattering on.

"Did you hear me?" Naveen asked.

"What?" I replied, not looking at him.

"I said you did a good job."

I scoffed. A good job? How patronizing. I rolled my eyes and checked my phone. No word from the guy cousins.

The rest of the performers were all amazing in their own ways, and I had total respect for their art. But based on how the judges and the audience had reacted, I'd say this guy who was leaning against the wall beside me was my biggest competition. He had everyone eating out of his hand, including the other competitors. While the rest of us were pretty darn good, he was practically untouchable.

Ugh. Why was he even here? How had he not gotten into a music college off the bat?

CHAPTER NINE
(Saturday Afternoon: Eight Days Until the Wedding)

#CompetitionGettingReal

Just as the last performer finished their solo, I turned and left with Naveen on my heels.

"Are you going home?" he asked.

"Yeah," I muttered. I had things to get done, parents to make an appearance for, and a room that I wanted to cry in without having this guy all up in my space.

I wanted to stop him right then and there and ask him where he thought he was going, but I didn't have it in me. Although the auditorium had been chilly enough, a fresh surge of AC blasted us as soon as we exited into the back hall. It was much quieter here, and we were away from inquisitive eyes, making it easier to calm down.

We walked past some people lingering in the halls by the glass trophy case jammed with awards and medals and plaques, and then around the corridor. I pushed against the double doors and moved outside, where the nice chilled air stayed behind and the muggy heat of Atlanta sizzled my skin.

"Hey, hold up." Naveen jogged around to stand in front of me just before we reached the courtyard, where bolted-down metal grate tables and benches were a popular hangout before school.

"What?" I snapped, annoyed that he probably expected a ride home, too.

"Are you upset with me?"

"You're kind of arrogant," I replied.

"What?" he asked, as if no one had ever accused him of such a thing. I highly doubted that.

"You tried to get in my head, like, *hey, just relax*." I mocked his low tone. "*It's no big deal. You've done it a hundred times*." Naveen scoffed, and I went on in my normal voice, "And then you so arrogantly acted like you did such an amazing job."

"Wait a minute." He guffawed. "So I shouldn't have been encouraging? And I shouldn't have been proud of my performance? Look, I get that you might be insecure—"

"Insecure!" I fumed, my blood turning into fire and scorching my veins.

He shook his head and took a step back. "Wait. No. I didn't mean—"

"Naveen. You can call yourself an Uber to get back."

He touched my elbow as I turned to stomp off. "Don't leave like this."

"Don't tell me what to do," I spat.

"Look. I'm sorry if I came off the wrong way."

I crossed my arms. "Tell me if you did it on purpose. And be honest. Do *not* play games with me during this of all weeks."

He twisted the corner of his mouth, and how a guy could look so adorable yet impish was beyond me. He knew, too. He knew he could probably get away with all sorts of trickery and schemes because of that face. "OK. OK. I did it on purpose. I didn't mean to. I'm just competitive, I guess."

"I'm competitive, too, but that doesn't mean I'm a jerk about it. You can be competitive and supportive."

"Well, I'm sorry. You did really great. Kind of mind-blowing, actually." His face flushed, and he scratched the back of his arm as if maybe he regretted gushing about his competition.

"Sweet words won't win me over," I muttered, and checked my phone to find a text from Meet. Finally. But then I frowned.

"What is it?" Naveen asked.

"My cousins said they need another half hour."

"Oh." He stuffed his hands into his pockets and looked around. "What do you want to do?"

Well, first off, he could do whatever he wanted for however long he wanted. I had never said I was going to give him a ride back.

I placed my violin case on a table and sat on the bench that curved around it. The metal was warm against my butt and the backs of my legs. Naveen, to my annoyance, sat beside me.

I groaned, throwing my head back.

"Before you tell me to shove off, please accept my apology," he said, but there went his voice, like before. Low and laced with mischief, saying one thing and meaning something else.

"I don't trust you, dude."

"I gave you a reason not to, huh? But I also told you a secret."

"What? That your parents don't want you to be a singer or know that you're out here? How do I know you're not lying about that?"

"I'm Indian?" he asked-answered.

All right. So I got that. His parents probably didn't want this for him.

"Can we start over?" he implored with doe eyes, which absolutely didn't work on me.

"Now that the competition is done?"

"We have one more level. It ain't over. I'll try my hardest not to throw you off. But I gotta admit, if that was you thrown off, then I'm definitely toast."

I spun my cell phone on the table, wondering about the results. People were pouring out the front doors. It'd been all of five minutes since the competition had ended, and already the suspense of where we ranked had diminished my sanity. "You think we'll get to the final level?"

"Are you kidding me? We had those scouts checking the floor for their dropped jaws."

I watched him carefully. Despite his confidence, he had this subtle twitch at the corner of his mouth, and there he went, playing with his ring. Why did that bother me so much?

"It was all a blur when I finished. I don't remember," I said.

"Take it from me, the scouts were eating out of your hand. That's not a performance they'll forget. I mean, didn't you hear them roaring with applause? And that section where you went crazy fast, I thought you were going to break your strings. And how do you dance while you play? I can't even wrap my head around the coordination."

I smiled, half fake. "Flattery only gets you so far."

"I'm being honest. Part of my competitiveness is not appreciating my competition, so it's hard to say this aloud to you. I usually try to find flaws to show myself I'm better." He stopped playing with the ring and tapped the grate surface of the table.

"You're twisted."

He crossed his arms and set his elbows on the table. "All right. So it's twisted, but I gotta do something, right? You know how it is."

I cocked an eyebrow, inviting him to elaborate. He sure had a negative way of dealing with stuff. Stress and anxiety were one thing, but picking apart someone else? That was too low for me to handle.

"The pressure gets to everyone."

"Doesn't seem to get to you," I countered.

He pressed his lips together and looked away. So maybe he wasn't as confident and cocky as he tried to make himself out to be. Maybe it was all an act to help him deal. Still. There had to be a better way than messing with other people's heads and mentally tearing them apart.

"How do you deal with it, then?" he asked quietly.

I shrugged. "The opposite. Appreciating everything my competition did well and empathizing with what didn't go well. They're people, too. They're trying to get somewhere, just like me. We have way too much in common to view them all as enemies. Besides, there's no room in my world for negativity. I'd rather be happy. I'd rather congratulate them and focus on their incredible talents than try to psych them out like some shady person." I eyed him.

He lowered his gaze for a second. "I guess that makes for a better mentality, huh?"

"No crap."

He laughed, and just like that, his false confidence reared its head. "All right. I'll try it your way." He pushed the ring around his finger once.

"Just don't get *in* my way."

There was a moment of silence between us.

Instead of simmering in this guy's negative vibes, I took my own advice and leaned on good sportsmanship. It was more for me than for him, though. "You performed really well. I'll have to keep an eye on you."

He looked up at me. "Same."

"So . . . where are you from in South Africa?"

"Durban. It's a city in KwaZulu-Natal Province," he replied with pride.

"That sounds interesting. I've read about Durban. How long are you here for?"

His brows shot up. "You mean, how long do you have to see my face?"

I waved my hand. "Or, ya know, be annoyed by it."

He grinned. "I'm leaving a couple of days after the wedding. Was hoping to sightsee a bit, but I doubt I'll get time."

"Probably not with a wedding and a contest. You double-booked yourself."

He poked a fingernail into one of the table's metal diamonds. "I want to try some local food, at least. I hear the burgers are a must."

"You eat meat?" I asked, not knowing why it was a surprise. I shouldn't have assumed all Patels were vegetarian.

"Yeah. Don't tell my parents, though."

"For someone I just met, you sure are telling me a lot of secrets."

He slouched over the table. "Guess I gotta earn your trust after earlier. Better be on my best behavior."

I smacked my lips, not buying it. "Mmm-hmm. By the way, what kind of song was that, the one you sang? The rhythm was sort of familiar but sort of not."

He beamed as he explained. "Ah. So, growing up in South Africa, you know we get American, Indian, and of course African influences. There was a little bit of hip-hop, some jazz, and Bantu beats. We grow up hearing it and study it in school. I like to build them on each other."

"That's just . . . wow." I couldn't even wrap my head around that. How did he know how to combine such different beats and make it sound like one flawless genre? "I can't believe your parents don't support you, knowing you can sing like that."

"Your family supports your musical ambitions?" he asked dryly.

I played my poker face, thinking of my cousins. "If the wedding wasn't about to happen, my family would be here. Does your brother know? I mean, he could've had his date afterward."

Naveen glanced down and pulled out his phone. There was a flicker of sadness on his face, like he wished his brother had come here instead of going on a date.

He checked his phone. "My brother hasn't texted. He must be having a good time."

"Does he like your singing?" I asked.

"Neelish thinks I sing well. He doesn't see it as a future, though. He and my parents want me to go into engineering. I don't mind. It's logical, and I'm good at it. But this was my shot at trying to make something of my music. I have to go for it, you know?"

I nodded. Oh boy, did I know. "Are you scared of failing?"

He scoffed and pushed his ring around. "Me? Did you hear my voice? No."

Yet the way his voice went up a level told me that he was probably as scared as I was.

"Did you apply to any music colleges here?"

"All of them," he replied with a nervous laugh. And that had to be the first time I'd seen him doubt himself. He had a great front.

"Heard from any?"

"Mostly rejections."

Well, so much for keeping the sting of Juilliard in the background. Just hearing the word—*rejection*—woke up the anxiety monster. Even though I tried not to take joy in the suffering of others, at least I wasn't the only one getting passed up. If Naveen, who was this phenomenal, had gotten rejected, then maybe I didn't totally suck. Maybe it was simply a matter of other applicants being more competitive.

He went on, "Trying not to check application status. Hoping to have a good time while I'm here. What about you?"

"No good news yet," I replied casually, not wanting to talk about colleges anymore. "Aren't you going to be in some of the wedding dances?"

"Yeah. We have one for garba and then another for the reception. We're supposed to meet with the bride's side to coordinate and bring our parts together. Are you performing the violin at the reception?"

"Yes. Of course. And speaking of reception performances, don't try to outshine me," I warned.

"What?" he choked out.

I explained slowly, "What you did in there? Don't try that at the reception."

"Are you that threatened by me? Wow, that's quite the compliment, to be honest."

I sucked in a breath. Nope. Never let the nemesis know how much of a threat they truly are. "You wish. Look. You're a good singer, but this is *my* sister's wedding and *my* moment to give her something special."

"I get it. Don't worry. My song is nothing like what I performed back there. It's way toned down, a love song."

I eyed him for a few minutes before he suggested, "What if we combine forces?"

"Not a chance. My spotlight."

"I mean, if you want to make it a little more interesting."

"Maitri doesn't like last-minute changes."

He raised an eyebrow. "Doesn't hurt to ask."

"Hmm. Maybe." I leaned toward him, my hands clasped on the table, and warned, "But I don't fully trust you. So don't try to pull a stunt."

He held a hand over his chest in mock pain. "Think I'd risk my parents' eternal wrath by ruining my dear cousin's reception? Hurts that you think I'm actually heartless."

"Just ruthless, huh?"

He tossed his head. "Oh my god. I'm sorry, OK?"

"Don't play those mind games or try to take my reception spotlight. Don't come for me again, Naveen Patel."

"Or what?" he shot back.

"Or I'll show you what ruthless is."

He grinned. "I doubt you have a mean bone in your body, much less a vindictive one."

Heat curled over my skin. "You don't know me. I *will* if you mess up my sister's reception or try to sabotage my audition."

He nodded, seeming somewhat impressed. "Noted."

I sat back, arms crossed.

Naveen's phone screen lit up. He read the message. "That's Neelish. He said . . . don't wait up. Ugh. Now I have to cover for him?"

"Sounds like your brother is having a *really* good date."

Naveen groaned. "He's getting desperate. My parents are worried that he'll never find a girl. It's drama all the time. You know how it goes."

"How old is he?"

"Twenty-four."

I waved a hand. "That's not a big deal. Parents worry way too much about marriage stuff. I'm just waiting for the hammer to drop. I'm ready."

His brows shot up. "Ready to get matched?"

"Oh, hecks no. I'm ready to withstand anything they throw at me. They're not going to make a dent."

Naveen tapped the table beside his phone. "Well, you know they're devising our match, right?"

I almost choked. "Say what now?"

He leaned in as if to tell me the world's biggest secret. His expression turned intense, brooding, and a half smirk revealed one single dimple. A tuft of otherwise perfectly styled hair curled down in a rebellious S over his forehead. Then he said, in the most matter-of-fact tone ever, "Zurika Damani . . ."

Oh crap. Was he going to propose? This was *so* not a Bollywood movie! Dude, please don't do this. Don't make me put you and your expectations in place and warp every encounter this week into cringeworthy awkwardness. I want to enjoy my sister's wedding. Is that too much to ask?

But then Naveen's superbly convincing face broke into a full-on grin.

"Oh, you had me going," I grunted.

"You thought I was going to propose, didn't you?"

I shook my head. "Thank god our parents are not seriously expecting us to get to know each other."

"Well . . . actually—"

"Seriously?" I groaned.

"Some aunties planted the idea in our moms' heads."

I rolled my eyes. "Of course." Meddling aunties . . . "Such noise, right?"

"Honestly? I thought it was nonsense, trying to get to know a girl now to maybe get serious with later. But then I saw your pictures and videos, and now in person? Not such a bad idea . . ." There was that small twitch at the corner of his mouth. I wondered if he knew he did that. How did he go from an amazing singer straight out of *American Idol* to this shy guy? Or was he just messing with me, and this was all an act?

I shrugged indifferently. "We're way too young. Get your hormones in check. You're here for what, a week?" I muttered.

"Well . . . I guess that means . . . that I have a week to make you like me."

I smiled with a wicked edge. "Sounds like a challenge no guy can handle."

"Guess the right guy has never tried."

I couldn't quite tell if he was serious, joking, or trying to toy with me.

Naveen Patel could play all the tricks he wanted, but there was nothing more satisfying in this moment than slashing his ego in half. I interlocked my fingers on the table and said, "Trust me, better guys have tried. You, my competitive, negatively reinforced, mind-tripping soon-to-be sort-of relative who just told me he wouldn't mess with me, are *not it*."

"*Ouch*," he said, his expression contorting in feigned pain.

CHAPTER TEN
(Saturday Evening: Eight Days Until the Wedding)

Once Krish texted to give the green light, the guy cousins and I quietly eased open the front door. Not that it mattered, because everyone was packed into the kitchen two rooms over, clanking pots, cooking, and laughing their merry heads off.

The perfume of the long-since-lit incense had faded, overpowered by the smell of spices and sweets, a deliciously intoxicating combination. Sweets heavy with jaggery and nuts, spiced with cardamom and saffron. Drool trickled out the corner of my mouth.

Krish took my violin case, and we hurried up the steps. Her brothers walked down the hallway and were hailed upon arrival. My family literally cheered their return, as if delivering the kankotri had ensured the wedding would happen.

We turned at the top of the stairs. My parents' room was to the right, next to the laundry room, and a short hallway on the left led to the other three bedrooms.

"Tell me everything!" Krish whispered as she locked my bedroom door behind me.

"I was so nervous," I confessed as I pulled my dress out of my backpack. I tripped over a pile of bright orange and pink fabrics studded with sequins.

Krish shoved the violin case back into place by the window while I swung open the closet door and reached for a hanger to carefully put away the audition dress.

A knock sounded on the door, and then the doorknob jiggled.

"Oh crap!" I mouthed, staring at the door and then at Krish.

Krish tossed my shoes into the closet, and I flung my dress in after them.

"Who is it?" I asked loudly.

"Neha. Why is the door locked?" Neha asked, jiggling the doorknob even harder, like she was one thrust away from smashing it open.

I tossed my backpack into the closet as Krish opened the door. Neha, being the ever-exuberant and entitled little sister that she was, barged in and eyed the room, then me, then Krish. If she could put her perceptive, curious energy into literally anything else, that would be great.

She crossed her arms and leaned against the wall. Neha was the loudest out of the four of us—she took after Mummie the most. Her filter was constantly off. She spoke her mind without thinking about consequences. She got away with it because she was the cute baby. But she was also extremely smart and scrupulous. One look at me, and dang, she knew.

I sighed and trudged through the pile of boxes to get to my hamper in the corner. "What's up? I have laundry to do and dinner to eat."

"Where'd you go?"

"I went with the guys. Why? Miss me while you had to stuff goody bags?"

She groaned. "Yeah. Guess who got put on ribbon-curling duty?" She lifted her hands as if to demand sympathy by showing off her nonexistent calluses.

I smiled. "Glad it wasn't me."

"Why'd you go over there?" she probed, crossing her arms again.

"To take pictures. Duh. You heard that when the parents let me go."

"Mmm-hmm . . ." She watched me with that intense indifference that made Neha as intimidating as she was pretty. Her favorite grape-flavored purple lip gloss was a stark contrast between her playful quirks and her cutthroat tendencies.

"You got something to say?" I asked, calling her bluff.

"Can I see the pictures?" She raised her brows and extended her hand.

"Why? Don't believe me?" I asked, telling myself not to swallow. Swallowing was almost always a sign of lying.

"I didn't see them posted on social," she replied, all innocent. She would, of course, be the only one to think about checking the social media account for an update on part two of this morning's ceremony.

Quick! Think of something! Aha! "I haven't decided which ones to post yet. Have to choose filters and edit and think of witty captions. It's harder than it looks, you know?"

She eyed me and replied without missing a beat, "It never takes you long to do those things, though."

"There has to be a certain elegance and tone to these. It's why Maitri asked me to take over," I reminded her.

I dragged out the hamper, struggling to get the overfull thing past the boxes. Krish helped by lifting. The hamper was flimsy plastic, anyway. It'd break before I could drag it out on my own.

"Can I see the pictures? Maybe I can help." Neha wiggled her fingers. Oh lord. Why wouldn't she leave it alone? She was never this "helpful."

Krish gave me a silent, pensive look as we lowered the hamper before she dropped onto my bed. She bit her fingernails out of habit but caught herself after a second and stopped. She pulled out her phone, pretending not to be in the middle of this.

"What are you getting at?" I asked Neha. "Just be direct. We don't have time."

"I think you bounced and ran off to that audition that I heard Mummie telling you not to go to."

I stilled, suddenly aware of how clammy my hands were. "You heard that?"

She smirked. "We *all* heard that. That's why Urvi and Maitri warned you to behave. But you didn't listen. I think you went anyway."

I really hoped Neha couldn't see any reaction in me, because what if she told everyone where I'd been? My mom would literally scream at me and watch me like a hawk from here on out. There went my last chance at Juilliard!

I said coolly, "You're speculating. And reaching."

"I had to come in here to get mesh bags and ribbons from one of the boxes, and I noticed that your violin was gone, too." She looked past me at the case, which had returned to its usual spot by the window.

I shrugged, my thoughts whirling around for a solid, believable response. "And? If I was getting out of the house, I thought I'd have a minute to play something, even if it was just during the car ride. You have your video games to help you relax. Maitri has books. Urvi has baking. I have playing the violin. So, what of it?"

She smacked her lips with that unruly attitude of hers, and I prayed she wouldn't make me straight-up lie to her face. She asked, "Are you going to let me see the pictures, then?"

"Are you going to tattle otherwise?" I countered.

She narrowed her eyes and got quiet. Yep. That got her. If there was one thing Neha hated more than not getting what she wanted, it was being called a narc. "I won't tell, but I don't believe you."

I pulled out my phone, because what else could I do? I'd had it on silent for the auditions, and I only just now saw two AirDrop notifications from the guy cousins. I didn't have to ask to know that Krish had texted them to send me pictures.

Thank the lord for plotting cousins who came prepared.

I immediately accepted the pictures and handed Neha the phone. "Well, to get you off my case, here they are."

She squinted suspiciously before going through the pictures. She cracked a smile at some of the funnier ones.

"Happy?" I asked, taking my phone back.

"I still think you're up to something."

"Don't you have ribbons to curl?"

"No. Unlike you, I'm a fast worker." She spun on her heel and skipped down the hall just as Jyoti and Sethal jogged past her and came crashing into my room.

They closed the door, and we all dropped onto my barely made bed. I could breathe now without worrying about Neha annihilating my cover story. For a second there, I'd thought I was toast. "Thank god they took pictures," I whispered. "Thanks for texting them."

Krish giggled. "For sure. OK! Tell us what happened."

"Just in time for the recap!" the other girls said, shimmying with excitement.

"Yeah. It was freaking amazing." I rubbed my fingernails against my leggings and blew on them, like *no big deal*. "I did what I do." They didn't need to know that I nearly barfed on the way up to the stage or that I might've made a fool of myself, given the lack of interest Ms. Ronald had expressed.

Krish nudged me with her shoulder just as Jyoti shoved me into the center of a growing cloud of laughter and applause and an ambush of hugs.

"Of course you did! Did the scouts announce you the best on the spot?" Sethal asked.

"I wish!" I forced a smile. My chest tingled at the memory of that Juilliard judge looking not one ounce impressed by me.

Not to mention that the cut from Juilliard's rejection was only a half-day old. What was I supposed to do now? Wait. Stress.

Pray. But I supposed the great thing about never getting much quiet alone time was that I didn't have many opportunities to dwell on the bad stuff.

"What happens next?" Krish asked.

I face-palmed. "Worst case is that I don't make the cut and I'll be a nobody the rest of my life. Slightly less worst case is that I make it to the next and final level . . . which is happening Saturday night!"

"During garba?" Sethal gasped.

I nodded, my lips quivering. "Yeah. It got moved. What am I going to do, guys? I can't just leave Maitri's garba. We have performances and photo ops and videographers."

The girls looked at one another in a fleeting second of dead silence.

"What time will it be? Maybe we can get the intro and dances done and get you out the door in time?" Krish said, hopeful.

My chest deflated. Just the idea of running around during the second-busiest day of the weekend had me feeling all kinds of exhausted. Evading a kitchen full of family wasn't the same as slipping away from two hundred garba guests. "That would be cutting it tight."

Krish took my elbow, sensing my apprehension. "You might be the last to perform, but you can make it. You have to try."

I rubbed the back of my neck, anxiety creeping up my skin like marching ants. Should I risk messing up my sister's dances or risk losing my last chance at Juilliard?

As I searched through and edited the photos from the guys, I admitted, "All the talent there was beyond amazing. There was a lot of intense competition. Even Naveen. I don't even know if I'll make it to the next round, so why am I worrying? I just don't know—"

"Wait. Who's Naveen?" Krish interrupted.

"Oh. Pranit's cousin from South Africa. I almost ran him over when he was trying to ask for a ride."

The girls snickered. I didn't have the best reputation with them for my driving, so I was sure it wasn't hard for them to imagine what had happened.

"Did you beat him, though?" Krish asked, her tone harsh. I absolutely understood that she wanted me to win and get my second chance, that she wanted me to reach my dreams without someone else cutting in front of me, that her competitiveness had brought her far and would take her through med school. But her dark side was rearing its ugly head, because Krish was scary competitive AF.

"I mean, I don't know. It's not like they gave us a rating on the spot, and neither will the rest of them." I gnawed on my lower lip, my brows creasing with worry.

"Don't fret. Naveen won't get that top spot. We know you did awesome with a fantastic, out-of-this-world performance."

"Magical," Jyoti added. "As it always is."

"Clubworthy," Sethal said in a sultry voice.

"Juilliardworthy," Krish said with her chin held high.

Jyoti giggled. "Moneymakerworthy."

"Hotlanta Mama!" Sethal hollered.

And the gushing went on and on. "OK, OK. I get it!" I said. Ugh. Could we just change the subject? Like how these new posts had already gotten a dozen likes?

"Do you, though?" Krish asked. "Because you're worried, and you shouldn't be. You made it out there and didn't get caught. Now, enjoy all the prewedding drama and prepare for the next level. Don't even worry about how to get there. Just stay positive."

"Easier said than done. What do you mean, not worry!" I asked.

"You've got this!"

"Yeah," Sethal and Jyoti added, and all three hugged me.

My fam? They really made me. They bombarded me with strength, optimism, and confidence, pushing away all the nagging doubts.

"More details. How did it feel up there? What did you play? When do you find out the results?" Krish prodded.

I'd barely opened my mouth when Maitri rapped on the door twice and let herself in. We tamped down the conversation real quick.

CHAPTER ELEVEN
(Saturday Evening: Eight Days Until the Wedding)

#DesiMatchmaking

Well?" Maitri asked, dressed in light pink designer pajama pants with a matching T-shirt. Her hair was still down and styled, but her face had been cleansed to reveal perfect dewy skin. The entire length of her arms was covered in shiny metallic gold, rose, green, and blue ribbons. She took center stage as she knee-crawled onto the middle of the bed.

All the girls gathered around. Except Neha. She watched from the door.

"Well, what?" I asked.

"Heard you met a certain young man from Durban?" she asked with a teasing voice.

I clamped down a gasp. Did she know, then, that we had left together? "You mean some random guy who is singing at your reception?" I bit out instead.

Her cheeks flushed. "Oh, yeah. I meant to tell you."

My gut sank. How could she? She knew how important this was for me, and he was just another cousin she'd probably never hear from again. He could perform at any reception; but why *this* one? "Maitri! He's going to outshine my violin solo. It's supposed to be my night."

"I think you mean *my* night."

I waved off her words and fumed. "You know what I mean. Me playing is a special, unique, personal, emotional gift to you, and now someone else, who isn't even that close to you, is going to share the spotlight."

She ambush-hugged me, and it was all I could do not to suffocate in a cloud of ribbons. "No one can outshine you! I'm sure he's a good singer, but you're an amazing violinist. Your gift will still be special for us no matter what."

She didn't even know how mind-blowing Naveen was. What if he stomped me out of the competition *and* out of the reception? People would be talking about this wedding for years—how beautiful it was, how extravagant and big—and instead of remembering the impressive violin solo cherry on top, they'd be mentioning some cousin from afar, never to be seen again.

Maitri sat back and said, "Mummie is all about this Naveen guy. Not that you should be thinking about anything serious with a guy, but how is he?"

Oh, how to say this? He was my mortal enemy right now.

I heaved out a breath. "You guys are ridiculous."

Maitri clapped twice. "He told Pranit that he liked you so far. And what? His mom and our mom are trying to make it happen? What world are we living in?"

I scrunched up my face and swept a hand down the length of my body. "First of all: What's not to like about me?"

Neha crowed. "The catch of the decade known as Zuri motha'-freaking Damani."

"Hey, watch your mouth," Maitri warned.

Neha shrugged with her telltale cunning smile that made her look both utterly adorable and absolutely devious. The world wasn't ready for the schemes that were to come.

I went on, "Secondly, you can't take Mummie's ambitions seriously right now. She is both joyful and destroyed over losing you, and weddings are on her mind twenty-four seven. She doesn't know what she's saying or doing at this point."

"Look. I have things to do, so you better spill the tea," Maitri said, readjusting the ribbons snaked around her arms. "We all know she's not serious about you getting married anytime soon, but she has a point that you can get to know a guy for a good long time. There's no shame in looking around early."

She said that now, but come to think of it, Mummie had suggested Pranit to Maitri back in her early days of college. *Just talk, get to know each other, be friends* was all she kept saying, practically programming his number into Maitri's phone for her. So Mummie did have an eye for these things. She wasn't all drama.

"He's OK . . ." I said, biting my tongue.

"Nah. Tell us the truth," Neha demanded. Oh, so now she was all about this. She moved to the bed and flung herself on top, bouncing on her knees and grinning like a fool. "We just stalked his social for the third time. He is kinda hot. And you're cute, I guess," Neha concluded.

We gawked at her. Neha had a no-shame honesty-to-your-face complex. If her mouth had a filter, we'd be hard-pressed to find it. So when she complimented anyone, it was a true moment of unadulterated praise.

"But you could do something with that hair," she added.

And there it was. The real Neha.

"Always in a bun or ponytail. The hairdressers must have something in mind for you during the wedding. Something extra to tame all that."

I tossed a pillow at her face, which she grabbed and spoke muffled, incoherent insults into.

"Did you decide which hairstyles you want for the wedding?" Maitri asked, reining in our soon-to-be pillow fight. Neither Neha nor I came to play when it came to fighting with stuffed items. She had ripped the arm off my favorite teddy bear once, and I'd beheaded her best toy. All was fair in sister fights.

"You should really make an effort if you're going to snag someone like Naveen," Neha crooned with laughter.

"Oh boy. He's also kinda conceited and cocky and narcissistic," I admitted. "If you want to know the truth."

"Swoon," Neha sang.

"No swoon! Don't *ever* fall for a guy that arrogant. Whatever pointless plot our moms hatched was ruined the second he started talking."

Maitri laughed. "Just as well. You're much too young, sweets. You have to wait until at least college graduation to decide something like this. Preferably law school graduation. Tastes change, and so will your patience with guys."

I flicked a piece of lint off my leggings. Law school seemed ever more present in my future if this Juilliard scout didn't make a move. "Yeah. Way too much to do before settling down. Why are we even talking about this?" I playfully tossed a pillow at Maitri, who dodged just in time. "You're always shoving me away from the mere idea of dating."

Her smile widened. "Oh, it's just funny to see the next sister being harassed by Mummie to meet the right guy. It will stave off her insistence that I have a baby within the next five years."

Peak elder sister deflection.

"Parents didn't get mad that I was gone, then?" I asked.

Maitri promised, "No. They were too busy cooking. Besides, we got an assembly line going after lunch and filled all the small mesh bags with snacks. Just have to tie ribbons on the goody boxes now." She eyed Neha. "Those nimble, skinny little fingers will work perfectly."

Neha dramatically threw her head back. "What even is my life right now?"

No one had missed the sister of the bride, huh? Maybe they wouldn't miss me if I got to the final stage of auditions. Could I actually sneak out of garba when there would be more than two hundred people there to get lost in?

"Are you guys staying late?" I asked.

"We're sleeping over!" Jyoti replied.

Oh boy. A bunch of people roaming through the house like a herd of gazelles twenty-four seven and most likely all up in my room. Mummie and Maitri were already letting themselves in and out at all hours getting this or that. Mummie had run out of space in her bedroom, seeing as she also had Papa's things, a heap of saris to pass out to all the women on the groom's side (count 'em, twenty-six!), plus the emblems the parents needed before and after the wedding.

And the bride couldn't have anything out of place in her room or she'd climb out of her skin with anxiety. Maitri needed everything in perfect order so she could easily find things and not feel cluttered and claustrophobic. Plus, she didn't want to get sick with dust allergens from having a ton of extra things in her space.

Urvi and Jijaji #1's room, the study downstairs, was small and already filled with their stuff. No one wanted to put anything in Neha's room, where Masi slept, so she could rest in peace. Neha would probably crash on the floor, because she had very violent episodes of kicking and punching in her sleep. She might even crash on my floor . . . which meant half of our cousins would crash on my floor, too. Guess *I* didn't need to be mindful of allergens and having my sleep interrupted or losing 85 percent of my privacy or feeling confined to a tiny corner and not knowing where anything was in this sea of madness.

All that on top of depending on this competition to get back into Juilliard's good graces, a situation on which all my hopes and dreams hinged.

I blew out a ragged breath. Nah. I wasn't stressed one single bit.

"OK. What's on the agenda for tonight?" I asked, trying to ward off the hundred worries swarming my head like angry gnats.

"Needlepoint and thread designs," Maitri replied a little too giddily as she took off the ribbons.

She and Urvi brought over the Styrofoam cutouts while I dug around the sleeping dragon of boxes in search of the DIY crafts container. I searched and searched, careful not to disturb the more delicately placed items. Believe or it not, some of the stacks were organized in order of event.

"I can't find it," I called behind me.

"What are you looking for?" Urvi asked.

"Thread and thumbtacks."

"They're in the garage," Maitri said. "Neha, can you bring up the plastic tote that says 'murals'?"

"Sure." She hopped off the bed and out the door.

Since there wasn't much space on the floor, we sat on my bed while Urvi took the desk chair, pulling it close to the footboard so she could work with us but still have her giant water bottle within reach on the desk.

We had three Styrofoam murals to work on: one oval and three feet tall and two peacock shapes about two feet tall. The oval surface had been painted gold while the peacock ones were painted a shimmery green. The oval one had a faint pencil drawing of Ganesh with a border, and the peacock ones had basic drawings of peacocks. Maitri's friends were working on the other three at their place, which would go to Pranit's house.

I'd seen thread designs before, and they looked pretty cool. Maitri's friends had done the base work of cutting the Styrofoam, smoothing it out, painting it, and drawing the sketches.

Neha returned with tote in hand. Maitri opened the container and pulled out several smaller containers. Each had a different-colored ball of glitter yarn: a dark red-orange, peacock green and blue, silver, deep purple, and of course gold. Then she set several boxes of clear tacks between us.

"Here's what we do," Maitri started. She demonstrated as she spoke. "Take a thumbtack and press it into one of the lines already drawn. Make sure it is directly on the line and almost touching the next thumbtack, so you can't see the drawing. And once all the thumbtacks are in, we're going to take the yarn, twist it around one thumbtack, then around the next one, then back and forth until all the thumbtacks are connected. In the end, it'll be a very pretty 3-D thread mural."

She showed us pictures on Pinterest, and she was right—it looked way awesome. But come on, when did DIY projects ever look like their Pinterest counterparts?

As if she could read my mind, Maitri assured, "Don't worry. My friends have done these before, and they always look the same. They'll come out great! They'll take up some of the white space on the wall in the living room for the house events."

What white space? "Because we don't have enough decorations?" I grumbled.

She shot me a sharp look. "No. Now get to thumbtacking, minions."

We mimicked her with a cartoonish high tone, a scowl, and a back-and-forth head bobble. But then we got to work. I took an entire peacock mural and a box of thumbtacks for myself, positioning my back against a stack of *my* pillows, because good lord, I'd have to fight Neha for them *and* struggle to keep them from my cousins. But the corner was also a great vantage point to get some more pics for social, glimpses of crafts and hands and glittering thread.

Maitri worked on the other peacock mural for about an hour before she put everything down and announced, "I'm headed off to bed for my beauty sleep."

I'd seen her enough times postshower in our shared bathroom to know her routine: slather herself with scented essential oils; smooth on charcoal toners, vitamin C serum, or retinol face and neck cream; pat on eye cream and velvety hand cream; and apply lip scrub. She'd get under a weighted blanket on top of a memory-foam bed with a hypoallergenic neck-supporting pillow in a temperature-controlled room with a dehumidifier. Then she'd turn on gentle white noise that would die down on a timer and sleep like an angel in a silk mask.

As for me? I was lucky if I showered once a day and owned a bottle of face wash. My body lotion was the same as my face lotion, and deodorant was a thing I sometimes remembered to apply.

About the same time Maitri left, Urvi set down her needlework on the partition cloth, the one that would separate the groom from the bride before the wedding. She leaned back and took a gulp of water before heading to her room with a yawn.

"Good night," she said.

"Night!" we called back.

I crawled over my cousins to get off the bed and traipsed downstairs for water myself. I really needed to keep a giant water bottle in my room to avoid running into my parents. Maybe Urvi was on to something.

Not that they noticed me, even as I took a few pictures of them for the social media account. Funny how sometimes pictures didn't do a scene justice, but then sometimes they really caught the energy of a room. Everyone was cooking and eating and baking and stuffing tins. It was as if they didn't have to be up early for mandir the next day.

I grabbed a bottle of water from the garage in hopes of evading them and succeeded in rounding the corner without being spotted, almost making it to the hallway before my ears plucked my name out of several conversations happening all at once.

"Ha. Zuri is too young to be matched," Mummie said.

Thank *god*. I walked down the hallway but paused when she added, "Although everyone is speaking so highly of this Naveen boy."

Oh no. Don't! Don't do it, Mummie! Don't get sucked deeper into this nonsense!

"I would pick him for her if this were the time."

"It's just talk," one of my fois said. "However . . . it doesn't hurt to get them started in getting to know each other. He seems like a good boy. Handsome and smart and from a wealthy, respectable family. If he's attached to her, then someone else can't grab him when the time comes."

"Silly things. She's too young. I don't want her focused on any boy yet." Yay, Mummie!

"Just thinking. Better to think on a nice Indian boy than someone else, huh?" Boo, foi of mine. What was she thinking?

"Well, it would be good if she picked a nice boy," Mummie chattered.

"What is this nonsense?" Papa asked. Ha! Yes. "Let the poor girl get through high school and focus on college studies first."

"Oh, we're just talking. Nothing wrong with thinking about a boy for her future," Mummie protested.

"She's not interested. He's only here for a week during a busy, busy period. She doesn't have time for this absurdity. And neither do you."

But then a foi interjected, "Let us handle it, huh? We have her biodata and nice pictures." Oh gods, no. *Not* the biodata!

Would meddling and matchmaking ever be a dying art with my people?

CHAPTER TWELVE
(Sunday Morning: Seven Days Until the Wedding)

#MindGames

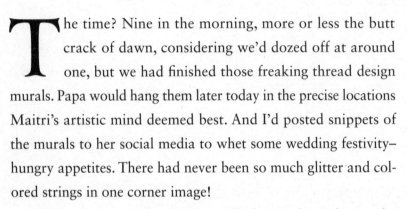

The time? Nine in the morning, more or less the butt crack of dawn, considering we'd dozed off at around one, but we had finished those freaking thread design murals. Papa would hang them later today in the precise locations Maitri's artistic mind deemed best. And I'd posted snippets of the murals to her social media to whet some wedding festivity–hungry appetites. There had never been so much glitter and colored strings in one corner image!

There were so many people in the house that I'd waited a grueling two hours before I could even pee, much less shower.

While I was running to the bathroom with my towel and clothes in hand, stinking Neha tried to strike like a ninja to jump ahead of Sethal and then tackle Jyoti. That girl could not simply rise from the dead of sleep and walk straight into the bathroom. That was not the natural order of things in this house! If one had to wait, all had to wait their turn.

We all had different routines. Neha was the quickest by far. She was in and out of the shower, hair sometimes washed, half a bottle of lotion and conditioner used and clothes all over the floor. She was the messiest of us. Urvi normally didn't take long, but pregnancy slowed her down. She, Jijaji #2, and Masi got to use Mummie's bathroom. Maitri had done her lengthy routine last night. Mine was fast (enough).

I had three types of shower days: in and out with soap and lotion; shaving day (every other day—darn these inherited hairy genes); and the ever-tedious weekly hair wash day. Today was the first kind. I was in and out of the bathroom in ten minutes, including brushing my teeth.

Neha was practically crouched in the corner of the hallway keeping her pee in. She rushed past me into the bathroom. Guess the downstairs half bath was also occupied.

I hung my lime-green towel on a hook on the back of my door and tossed my clothes in the vicinity of where the hamper had last been seen.

Today was the day I'd find out if I'd made it to the next stage of the competition. What if I *wasn't* exceptional enough, though?

"Ugh, stop that. Get out of your head," I chided myself.

Besides, there was so much to get done: finishing the last of the decorations for the house, finally moving these boxes into the garage so they could travel to the hotel rooms with us, organizing my room for the millionth time, working on my reception performance, and meeting up for dance practice. Which meant seeing Naveen again.

I made the bed and dropped my phone onto it. It lit up with a message notification. My heart fluttered, and yet it prepared for the worst-case news.

I plopped onto the bed, closed my eyes, held the phone to my chest, and said a little prayer. I'd never been religious, but boy, when I wanted something bad enough, suddenly prayer was all the rage.

But it wasn't the email I'd been waiting for. It was a text.

Naveen: Hope you slept well. And that you don't mind me texting you.

I tapped a fingernail against the screen and deliberated about what to say, if anything at all. I decided I should respond; Naveen was almost family, and we'd be seeing a lot of each other. Sounded gross, considering our moms were trying to hook us up for a twenty-to-life sentence.

Me: I slept OK. It's fine if you text. We're practically family, right?

Ha! That should slow his roll.

I lay on my bed, arms splayed over my head, and enjoyed this time of quiet while my cousins were either in search of a bathroom or eating breakfast. As in, no one in my room. Conversations went on outside and downstairs, muffled by my door. The phone pinged with another text.

Naveen: Not even. Pranit is my cousin. Either way, we'll never be BLOOD RELATED. Our moms know what's up.
Me: I think of you as fam, though.
Naveen: Not for long.

I laughed. Ha! If he ever denied being cocky again, I had actual proof to disband his futile argument.

Me: And you denied being arrogant?

Naveen: Confident. Big difference. I'm always like this.

Me: I don't think I want to deal with that.

Naveen: ☺

Me: What are you up to today? Touristy things? I don't imagine the groom has a ton of things for you to help with.

Naveen: Little do you know.

Me: Then tell me.

Naveen: I can't. Sworn to secrecy.

Me: Can't keep secrets from your potential prearranged bae.

Naveen: So you are potentially thinking about being my potential?

Me: Not even. Actually think you're upping your game to take me out at finals.

Naveen: Ha ha!

Me: Have you heard from the contest?

Naveen: Yes.

I shot up in bed and checked my email, my missed calls, my voice mail, and my texts. Ugh. Nothing! Not a single notification. What even? How the crap had he gotten a notification? Were they contacting the winners first, and if any declined, then they'd contact the runners-up? Was this just a big game to everyone?

I furiously texted Naveen as anxiety rose up my throat like bile.

Me: Well? Did you get to the next level?

Naveen: Tell me if you did first.

Me: Why? So you can say you didn't if I didn't so I won't feel bad?
Naveen: No.
Me: So tell me.
Naveen: Yep. I got invited to the next level. Once all the competitors are notified and acknowledge, they'll let us know the next step.

My head hurt. I glanced around my room, which seemed to get smaller and stuffier by the second, my gaze landing on the dresser against the wall. There was a new bottle on the end, one I didn't recognize. Maybe just one of many lotions we had around the house. Neha liked the small ones she could carry with her. Must've been hers, seeing as she was always in my room.

Naveen: Zuri?
Me: No word.
Naveen: Hey, no worries! They're not done yet.

Yeah, but I'd performed before him. I should've been notified first. If they went in alphabetical order, then Damani came before Patel, so I still would've known first. If they went by location, Atlanta came before Durban. And if they went by country, well, the U.S. didn't come before South Africa, but we were local, so we came first.

Jealousy wasn't a tendency of mine. I was almost always happy for a person who succeeded, as long as they earned it. And I was genuinely happy for Naveen. He had an incredible voice.

This competition could seriously be his one and only realistic way of going to college in the States and pursuing his creative path. But he didn't even live here. He hadn't worked years and years for this. How was this fair, universe?

"Stop that," I muttered.

Who was I to assume that he hadn't worked as hard as I had? That he didn't deserve his shot? And anyway, hadn't I just given him a big ol' spiel about good sportsmanship and appreciating the competition and yada yada? Me not making it shouldn't detract from his feeling of accomplishment, but more importantly, it shouldn't make me feel like something less. Jealousy and envy had no place in my world.

Me: I'm excited that you got to the next level!
Naveen: Thanks. But I'd rather have you there to compete against. Otherwise, it'll be more of a slaughter than a competition. 😉

I smiled, my shoulders slackening and my negativity level dropping.

Good. My heart was moving back into the right place. It was good karma. Maybe, just maybe, someone had noticed me last night and thought I was good enough for them, even if I didn't get to move forward. I still had that chance. Right? It wasn't unheard-of for judges at competitions to offer admission to contestants who hadn't won, even if there weren't scholarships attached.

Naveen: Let me know when you find out.

Me: ☺

My turn to send gushy emoticons, because what else could I say? My heart would break if I didn't make something out of this audition. C'mon, world. Give me a freaking break. Give me just one judge who wanted me as badly as I wanted them to.

Instead of another text, Naveen sent a picture. A selfie. Of him hugging the crap out of a giant stuffed monkey, his eyes squeezed tightly closed and a smile wider than wide.

Me: Already have a gf, I see.

Naveen: Ha! She wishes! You've got this.

Me: LOL. Thanks!

Naveen: Wonder why Pranit has this huge monkey in here. Or is Maitri already bringing her things over?

Me: Oh, that's not Maitri's. That's Pranit's.

Naveen: No way. What!

Me: Yeah, my sister won that for him at the carnival. She's crazy good at basketball and shooting plastic ducks.

Naveen: Way to break gender norms.

Me: Pranit had to wrap its arms around his neck and carry it on his back to the car, and some random dude came up and poked its nose, and Maitri yelled, "Hey, stop playing with my man's monkey!"

Naveen: LMAO!

I smiled to myself, remembering how serious she'd sounded, how protective she was of that stupid monkey, and how everyone around them had paused before cracking up.

Naveen: Hey, I'll see you later today for dance practice?
Me: Yeah.
Naveen: But text me when you find out the good news.
Me: Sure thing.

Ugh. There was no way I'd be able to concentrate on choreography for a bunch of dances with the unknown results following me around like some cryptic Grim Reaper of music school admissions. Again, I updated my emails and checked through my missed calls, voice mail, and texts. Still a big fat nothing since the last time I'd checked approximately six minutes ago.

Krish: News?
Me: OMG. Are you texting me from another room?
Krish: Duh.
Me: Nothing yet.
Krish: It's still early in the morning! No worries!

I scratched my tooth with a nail. Sometimes I had gut feelings about results, and gut feelings were almost always accurate. Mine was leaning toward a big nope.

Me: Well, Naveen got in. And I auditioned before him. I'm also alphabetically before him. I don't think I got in.
Krish: Are you sure he's not lying?
Me: Why would he?
Krish: Weren't you saying yesterday that he was trying to get in your head?

Me: He told me he wouldn't do that again.
Krish: And you trust him just cuz he said so? You know the rules. Don't. Trust. Boys. Why else is he getting so chatty with you?

I rubbed my chin. It was best to believe the good in people and not jump to negative conclusions. But Krish had a point. We'd been burned by guys before, especially Krish. There was a reason why she didn't like guys getting near us. There had been some gossip and twisted tales and a whole ton of woes because of boys. She made sure I learned from her experiences so I wouldn't ever go through what she had.

Boys lied and destroyed reputations, leaving mental and emotional trauma in their wake.

CHAPTER THIRTEEN
(Sunday Morning: Seven Days Until the Wedding)

#Fair&Lovely

I rolled out of bed in the most guest-appropriate pair of sweat shorts I had and passed my dresser, eyeing the out-of-place bottle next to my hair and makeup organizers. When I realized what it was, I screeched to a dead stop.

Oh. My. *Gawd.* This wasn't lotion at all! It was that hideously grotesque, offensive lightening cream from India. The brand that had been around for decades, telling all of society that we dark-skinned girls needed to lighten up. Literally. They may have changed their product name, but it still did the same freaking thing and reinforced the same systemic bias.

And I absolutely seethed. I snatched it so fast and so hard off the dresser, it could've imploded in my death grip. I stormed down the hallway, looking for the culprit. I so very, very much wanted this to be an obscene joke.

Mummie waltzed out of her bedroom as she adjusted a pair of chandelier earrings, her set of two gold bangles clinking with every movement. She was dressed to impress in a red-and-green salwar kameez, even though we weren't hosting anything today.

She dragged her disapproving gaze down to my shorts and tsked. "*What* are you wearing?"

"Shorts. It's hot," I replied, totally aware that my mom thought exposing anything above the knee could be misconstrued as scandalous.

"We'll turn up the AC, but you have to put clothes on."

"I do have clothes on."

"Actual clothes. You're half naked. No shame?"

I groaned. While my cousins ran around all of Hotlanta in booty shorts and tank tops, my mom flipped her lid if I showed any knee, much less some thigh.

She explained, "Your papa's Masi is here. What will she think? That we raised shameless girls in America?"

"Fine. OK. But first, *what* is this?" I asked, trying my hardest to keep the anger out of my voice out of respect for my mother.

"What is it?" she asked and took the bottle, squinting to read the label. She always forgot that her reading glasses were on top of her head.

"Who put this in my room?" *Don't let your tone get any sharper*, I warned myself.

She scoffed but kept the bottle in her hand. "Ah. I see why you're so upset. Beta, don't take it personally. Masi must've brought this from India. She doesn't know any better."

I politely waited for Mummie to walk away and give Masi a talking-to, but I thought better of it. Maybe it wasn't fair to say something. Correcting Masi was like correcting my grandmother, and that was a weird, awkward position, because I'd feel bad if I made her feel bad.

"What the hell?" I mumbled out what could've been a scream and returned to my room.

"What's wrong?" Maitri asked as she zipped out of her bedroom and into mine to spread pictures across my floral bedspread.

"Did you get a 'lovely' gift from India on your dresser?" I asked, making air quotes around the word *lovely*. There wasn't one desi girl out there who didn't know what this product was all about.

It took her a second to catch on. Then she sneered. "Masi? Ah, yes. I did get a *lovely* gift. She means well. Don't worry about it."

"That's not an excuse." My eyes sprang wide-open with disbelief. How could Maitri seem so blasé about it? Sure, my sisters followed lots of traditions, but they were also modern feminists. They supported women's rights to be who they wanted to be, which included stomping down the idiotic idea that we had to look a certain way to be perceived as attractive.

"She's old and old-school. You can't really let loose your rage on poor Masi. To her, this is just a standard gift."

"Still not an excuse. It's like she's passive-aggressively telling us that we're ugly and unacceptable and need to be lighter-skinned." I guffawed, extending my hands. "The product pretty much says all that on the label!"

She looked up from the display of photos and sighed. "Just let it go. Please? We really don't have time to school our elders on the long-lasting detrimental effects of colonization and how they negatively impact beauty standards. It's a fight all of India and most of the world struggle with, and this week, my sweets, is not the time to take on that challenge. We will fight the good fight on many fronts, but not this week. I need help narrowing these pictures down to twenty for the reception slideshow that will play while people eat."

I sank onto the bed across from her, fuming and mumbling, "Fair & Lovely, my dark and gorgeous behind."

She coughed out a laugh. "That's a far better name for this heinous lightening so-called beauty product. Even changing it to Glow & Lovely doesn't change what it does or what it implies. Your sisters and our parents are the last people on the planet who would ever think that your dark skin isn't lovely."

I smirked, studying the bronze tone of my forearms. People paid lots of money on tanning to get this color, and yet we who had this color naturally were told to change. "Whitening creams should be outlawed. First white people colonized us, then they jammed their Eurocentric ideals of beauty down our throats that still remain to this day? It's like Masi is spitting on our Trinidadian heritage, too. We should change what we are to look more like our former enslavers?"

Maitri snapped her fingers so that I'd look down at the row of pictures. She said in a lowered voice, "She's old, OK? And we love her dearly. We don't want to hurt her feelings or make her feel bad, especially when she traveled halfway across the world for my wedding. Do *not* take up arms with her. This is not the hill you want to die on. However . . ."

"Oh boy, what now?" I crossed my arms, vaguely aware of which pictures she kept tapping on.

"There is one thing I'm going to ask you to do that I promise is not based on Eurocentric beauty standards."

Yet I had a feeling it might be. It was like when people started a comment or question with, *I'm not racist/sexist/misogynistic/bigoted/etc., but* . . . "Hmm. What?"

"Straighten your hair?"

I scoffed. At first I didn't even have words for her. She knew me, right? She couldn't be serious. "What the heck? Nope. I'm proud of my dark skin and curls. And you're wrong. Either you're lying to yourself or to me if you think preferring straight hair over curly hair isn't Eurocentric. Just be happy that I'm letting someone even *touch* my hair," I snapped, anger rising in my tone.

"It doesn't have to be straight to look nice, and you definitely don't have to do it the entire week. It's just that changing it up once in a while makes you look astonishing. That in itself isn't Eurocentric. Curl straight hair, and it's a bombshell. Straightening curly hair once in a while is also a bombshell. I just need you to rock a different style for each major event, because we have five of them. We all have to. Different outfit, different jewelry, different makeup, different hair."

She wound her hair around her finger, but the curl instantly fell flat. She went on, "We're doing professional pictures for everything, right? It's just like how we agreed that we would wear different colors for each event. You've got green, purple, pink, orange, and blue. So make sure that you have your hair different for all the events. You straighten your hair once in a while anyway, not to fit in or look quote unquote nicer or tamed but because you want a different look. Can you do that? Can you calm down and bring your once-in-a-while straight hair into this weekend? For the other events, we'll do your curls in an updo, a half updo, an intricate braid, and fully down. Just one more style?"

I rolled my eyes and tamped down my temper. Maybe it wasn't asking for too much? But I'd always straightened on my own terms.

"What about wavy?" I conceded. "I don't want to do pencil straight, but I could compromise and do waves."

She sighed. "Yes. That would be lovely." She gently touched my hair. "I adore your hair. I've spent hours trying to replicate it on my hair, but I have this. It won't hold a spiral for anything, and curls go limp in a matter of hours. Your hair is easy to envy. I would never ask you to change it for anything other than looking a little different for back-to-back events."

"Sure," I mumbled. I totally understood her viewpoint, but I also hated damaging my hair with heat and flat irons. I took care of my curls the way Maitri took care of her skin.

"And makeup?" she went on, reminding me that I had to succumb to letting someone do my face up.

We both knew I was horrible with makeup, just as I was horrible with any other sort of visual artwork. I'd even watched video tutorials with Krish, and while she mastered contouring and blending, I couldn't get past foundation 101. "How does one do different styles of makeup?"

"That's what the makeup artist is for. The high-def makeup will enhance our pictures, and you're sister to the bride, so you have to look almost as bomb as me. OK?"

"I can't just do it myself?"

She laughed. "You? Do your own makeup? Nah. It's way too late to back out. Besides, the pros are hired. They're scheduled to come and make us look like models. They've already been paid. Don't waste my money. They weren't cheap."

"You're lucky I love you enough to do all of this for you."

Maitri pinched my cheek. "I am lucky! You're behaving so well and taking everything in stride. I know it's a lot, but the amount of effort you're putting into all this makes my heart swell. Not everyone would go through this much trouble for their sister."

I gave her a small smile. Making Maitri happy this weekend was a reward in itself. We didn't get along every second, but we did for the most part, and I wanted her to have a flawless dream wedding weekend.

"Now narrow these pics down, and if you have some nice ones from when I was little, hold them aside for me to see if we might want to use them. Then, if you could upload these and email them in a single file? That would be great."

She hopped off my bed and called back from the door, "And don't go all feminista on poor old Masi."

I grumbled absolute nothings into the air, grumbling just to grumble, as I changed into a pair of loose boyfriend jeans and looked over the pictures. They were all of Maitri growing up, from full-on chipmunk-cheek baby photos to college graduation.

She smiled in every one of them, just living her best life and not letting the world get her down. She had a forced smile in all the staged pictures, the kind others wouldn't immediately recognize, but I did. It was a smile that was pulled back a little too far.

I went through some of my pictures of her, adding in my personal picks, namely the ones where she was with family or all dressed up, always glowing. To get my mind off Masi, I scanned all the pictures I'd chosen, creating a second folder for the ones I'd found on my own. We didn't have time to go back and forth with this last-minute stuff. Maitri could pick and choose more easily when everything was already on the computer.

By the time I'd finished my first errand of the day, it was already eleven and time for lunch. I'd missed morning cha and breakfast.

The entire downstairs looked weirdly empty devoid of furniture except for the table in the breakfast nook. The blankets we'd sat on for yesterday's kankotri ceremony had been folded and put away, replaced with a throne and backdrop for Maitri's mehndi party this Friday.

Mummie was finishing up cooking the last roti as Urvi placed the rest of the food on the table for . . . I didn't even know how many people. There was just a stack of plates, and everyone would serve themselves. I picked up a plate and took some steamy bhinda ni shaak (it was the only way I liked okra, to be honest) next to buttery roti and planned on coming back for rice and tangy dhal later. Unlike everyone else, who'd most likely had breakfast, I was starving.

Unfortunately, I had to sit next to Masi while she ate. I really wished Mummie would let us eat upstairs, but nope.

Masi's face lit up when she saw me. She smiled and patted the seat beside her.

I gave Masi a smile and hoped it was enough to cover my RBF for once. Here was the thing: It was exceptionally shameful to speak out against our elders, especially one as old as Masi, who knew very little of the world outside her small-town home in India. We were generations apart. While my parents had instilled in me a deep respect for elders, I was also stirred by the evils of the world and moved to speak out and take a stand.

I needed to say something to Masi about her skin-lightening gift, but no matter how I did it, it would be considered highly offensive. Which would not only make me look like a disrespectful, insolent heathen but also bring reproach and shame to my parents and entire family. On this of all weeks.

"How are you, Masi?" I asked in Gujarati, focusing on her plentiful goodness.

She smiled big and bright and did that side-to-side head bob thing, her eyes glistening behind her horn-rimmed glasses as she patted my head. That was one of those nostalgic and heartwarming things elders tended to do, as if we were still kids, and it almost had me thinking she was my grandma.

Masi's snowy hair was pulled back in its usual simple but elegant bun. She wore a tan sari with a light pink floral pattern and her everyday set of two golden bangles with matching earrings and a thin chain necklace.

Maitri pranced around the kitchen to get this and that while Papa and cousins finished hanging up the last mural in the living room behind us. So that's what the girls had been doing.

I sat down beside Masi, hoping to scarf down my meal before she said—

"Have you been using the Fair & Lovely?" she asked with a genuine smile, void of condescension, referring to the product by its former infamous name. "Did you see it in your room?"

I side-eyed her, the scent of bhinda so deliciously inviting that my mouth watered. I swallowed hard and said, my food still hovering at my lips, "Um, Masi. Do you think I'm ugly?"

"Zurika!" Mummie hissed from the kitchen.

Simultaneously, all who were present froze and gaped at my rudeness. But didn't they think it was rude that someone had basically told me to be whiter? That the darkness of my skin should be changed?

"No, beta. Why would you ever say such a thing?" Masi asked in a sweet, raspy voice. She frowned, looking genuinely concerned that I would ever suggest something so vile.

I bit my tongue as the glares of my mother and elder sisters cut right through me. But nah. It came out anyway. "I appreciate the gift, but giving me that cream is the same as telling me that lighter skin is prettier."

"*Zurika*," Mummie growled, sending shivers down my spine. I ducked my head and ate. Fast.

"No, no, beta. That's not what it means, although you'll attract more boys for marriage with creamy skin, no?"

Son of a . . . I just had to open my mouth. At least that mouth was now full of food and unable to spill any more unfiltered thoughts to my elders. But judging by the scorching gazes of my mom and sisters and, I was 100 percent sure, my dad behind me, I was going to *get it*.

And as I'd expected, the second Masi was out of the room, Mummie yelled my ear off. I flinched with every word, but her anger was short-lived, and it wasn't long before she sputtered, "Eh. This is a happy time. We will not ruin it with anger."

She rubbed her temple, as if I were vexing her to no end. "We must be joyful lest we invite bad karma into Maitri's marriage."

Then she lowered her hand and looked me dead in the eye. "Do not ruin your sister's wedding."

CHAPTER FOURTEEN
(Sunday Afternoon: Seven Days Until the Wedding)

Beta?" Papa asked, rapping on my open bedroom door.

Oh, crap.

"Yes, Papa?" I straightened my shirt and tied my hair back loosely, preparing for upsetting words.

"You do understand that Masi is old, correct? And that your mummie only yelled at you because she thought you'd hurt Masi's feelings?" he asked calmly.

"Yes," I mumbled, mortification prickling my neck.

Papa paused and watched me, which, of course, had me sweating bullets. He was the quiet type. His anger was delivered in a more thought-out way, the kind that made me think instead of cringe. While Mummie always lost her crap and yelled right away, Papa waited for the best time to talk. The waiting was the worst part. You knew it was coming and that it would hurt.

He examined the lightening cream. A white bottle with a very light-skinned model claiming her melanin had faded over time. "She doesn't mean anything by her gift. She has a very old-school mentality, and that's hard to change, but she loves you for you.

The older ones will always have something to say. Don't take it personally. Forgive her."

My shoulders slumped. The way he asked for my forgiveness broke my heart, as if he thought I truly despised my dear old masi. "Of course. I wasn't mad . . . I just . . ."

"Thought she wants you to be whiter? Well, I think you're perfect," he said matter-of-factly. He lowered his hand, keeping the bottle in his grasp.

I rolled my eyes and tried not to smile. "Papa . . . that's so cheesy."

"I thought you loved cheese."

I laughed, the weight of the world crumbling off my shoulders. "You, um, understand my response?"

"Ha," he said with a nod of his head. "Shouldn't surprise you, should it?"

"Thanks, Papa. Is it OK if I leave now? I have to go to dance practice."

"Make me proud. You always do." He gave a soft smile and left my room with the bottle.

I watched his back for a minute, knowing that product was going into the trash where it belonged, or maybe back to Masi so he could explain why I'd said what I'd said. 'Cause that stupid lightening cream was offensive AF. Chances were high that he'd be tactful and help her understand, unlike how I'd come at her.

Papa really was the best.

Still, thank goodness we had to get to Priyanka's house to practice our routines. Anything to hide from Mummie.

I met my sisters downstairs, and we quickly shuffled into Maitri's car. Neha brought her backpack, the one with the big fluffy teddy bear head on it, to store our water bottles.

I sat in the back beside Neha, eying Urvi and waiting for her reprimand. She just quietly sipped from her giant water bottle and told Maitri, "I still have six weeks left till this baby comes, and my back is killing me. You know what Mummie said?"

"Food!" we all instinctively shouted.

Urvi shook her head. "Yes! Food cures everything. Backache? Eat. Arthritis? It's because you don't eat. You know what food does work for?" She twisted in her seat and looked back at me. "Stuffing your face so you don't say things like that in front of your elders, the last of our grandparents' generation."

I shrank into my seat.

Neha crowed, "So what? We can't ever correct our elders or let them know they did something wrong or hurt our feelings?"

"It's called picking your battles and being respectful, especially to someone as old as her," Urvi said in that stern, motherly voice. She had that tone down.

"We can't say anything respectfully then?" Neha countered.

Urvi rubbed her brow, exasperated. "I can't with either of you right now." Which meant that was the end of that until further notice. Wow. She was already in mom mode.

Priyanka's house was only eight minutes away. Our arrival helped shift everyone's focus, defusing the tension. Maitri parked on the street, already crowded with cars, so that we could utilize the driveway in front of the open and empty three-car garage and multiple groups could practice at once.

All the siblings, cousins, and friends of the couple who were dancing or choreographing were here. I was still in my jeans with a short-sleeved shirt, my hands on my waist as I awaited my turn in the shade of a tree. They'd already begun practicing their small-group performances. Fans in the garage blew out refreshing air.

I was only in three dances, one of which was solely us Damani girls and was just a quick garba night performance. Since there were so many people willing to dance, I didn't need to embarrass myself any more than that. We were going to perform to a Bollywood song.

I happened to look over my shoulder just as Pranit and his brother and cousins walked toward the house from where they had parked way down the street. There was excitement in the air when the groom arrived, because the bride hadn't seen him in days, but also just because he was this week's costar. He and Maitri immediately went to each other and embraced and got all doe-eyed and lovey-dovey. But they didn't kiss. Not with all of us gawking.

Everyone took a break to mingle. And when Naveen caught me staring hard, his face flushed even as he smiled.

"OMG, is that Naveen?" Neha asked, poking me in the rib with her bony elbow. "He *is* fine."

"Hush," I told her.

"And he's looking at you like he wants some of this Georgia peach."

I dropped my head back. Why was my sister like this? "Ugh. Can you not?"

"Does he have a younger brother? I don't know if I could control myself if someone were looking at me like that."

I slapped her arm as subtly as I could. "Stop. Now. Go say hi and be appropriate or something."

"Ow." She rubbed her arm but took Sethal with her to meet all the visiting family.

Once the girls had fawned over Naveen for a good two minutes, they had the sense to move on and not humiliate themselves and bring shame to our family.

Krish and her brothers arrived just in time, hurrying toward the driveway in sneakers, eager to socialize.

Everyone greeted each other with long-winded Indian-style introductions: name, relation to the couple, location, and, for some reason, occupation. It was the norm for us.

Krish hugged me and said, "Are you wearing jeans because your mom caught you wearing shorts again?"

I groaned, envying her short shorts. "I'm so hot."

"You should've told me. I could've brought you a pair to change into."

I fake-cried, "Wah."

"Where's the competition?" she whispered.

I cocked my chin toward Naveen, who came to me last, greeting Krish first with, "Hello, I'm Naveen."

She smacked her lips, unimpressed, implying he was the enemy so hard that I felt it. Salt level: Dead Sea.

He frowned before turning to me, fiddling with his ring. Krish noticed it right away and gave me a WTF look. I dug around in my brain before it clicked, my gut suddenly plummeting. Whenever her ex, Adam, was lying to Krish, his telltale signs were playing with his ring or jacket zipper.

Adam had been Krish's epic high school crush. He was cute, smart, and on his way to becoming something after graduation. He had seemed nice and charismatic and cocky—so yeah, totally saw the comparison—but then he'd turned problematic by telling his friends they'd slept together and playing up the whole "hot, Indian, exotic" crap. I had almost punched him, but thankfully the principal had taken Krish's complaint seriously, and Adam had stopped. But the damage had been done.

"Krish!" someone called, pulling her away, although she kept glancing at us.

"What's that all about?" Naveen asked, watching Krish watching him from afar.

"You're the competition," I explained.

He drew his gaze back to me, lowering his chin. "You never texted me back."

"I never got an invitation," I replied curtly.

His jaw dropped, although I couldn't tell if he was shocked or being dramatic. "No way. Not even a rejection?"

I cringed at the word. "No. Are you playing mind games with me? Did you really get an invitation, or are you just trying to make me think I didn't get in?"

He held his hands up. "Wow. Where is this coming from?"

I planted my hands on my hips and looked him in the eye. "Oh, I dunno. You being you."

"You've known me for, like, all of twenty-four hours."

"And those first few hours proved a lot."

"I told you I wouldn't mess with you again."

I eyed him suspiciously for a good long minute to make him sweat. I didn't know what to believe. His negative take on competition was getting to me, like the dark side leaking into the goodness the Jedis were supposed to represent. Like, I felt it oozing into my soul and cracking my karma.

He let out a rough breath. "Maybe something happened. Did you check your spam folder?"

"Really?" I scowled. "You think I forgot to check my spam folder?" I mocked, rolling my eyes and bobbing my head.

"Well? Did you?"

I thought for a second and tried to recall if I had or not. Ah, shoot. I couldn't remember.

"See? Important things almost always end up in spam."

Ugh. I was going to be so furious with myself if that email had been in my spam folder all day. But I had to wait until later to check, because Urvi clapped her hands, and we quieted.

"Let's get started!" She nodded at Priyanka, who whipped out her phone and went through the dance schedule.

Our big number, the one that included all the dancers, was the second of the dance combos. Since the other dances would be performed by small groups of people who lived near one another, they'd had months to practice. This time was dedicated solely to the combos, since we hadn't danced with those from far away.

I snapped a few pictures for the joint social media before trotting into place.

"Hurry!" Priyanka called. "Over there."

"OK! OK!" I slid toward Naveen.

"First up is the group garba night performance," she announced before turning on the music.

We . . . did not sync up right away. Naveen and I stood next to each other, and I glanced up at him. His jaw was rigid as he paid attention to Priyanka's cues and choreography adjustments, but he also knew I was watching him, because his stoic expression broke into a twitch. Hmm. I wondered if the twitch was real—maybe nerves?

I rolled my eyes. Why was I watching him like he was the last slice of cake, anyway?

We stayed in our own space for most of our moves, no touching, but one too many involved his arms wrapped around my waist to spin and sway and dance with me. His touch was a warmth bomb exploding on my skin, making my stomach flutter. I loathed the way he was making me feel when every gut fiber told me he was bad news.

Once we'd gone through the routine a few times, we moved on to the collaborative reception number. Thank god. No more touching Naveen.

You didn't know the meaning of grueling, cutthroat practice until you were in the final days before a wedding with a bunch of meticulous cousins and friends-turned-choreographers. There was always someone on the verge of yelling or rubbing their temples out of stress. This, *this* right here was why most people didn't do these big, elaborate dances. Urvi knew that! Why didn't Maitri?

Although most of us had our routines down to the very last sway of the hip and flick of the wrist, bringing together two sets of strangers who had never practiced together was something else. Separately, we looked good, even if half complete. Together? We were a bubbling, hot mess. We kept glancing at one another to make sure we were in the right position and ready for the correct sequence. The stars of the act? Naveen and I portraying the bride and groom. We kept ungracefully walking into each other.

I spun and smacked my face into his armpit at one point. How did that even happen?

"Are you OK?" he asked, reaching out to touch my cheek.

I pulled back before his fingers made contact. "Yeah, I'm fine. Try not to bruise my face before the weekend is over, huh?"

Once I even stepped on his foot, but instead of *him* hopping around in pain, *I* nearly tripped. He caught me around the waist before I fell.

"OK. Now I know that you're literally trying to trip me up," I grumbled, fighting off the rumble in my belly from his touch.

He smirked. "Am I?"

I practically growled under my breath. So he *was* messing with me!

And it was one mishap after another—I even lowered myself to his level and "accidentally" smacked him in the mouth and elbowed him in the back. People were starting to stare at us. Notably, Priyanka kept whispering to Neelish, and their giggles made it plain as day that they were laughing at us! Were we now the entertainment?

"Ow!" Naveen said, feigning pain and cradling whichever body part I'd managed to hit.

One week, he'd said. Well, I didn't believe there was any *like* to be had between us at this rate, at least not on my end. But I knew one could acquire an archnemesis in a much shorter time frame. That seemed more likely.

We paused, heaving and sweating, and then took it from the top.

Pranit raised a pretend mic and said, "So many people have asked us how we met and when we fell in love. To set the story straight, the *entire* story, we're going to tell you."

"But Pranit," Maitri said, taking the pretend mic from him, "wouldn't our guests prefer to *see* the story instead of just talking about it?"

Yeah, they were *not* the best actors, to the point where a few people were snickering at the sheer cheesiness.

Pretending that our applause and whoops was the sound of three hundred reception guests, Pranit replied, "Then here we go . . ." After which the couple would sit back down on their throne-like chairs in front of the makeshift dance floor in the hotel ballroom. The hosts, the guy cousins, would begin the tale, and the DJ responsible for starting the recording would hit play as we all got in position.

This giant dance troupe of twenty people relayed the epic tale of love that had brought Maitri (played by me) and Pranit (played by Naveen) together. Part of it was the untold story. Most people, especially the parents and older generation, believed their union had been created by mutual auntie friends. Each dancer played a role of someone in the story, but instead of just acting it out to recorded narration—because that would just be *too boring*—we partly acted (during prerecorded commentary) and partly danced (during songs) straight-up Bollywood style.

The gist of their epic love story was this: Our mom's best friend was also best friends with Pranit's mom, who, in turn, was coincidentally the mom of Pranit's best friend, who was married to one of Maitri's best friends and was the sister of one of Maitri's other best friends. Wild, right? One day, this auntie suggested Maitri to Pranit's mom, and she liked the idea, so she had a chat with our mom, who also favored the idea. With not-so-subtle hints from our parents and Pranit's parents, the two were nudged toward considering one other.

At first, they pushed back against the idea, claiming they weren't ready. But after weeks of parental harassment, our mom telling Maitri to stop being so lazy (depicted by me lying across a few chairs, pretending to watch TV), and Pranit's dad telling him to make a move before someone else snatched Maitri away, the two had changed their minds and decided they were ready to consider someone for marriage. And Pranit finally texted Maitri. Which turned into long phone calls. Which then turned into group outings and activities like bowling, playing tennis (which earned a few giggles as we gingerly bounded up and down with rackets), watching movies, going out to eat, and so on, all the while keeping it low-key so not even their close friends were suspicious.

Our moms thought that if the kids liked each other enough, why wait? But the couple made the parents sweat it out for a bit while they secretly discussed their future together. And just when the parents were about to lose their ever-loving minds, the couple announced that they had agreed . . . to date. There was a bunch of eye-rolling and sighing, the moms asked what the holdup was, and our mom even threatened Maitri that she had exactly two weeks to say yes to marriage. But the couple set a firm boundary called "Calm the Heck Down and Wait." The parents didn't have much of a choice.

Months went by before the couple told the parents, who'd turned gray and old from waiting, that they were ready to announce their intentions. Which basically meant they were 100 percent certain they wanted to get engaged. As the parents rejoiced and told our aunts and uncles and everyone within a fifty-mile radius, plus everyone else they'd ever met, the couple told their friends.

Gasp! No one had known they'd been dating all those months? Nope. My sister knew how to play it so low-key, she could've been creeping around with a celebrity and no one would've been the wiser.

While it seemed odd that they had said they weren't ready for marriage one week but changed their minds two weeks later, there was the real story of how they'd been low-key texting and chatting for *months* before any auntie stepped in to play matchmaker. A surprise twist thrown in at the end. When they had said they weren't ready for marriage, they'd meant they weren't ready for the parents to get wise and ambush them.

After their match was blessed (this part wasn't acted or danced out), Pranit surprised Maitri with a romantic proposal on a Hawaiian beach during a "quick getaway." Bam, a giant diamond ring landed on her finger, and she ugly-cried all over video chat with us later. I mean, she'd known it was coming, but OK . . .

The audience knew the story from there. And here we were, ending in a bigger-than-life collaborative dance routine, at the end of which the bride and groom joined us.

After that, they'd have their slow dance to my violin composition, cut the cake, and invite everyone else to dance the night away.

CHAPTER FIFTEEN
(Sunday Afternoon: Seven Days Until the Wedding)

#SpamFolder

By the time we finished practice, I was a sweaty monster. My curls were in a barely tamed high ponytail on the top of my head. I wiped perspiration from my temples and neck and stood with hands on my hips while most everyone gathered their stuff and left, leaving the core of our soon-to-be united families behind as the evening cooled down.

Naveen slipped up beside me, his hands clasped at his waist. His closeness brought a wall of heat, the sweaty kind. "Check that spam folder yet?" How was he not out of breath?

"I've been dying to check it for the last three hours." I dug my phone out of my back pocket and refreshed my emails. Still nothing in the main in-box. I tapped on the drop-down for all my folders, including junk mail. And . . . what do ya know? Right there beside the junk folder was a big ol' number three.

My shoulders curled in, and my chest deflated. Had I really been this dense?

"Yes," Naveen said out of nowhere, answering a question no one had asked.

"Huh?"

"You're thinking what a silly girl you've been all day, fretting over nothing because you forgot to check the spam folder."

My blood boiled as I hissed, "*Silly girl*? Listen. Just because you have an adorable accent doesn't mean you can say whatever you want."

The corner of his mouth quirked up. "So I'm adorable, huh?"

I grunted. "No. Your accent is."

"But my accent is part of me, and therefore you find a part of me adorable."

"Unfortunately, the bigger part of you is annoying."

A sort of hurt crossed his eyes, but he laughed it off and cocked his chin toward my phone. "C'mon. I need to know if I've actually got competition."

Clicking on the spam folder, hyperaware of the sweaty guy beside me, I gasped and held my breath as we both skimmed the short email. Short letters were almost always rejections. Ones that began with "We regret to inform you" or "Thank you for auditioning/applying, but unfortunately . . ."

This was not one of those heart-crushing emails. This was nothing like Juilliard, and thank the lord, because I honestly didn't think I could take another big hit so soon.

I paced across the yard away from others and read it twice, just to make sure I'd read correctly and wasn't mixing up words.

Dear Zurika Damani,

Your performance this weekend at the Atlanta Musical Scouting Competition was extraordinary. We were impressed by your talent and would love to extend the opportunity to compete in front of our panel of judges in a final performance for full tuition coverage, pending acceptance to any performing arts college in attendance.

"Oh . . ." I breathed, my throat suddenly dry and tight, my vision blurry.

I still had a chance? More than that, I could end up with money so that my parents wouldn't think I was wasting theirs. Winning this would be better than mere acceptance into Juilliard. This held more weight, would give me more leverage to get my parents to agree. Plus, if I won this contest, schools would be more willing to consider me next semester.

There were instructions at the bottom about how to reply and what to sign. But I kept reading and rereading the first few lines. I'd made it. Music college scouts, actual professionals, had deemed me special enough to move on to the final level! The devasting sting of Juilliard's rejection dwindled as a new hope lifted those shredded goals and breathed life back into them.

"Ah! Zuri! You did it!" Naveen said.

The authenticity of his response startled me, or perhaps he wanted me to lower my guard because he had an ace up his sleeve. But I was too excited to care.

My squeal came out high-pitched and short before I muffled it behind a fist. I couldn't help it. I bounced up and down, hidden from view behind Naveen's frame.

"Shh!" I said before realizing *I* was the one making all the commotion.

"Yeah. Hush before we both get caught."

Krish grabbed Sethal and Jyoti from the driveway and immediately ran to us.

"Did you get in? Let me see!" Krish grabbed the phone.

"Yes! Yes! Yes!" she hissed. Then she glared at Naveen. "You better watch your back. Zuri is coming for you."

He smiled with a careful nod. "I'm glad to hear it."

She spun toward me and blessed me with a giant smile that squished up her eyes.

A flood of hushed congratulations and embraces rained over me.

"Hush! Don't tell! Don't tell on us," I gasped as the girls made a semicircle in front of me to block me from the others, in effect pushing Naveen farther away.

"We won't," Jyoti promised. "You better do us proud."

"We'll work it out," Krish promised, her arm around my shoulders. Then she cocked her brows at our cousins, her face full of that Damani girl conviction. "Right, ladies?"

"For sure," Jyoti said, and Sethal nodded.

"Ugh. But these times?" I protested. "We've got the dances and games, and I can't miss a minute of it. One, I don't want to, and two, my fam will definitely notice."

"It's at eight, but we have to check in half an hour early," Naveen interjected.

Krish said, "It'll be tight, but you'll make it."

Sethal added, going over the schedule, "Garba officially starts at five. The couple makes their entrance at five fifteen. Performances and games from five thirty to six thirty, including yours. Is it at your school again?"

"No, but it's close to the hotel where the garba will be." My mind raced as I opened the map app on my phone and checked the route. "Seven minutes away from the hotel."

"Not bad! Totally doable. Your garba performances are midway through, so you'll be done by six thirty. And Maitri's friends are going to make sure things are on time. This isn't going to be running on IST."

"You're going to be at the hotel Friday through Sunday, right?" Krish asked, and I nodded. "That's perfect. Easier to sneak in and out. Bring your audition clothes and violin to the hotel room, and you can change there. You can take my car. That way, your parents won't notice your car missing, and you won't have to depend on an Uber. You're going to do what it takes, and look, timing will be tight, but you won't mess up anything with the garba dances. We got this."

Krish hooked arms with me, tugging me away from Naveen.

I felt a tinge of sadness for leaving him there. "Why are you being so mean to him?" I whispered, glancing at him over my shoulder. He stuffed his hands into his jeans pockets and pressed his lips together, looking entirely innocent and left out. While I at least had close friends to support me, he didn't have anyone.

"I don't trust him. He gives off strong Adam vibes."

"Oh boy . . ."

She said in a louder, normal voice, "You're doing this, and you're going to do so well that you're going to give Naveen here a run for his money. I'm on to you." She eyed him.

"What did I do?" he asked innocently, still stuck to the spot where we'd left him a few feet away. "I'm not getting in her way. Can't afford to get bulldozed." Then he looked to me. "You're doing this, right? Because seriously, I need actual competition."

"Of course," I said. "You're not having all the fun."

"Good." He gave a small smile and walked off as Pranit beckoned to him from across the yard. I watched him until he was out of earshot. Then the cousins departed with a hug, leaving Krish and me.

Krish nudged my shoulder with hers. "Don't even think about it."

"Think about what?"

"That he's cute or innocent or that you can let your guard down with guys like that. Adam used to smile at me like that. There's venom beneath that heartthrob smile. He seems like the type to weasel out all of your secrets and then destroy you with them." She ended with a sharp tone, her voice shaking.

"That's way harsh," I said, yet a part of me believed her,

because I'd seen her go through a miserable few months because of Adam and his friends. I'd seen Krish a wreck, miserable and worried and depressed and feeling like she had her hands tied.

"What's he got riding on this?" she asked.

"He wants to be a singer. His fam will never just let him go to music school. So this is his shot to show them that top colleges take his talent seriously."

She scoffed. "And this is your shot to do the same, to make up for the . . . ya know."

"Did you tell anyone?" I whispered.

"Of course not."

"Thanks."

She elbowed my side making me flinch. "And that's why you gotta take Naveen out."

"Sound more cutthroat, will ya?" I simply didn't like the sound or the feel of being this competitive. Yes, I wanted music college, but no, I didn't want to sacrifice the goodness of my soul to get there.

"Everyone competing at the final level is the enemy. Remember that."

I nodded quietly. I hated to think of anyone as an enemy. I just wanted to be astounding enough to get noticed.

Her tone relaxed with a sigh as she hooked her arm with mine again. "Don't stress too much about garba and timing and your fam, OK? We'll help you. Just do what you gotta do and get it done. Be fearless."

Fearless, huh? Definitely the right word when sneaking out of my sister's wedding events.

Behind us in the garage, Maitri slow danced with Pranit just for the heck of it, and he twirled her and joked about how he'd like to be twirled, too. Her laughter was like a song, so melodious and ethereal and joyous. It practically sang, "Everything is so perfect . . . don't screw this up, Zuri."

CHAPTER SIXTEEN
(Sunday Evening: Seven Days Until the Wedding)

#HotChocolate

After practice, the core of our group went to a diner for a late dinner. It was just the couple, the siblings, and a few cousins.

Every minute or so, I went to bite my nail and then stopped myself before Maitri caught me.

Krish was sitting to my right and asked, "You're freaking out, aren't you?"

Yeah. I was all up in my head.

As if being tangled in my thoughts wasn't enough, Maitri winked at me from across the table and said, "I'm so proud of you, you know?"

"What? Why?" I asked.

She tilted her head as conversations from others rose around us. "Growing up and doing so well. You really do have a good head on your shoulders, and I just wanted you to know that. I know you'll continue making us proud. That's all. You danced really well, and I appreciate you stepping out of your comfort zone to help make this weekend perfect."

Pranit nudged her with his shoulder to look at something

on the menu. Meanwhile, my stomach sank. *Be perfect. Don't screw up.* If I didn't execute Saturday night just right, Maitri might never forgive me.

"You need chocolate. Shh . . ." Krish held a finger to her lips and cocked her head toward Maitri.

Maitri had put herself on a strict diet for the wedding, but we all had to maintain our body weight simply because it was too late to get anything altered. There was no shame in being thick, but no one wanted to walk down aisles or dance in front of hundreds of people in stomach-baring bodices too tight to breathe in. We couldn't bring bad vibes to a wedding weekend by passing out from too-tight cholis, could we?

But forget that. I definitely needed chocolate.

After our orders came, our long table filled to the edge with food and drinks, I stood and took a picture of our group, swatting at the air, indicating that everyone should squish together.

I grinned at my handiwork. Perfect. Posted.

When I sat down, Naveen took out his phone and took a selfie of all of us, with him and me most prominent before asking the waitress to help us out.

"Really?" I asked.

He nodded and, a few seconds later, AirDropped the pictures to my phone. He leaned over my arm to check them out and muttered, "Are we cute or what?"

"Stop," I scoffed.

"What?" He shrugged.

"You're doing it again."

He kept his intense gaze on me. "What exactly am I doing? Being charming?"

"Being full of it."

"I'm just trying to be nice. You got me all wrong."

"You're trying to get in my head again," I whispered. "I will end you, Naveen."

"What are you two whispering about?" Maitri teased from across the table, and suddenly all eyes were on us.

Naveen's face turned red. He didn't like this attention? Well, that meant I had the upper hand. Finally.

"Oh, everyone knows our moms want us to hook up," I said, silencing everyone and making a red-faced Naveen even redder. "We're just trying to get to know each other."

"You better be joking," Urvi said.

I leaned my head against Naveen's. "We are cute, though."

Urvi pointed a fork at him. "You better move away from my kid sister."

Naveen put his hands up. "I'm not doing anything."

"You're sitting too close," she warned.

He scooted away from me, his eyes downcast, before shooting me a scathing look as everyone burst out laughing.

"You started it," I whispered. "But I look good in that picture, so it's going up."

I posted the picture on social as I playfully smacked my lips in a light, audible, "Boop. Boop. Boop."

Pranit, looking at Naveen with pity, said, "So, Naveen suggested a song changeup for the reception."

"What?" Maitri asked, her eyes getting big and practically showcasing her descent into panic.

Pranit placed a reassuring hand on top of hers between their plates. "They would just combine their solos. See, Naveen is a fantastic singer. And he knows Zuri is an incredible violinist. What do you think of letting them combine their acts?"

I eyed Naveen. Oh, he'd actually had the guts to ask?

"Which song?" Maitri asked.

"It's something I've been working on. I was going to sing it anyway, but when I saw Zuri play—" He caught my *oh crap* look in time to clarify, "—on social media, her excellent style, I, um, thought, what if we got together and did a mash-up of our solos?"

"Let me think about it," Maitri said after a moment of deliberation.

Please look at me, sister, and say hell no.

Naveen winked at me, and I slowly sipped my hot chocolate. It was in a big ol' mug with a full, fluffy layer of whipped cream, chocolate shavings, and a toasted marshmallow.

Naveen studied the drink curiously. "Is that . . . ?"

I answered, "Hot chocolate. Never had it?"

"No."

"Dude." I pushed the mug toward him.

He took a tentative sip. "I love it," he said after a moment.

I chuckled. "You have whipped cream on your nose."

"Do I?" He crossed his eyes and stared down his nose at the little dollop of cream, looking stupidly adorable.

I swiped the whipped cream off his nose.

"No," he crowed. "You did that all wrong."

"Was I supposed to kiss that off?"

"Yep."

"Kiss your nose? Who does that?"

"Isn't that what they do in the movies?"

"No, weirdo. And my sister is watching you. She will drive that fork right into your hand if you keep flirting with me."

He guffawed and looked genuinely terrified of Urvi. "You started it."

"Did I, though?" I swiped the back of my spoon across the layer of whipped cream on my drink. Messing with him was fun.

He smiled as I took another sip.

I came up from my mug with whipped cream lipstick and made a duck face at Krish. "Do I have something on my face?"

She cracked up, took a picture for me, and there it went, up on the couple's social media right after the dance sneak peek and the last prewedding dinner out.

After we ate more than we should've, Krish and I slumped in our chairs with our knees apart, not even caring how we looked. I rubbed my big ol' food baby. "I think it's a girl," I told her.

"Another Damani girl for the win!" Krish cheered, and patted her own belly. Then she leaned over and whispered, "Hey, after this, maybe I can help you practice? Give you some feedback? We can study past performances, too."

I smiled and leaned my head on her shoulder. "What would I do without you?"

CHAPTER SEVENTEEN
(Tuesday Afternoon: Five Days Until the Wedding)

#LoveSongsAndRomComs

By some miracle, we'd finished all the little things. There were no more goody bags to stuff or gift boxes to fill with chocolates, only the decorative tins in which the sweets could be packaged on Thursday. Mummie and the fois would cook and cool pista baklava and sweets tomorrow.

The murals were hanging in both houses; the partition sheet had been needlepointed to death and lay folded and ready. Any last-minute tailoring to our outfits was finished. All the clothes hung in our closets in order of event. Jewelry and shoes and accessories were sorted and labeled.

Whew!

More people were arriving, making our space tighter and forcing me to interact with everyone multiple times an hour. And now, every time I walked past Masi, I felt pretty awful—like, bile-gurgling-into-the-back-of-my-throat awful. So I hugged her as often as possible. She hugged me and kissed my forehead as if nothing had happened. Also, Mummie kept throwing me shade.

Masi was as sweet as ever. I didn't know if my parents had

explained anything to her, but she continued to smile kindly at me. I couldn't help but hug her when she patted my head and sneaked me sweets.

"These will make you stronger," she said.

I laughed with her. So, food being the cure for all wasn't just a thing my mom insisted on?

Neha and the cousins were upstairs doing god knew what. Urvi and her hubs had gone out to visit friends. Maitri was out and about. I needed to practice for the wedding *and* the competition, but all the aunts and uncles coming and leaving and all the girls making noise had my eye twitching.

Neha burst through my bedroom door without knocking to get something for the millionth time. I accidentally cut my bow across the violin strings, letting loose a warped noise. I gritted my teeth.

She bumped into my dresser on the way out, lunging at the bottles in my organizer to catch anything before it fell.

"What are you practicing for?" she asked instead of apologizing.

"Nothing. Ugh. Can you knock for once in your life and actually wait to be invited into my room?" I asked, shoving her out.

"Is that the song for the reception?" she asked, turning in my arms.

"Maybe," I grunted and forced her out.

"It's nice."

I paused. We stood toe-to-toe while she looked around me at the instrument on my bed.

"But boring," she added. Ah. Her niceness had lasted as long as it could.

"Ugh. Out," I demanded, gently pushing her back.

She was dead weight and barely moved an inch. "I'm just saying, why not add some of your style to it? Don't put us in a coma."

I let up, stepped back, and rubbed my temples. I absolutely agreed with her, but there wasn't much to be done. "Everyone is expecting classical."

She shrugged and hurried to her room, calling over her shoulder, "Did you ever ask Maitri and Pranit what they wanted, though? She likes your music. Also, she probably doesn't want to fall asleep in the cake."

I swung the door closed and went back to practicing, just before my phone pinged with a text.

Maitri: So Pranit and I talked it over, and if you and Naveen want to do a song together, I think that would be fine. Just try to practice together beforehand.

No! How could Maitri fall for this? Why was she taking away my spotlight and diluting my gift to her? I frantically replied.

Me: What?? I don't want to share with him.
Maitri: Please? Can you work with him?

Me: But this is my gift to you.
Maitri: And I'll love every second of it. Will you just consider it? Try it out.

I puffed out a breath and searched long and hard to find my calm, hating that she wanted me to compromise, hating that Naveen now got to share my special gift. But in the end, it was her reception, and I didn't want to stress her out. So, with a disgruntled huff, I bottled up all those negative feels and responded.

Me: No promises.
Maitri: Thank you!!

I seethed when another text came.

Naveen: Whatcha doing? Practicing?
Me: Are you stalking me?
Naveen: No! I'm not a creeper. But great minds think alike. Whatcha practicing?
Me: My songs.
Naveen: Which ones?
Me: Nice try.

The sound of Neha and the girls cackling in her room next to mine permeated the thin wall. Downstairs, the adults had turned up their dramas on the TV to eardrum-implosion volume. I couldn't think straight. My eyes started crossing.

How was I supposed to concentrate on the audition performance of a lifetime with all this noise driving me up the wall?

Someone screeched, and then all the girls erupted into laughter again. I groaned. That was *it*. I had to get out of here. I packed my violin just as my phone pinged again with another text. And why was I even responding to this guy?

Naveen: Pranit said we could do a duet.

Me: First of all, kinda annoyed that I have to share my reception song with you.

Naveen: I'll drop out if you don't want to.

Me: I told Maitri I'll try. But don't expect much.

Naveen: Fair enough. Wanna practice? I have literally nothing else to do while Neelish goes on another date.

Me: Same girl or different?

Naveen: Same. Guess it's going well. So . . . wanna meet and practice?

Me: I never agreed to a duet.

Naveen: You don't want to? Why miss this chance?

Me: To play with you?

Naveen: That too. But I mean wowing the audience with the music inside you. Not the classical they're expecting. Give them something to move to, get them amped up.

I gnawed on my lower lip. Maybe Neha and Naveen were right about boring everyone with classical. There was no denying that doing a duet with Naveen would be something else. As much as he sometimes irked me, he had one of the most knee-wobbling voices I'd ever heard. When else would we ever get the opportunity to play together and, not to sound egotistical, blow everyone's minds?

I'd rather do an explosive duet that people would talk about for years than a sleepy song followed by a performance by Naveen. I couldn't stand the thought of people remembering his gift instead of mine at my own sister's reception.

We were each great on our own, but maybe we could be phenomenal together. Maybe I owed it to Maitri to give her the best, if this guy was performing at her reception either way. Everything else about her wedding weekend would be extraordinary and out of this world. Why not this?

Me: Fine. I'll consider it. I have to get out of the house anyway.
Naveen: Sweet! When and where?
Me: How about the park?

I added a map link to a nearby park.

Naveen: That's close. Neelish said he'll drop me off.
Me: Gotta stay out until he's done again?
Naveen: Yeah. Can't be too long, though. We have dance practice.
Me: Cool.
Naveen: Neelish said we'll leave in about fifteen.
Me: See ya there.

After notifying my sisters via text where I was heading off to in case they needed me, I waved at my parents to let them know I was heading out. They barely noticed me.

I didn't have my own car and instead hopped into Mummie's—a silver four-door sedan that was practically mine. Mummie let me use it to get to and from school, recitals, and practices and to drive Neha to her many, many school clubs. Maybe I would get a car of my own in college. Although a great selling point of Juilliard was that I wouldn't need a car in New York City.

The park was a short and quiet ride away. The absolute dead silence made my ears buzz—it was sorta weird and creepy being alone.

In the middle of day during spring break, there were lots of kids out. Plenty were at the park, hanging around or playing football or soccer. Couples sat on blankets in the tall, uncut grass or lay across benches and tables.

I hurried with my violin case to an old, faded picnic table on a hill that was slanted by roots pushing up through the ground. The table stood beneath a giant magnolia tree near a cluster of cherry blossom trees. The canopy was draped in light pink flowers. Petals scattered across the table in a soft breeze as I set my case on the splintered surface and took out my violin.

Naveen: Pulling up.

I sent him my exact location via Maps, stuffed my phone into my back pocket, and positioned my violin on my left shoulder. I closed my eyes and rested my chin against the wooden extension of my being. There was no better Zen moment than first positioning. No better soul-moving fire than gliding my bow against strings, feeling the sounds thrum through my veins and the music hum through my ears. No better sense of control and elegant, creative power than the faint adjustment of my wrists, the dance of my fingers, the slight pressure against strings, turning one movement into a myriad of cadences.

I began with soothing classical segments before transitioning into something upbeat and modern. This was my warm-up. Sophisticated and slow, then faster until my arms, wrists, and fingers were limber. It wasn't until I'd finished that I realized how long I'd been playing. Naveen should've been here by now.

Lowering my violin, I glanced across the water as the breeze danced over my skin. Naveen wasn't on the trail farther up the slant of the hill where I expected him to come from. I turned around to place my violin on the table and check my phone, then startled. There he was, sitting on the table beside my case, his feet on the bench and his arms crossed.

"Why'd you stop?" he asked in all sincerity, his brows furrowed.

Why did he make my hands shake?

"I'd love to hear the song you're playing at the reception," he said, hopeful.

My thoughts sort of tripped around my head when he looked at me like that, all intense. I shook off this ludicrous feeling and concentrated on the music.

He cleared his throat and scratched the back of his neck. "Do you have sheets?"

My musical memory was both visual and auditory. "No. I don't need any. I can play any music I've read or heard. I compose by heart and mood. That's what the reception song is based on—a mood I captured when I first took a picture of Maitri and Pranit. They hadn't announced they were dating, but we knew."

We knew by the excited whispers of our mothers and the pride of our fathers. We knew from the way Pranit grinned around Maitri and cast her a wink or two when he thought no one was looking. We knew from the way my sister's cheeks blushed and her skin glowed.

Every time they greeted each other, there was a flutter in the air around them. When he leaned in to whisper something and she smiled shyly, thinking no one saw. When he pulled away and, for the quickest of seconds, brushed his knuckle against her jaw . . . *that* was the moment. The moment we knew these two had not only rationally, methodically chosen each other for their future lives, but that they were wholly and irrevocably in love.

They had something that I'd never really thought happened in real life. There were arranged marriages: ones that had been orchestrated and approved by parents and families and communities. And then there were what some called love marriages: ones based on emotion, with or without the approval of others. But here, Maitri and Pranit had found both. They had an easy tale of love meeting tradition, hitting all the right notes, and now that story would come to a climax with an all-out, cinematic fairy-tale wedding.

And that was the basis of this melody. A romantic, dramatic, soul-piercing, eye-watering, hand-trembling, make-you-believe-in-love-when-you-didn't, make-you-appreciate-love-when-you-couldn't-fathom-it, make-you-*want*-to-fall-in-love type of song.

As I played, swaying along with the music, my eyes wandered all over the place to truly appreciate the day. Sunlight shone through the clouds and pierced the canopy of blossoms. Squirrels chased each other up trees; birds cackled in the sky. A deep wind rushed by, rustling the leaves overhead, sending a spray of light pink cherry blossoms and magnolia petals floating to the ground. They took their time, though, dancing in the changing breeze like a curtain between Naveen and me.

As my gaze followed the blossoms, I caught sight of Naveen looking at his phone, which he held up near eye level. When my song concluded and my violin hung by my side, he looked up over his phone at me with a heartrending expression filled with awe and respect. It was how I'd imagined my future guy would look at me, but that was a fantasy bred from love songs and rom-coms.

Still, my breath hitched.

We stared at one another, neither knowing what to do. I'd never really been smooth around a guy, and trying to play off what his look did to me was only going to prove how he made me feel.

This was not a rom-com.

We would not fall in love under giddy and hilarious circumstances and dance off into the night.

Say something. Say something first, Naveen, to break this silence. Stop making that expression that sees so deep into my being that it's got me shaking.

His cheeks flushed when he finally looked down at his phone. He chuckled and said, his voice cracking, "That was incredible. You're . . . incredible."

"What?"

"Um . . ." He scratched the back of his neck and left his hand there, focusing on the phone.

When I'd caught my breath, I walked toward him as nonchalantly as possible, hoping that he wouldn't notice my fast breathing or detect how my pulse pounded. "I know."

He laughed, and suddenly we went from hot-and-heavy tension to getting-down-to-practice mode. "So, that's a Zuri original?"

"Yep," I replied proudly. "Some people see the world artistically, others in numbers, some as stories. I see the world in musical notes."

"Very cool."

"You understand that?" I asked.

"Yeah. I see it the same way."

I regarded him for a moment. That seemed like an honest response, which meant maybe his brain was hardwired for music, too. "I don't think I've ever met anyone like me."

"Didn't Pranit tell you that we had a lot in common?"

I nodded, then changed the subject before I lowered my guard too much. "Let me see what you recorded. You're supposed to ask permission, you know?"

"Sorry."

"Stalker . . ." But I didn't mind too much. I was used to people at recitals and performances recording me.

He smiled and handed me his phone. I expected a video and looked forward to seeing it, since I hadn't played the song in front of anyone and wanted to see and hear for myself what I needed to work on. I was surprised to find that Naveen hadn't taken a video but a bunch of very nice pictures. Some were in portrait mode, some already in filters.

Naveen scooted to the edge of the table and leaned toward me to swipe left a few times, landing on a picture that took my breath away. I had just swayed, my violin against my shoulder, my head tilted downward, my elbow out, my fingers moving across the strings, my eyes looking away in deep concentration, and the breeze had just picked up, showering blossoms all around me. Some were out of focus, especially the ones closest to the camera.

"That's my favorite," he said.

"Nice shot." Amazing was more like it. I'd never seen myself as pretty as Maitri or as free as Neha or as secure as Urvi, but I saw all those things in myself in these pictures.

"*Nice* isn't the right word."

I frowned. "Pretty?" Dude, at least.

"Drop-dead beautiful," he corrected, his voice low and close to my ear.

I tried not to grin, but darn it, a stupid smile hiked up the corners of my mouth anyway. "Maybe it's just the shot, the camera angle, all the flowers falling at the exact right moment."

"Or maybe it's just you." He immediately looked down at the phone in my hand.

"That's sappy, you know?"

"Yeah?"

I AirDropped the picture to myself and handed Naveen his phone back. I said jokingly, "Don't let me catch you taking unsolicited pictures of me again."

He tucked his phone into his jeans pocket. "Be more clandestine next time. Got it."

"Hey!" I playfully pushed him and he clutched his chest in mock pain. I hopped onto the table beside him, closer than I meant to, with just enough space for our hands to sit side by side between us.

"So. What do you think? Am I worthy enough to share the reception song?"

"You'll have to really bring the lyrics and match my notes. I didn't compose a heartfelt song for nothing." I crossed my arms. "That's the only way. You have to level it up, otherwise I'm going solo."

"Fair enough. You know, I'm not trying to steal the spotlight or mess up your gift to the couple. But if we combine our talents, it'll be incredible. If we posted it, I'm scared we might actually break the internet."

I laughed.

"Let's try?"

I nodded and picked up the violin. We went through the song four times. He mumbled lyrics the first time around, but it wasn't until the fourth time through when things sorta started to make sense.

"OK," I said. "I can kinda see this coming together if you practice a lot more."

"Yeah. I'll get it. I know the notes now. I have an idea."

"I'll need to hear it, and we need to be able to sound flawless together before I agree to perform a duet."

"Of course." Naveen smiled at me, his gaze constantly flitting away the second he made eye contact. "So, Zurika Damani, violinist extraordinaire and composer of reception songs. What's your plan after graduation?"

I shrugged. Avoiding college talk had become a skill.

"Ah. Still think I'm gathering intel in a plot to take you out when you least expect it?"

"I don't really know what to make of you, to be honest."

"Well, whatever goals you have for college, music, everything after this weekend . . . I hope they come true. You deserve it. Your talent should be shared."

My breath caught in my throat. "Thanks. Um, what about you? I know your singing goals, but what are your college plans?"

He sucked in a breath and said, "I haven't told my parents that I didn't apply to any universities in South Africa."

I almost choked. "*What!* Why? Dude, that's playing Russian roulette with your future."

"To reduce options," he protested.

"Or sabotage yourself."

"Sometimes you need to corner yourself to get things done. I want to move to the States. I want to pursue music. If I take local options off the table, then my parents will have to agree to let me go."

I shook my head. No way was it that simple. "They're going to make you stay in South Africa and get a job or something until next year or next semester, however it works over there. But first they're going to kill you."

"Probably."

I bit my lip, sorta knowing the answer, but asked anyway, "Did you get into any schools here?"

"I applied to twenty. I got into two."

Oh my goodness. Even Naveen, from out of the country, had gotten into colleges here? What the crap was wrong with me, then? I pushed out, "Congrats! That's amazing."

"I didn't get into Juilliard," he admitted, his shoulders deflating. He pressed his lips together, his dimples deepening. Sorrow and failure creased his forehead, and my gut clenched.

I knew that feeling all too well. I knew having my dreams dashed, being forced into something as tedious as law, would make my creative soul wither. People like us? We needed our creative outlet more than air. It wasn't a hobby; it was life. Putting it behind us was a death sentence.

My hand reached over to cover his. "It's OK."

"Sure."

I squinted past the petals floating on another gust of wind and found myself giving him the pep talk I'd needed myself. "Maybe the other colleges have great music departments. You can always transfer later. And who knows? Juilliard doesn't guarantee anything, and the other colleges may lead to something bigger and better."

"I know. But Juilliard was the dream."

I watched the ripples in the water ahead and leaned forward. "Where did you get accepted?"

"Rice and Yale."

"Yale!" I slapped his chest on instinct with the back of my hand. "Oh! Sorry!"

He hissed, touching his chest. "That's OK."

I gestured wildly, swinging my arms out. "Yale is . . . well, it's *Yale*! And it has one of the best music programs in the country. Plus, it's Yale. Hello? Your parents are going to sing your praises. They won't be able to shut up about it to every person they ever come across."

"Are you done?"

"Are you freaking serious? Uh! What I wouldn't do to get into Yale. And Rice isn't a joke, either!" I scowled.

"Did you apply to Yale, then?" he asked matter-of-factly. Like it was that simple. Want something? Just apply.

"No. It was a *long* shot. My uncles hammered in the importance of the Ivy League schools. But there's no way. I don't have the grades or the money for that. Dude, you going to Yale . . . Stop frowning, forget Juilliard . . . Your mom is going to try to arrange your marriage to the next, I dunno . . . first female Indian president of the U.S."

"I didn't know you were into politics." He winked.

"Not me," I muttered. "Your parents will think I'm way below your level."

He nudged my shoulder with his. "No, they won't, and I definitely will never think that."

"Whatever." My phone alarm went off. I dug it out to turn it off, then slipped it into my purse. "Better head over to dance practice."

He offered to carry my violin case. We walked the few minutes it took to get back to the trail and then the parking lot. He placed the case in my trunk and closed the door.

"So, are you going to come up with a Zuri original for the final competition and blow everyone's mind?" he asked.

"Maybe, but probably a rendition. What about you?"

He squinted down at me. "Oh, I've got ideas."

CHAPTER EIGHTEEN
(Wednesday Morning: Four Days Until the Wedding)

#AnotherDamPatel

Another Dam(ani) Patel. Some cousins were married to Patels, Urvi had married a Patel, Maitri was marrying a Patel. And if Mummie had it her way, I'd be the next in line to get Patel-inated.

The giant and expanding contingent of Patels was invading our backyard.

Even though Pranit wasn't supposed to cross our threshold, there was no rule about him going straight to the backyard and circumventing the entire system. My parents immediately showered him with hugs and pinched his cheeks and, of course, forced food galore upon him. I mean, why not feed your own starving children, Mummie? Just kidding. There was enough food to feed . . . well, to feed a wedding!

Mummie and aunts and aunties, including Pranit's and Naveen's moms, cooked away in the kitchen, preparing numerous sweets, from the nontraditional but cult fave baklava to the expected condensed balls of laddoo and barfi squares sprinkled with almond slivers and kesar kaju katli diamonds covered in edible silver foil.

Then the inevitable happened. Mummie cocked her chin at me. I dragged Neha with me to water down the awkwardness of finally meeting Naveen's mom.

"My youngest daughters," Mummie proudly introduced us. "The baby, Neha. She's a freshman in high school. Very smart, top of her class. And this is Zurika. She's a senior in high school. Very talented and smart. She's starting college in the fall."

I swallowed. Was I, though?

"My Naveen is starting college next year, too. Which school are you attending?" his mom asked, her focus homing in on me, the most eligible girl, while Neha wagged her brows at me and slunk away. I wanted to grab her by the shirt and force her to stay, but she'd already made it to the back door. Past her, Naveen raised his brows at us through the open windows before turning away.

Deserters!

"We haven't decided yet," Mummie answered.

"What will your studies be?" his mom asked.

"I hope music," I replied, but Mummie tsked at my response.

Naveen's mom looked from Mummie to me, like maybe I was kidding and she couldn't tell why I'd make such a joke. She quirked a brow, that very muted yet clear and condescending response that most gave when someone wanted to major in things like music or art or writing. She didn't say anything, but I knew that perched on her tongue was a tirade about how such degrees were a waste of time and money, were never put to use, and how those who received them nearly always ended up in jobs in other fields and often had to settle for low-paying ones.

Well, good. Maybe she'd change her mind about trying to prearrange my marriage to Naveen. But also, wow. I totally got where Naveen's sadness came from whenever he mentioned his parents not approving of his ambitions.

Mummie chimed in, "As you know, my eldest two are lawyers. While Zurika plays the violin—she's going to play during the reception—she will hopefully go to law school. Her interests seem to point that way."

As in, I didn't really excel in anything else. I was OK in every subject across the board, but nothing stood out.

At this, the auntie smiled proudly at Mummie. "Pranit and his family cannot stop bragging about Maitri being such a smart, accomplished lawyer."

"Maitri and Urvi were top of their classes! I wanted them to be doctors"—Mummie always downplayed my sisters' achievements—"but they were set on upholding justice."

Yeah, how could I meet their achievements? My sisters were changing the world, and I wanted to play music. They were going to leave behind a legacy, an impact. What was I going to leave behind?

"Admirable," the auntie said with a nod of her head, impressed. "We Indians are so successful, not a surprise."

I rolled my eyes. Oh, brother. Could she not with the complex? Could we Indians just live and let live? Not be considered failures and disgraces if we didn't reach those particular goals society at some point deemed the only worthy ones?

"So, Zurika, you will follow your sisters?" she asked me, her brows up, her expression pressing.

I shrugged, my heart palpitating. "We'll see where college takes me." Because I couldn't lie, not when my mom knew me so well, and apparently declaring my love for music wasn't enough. I had to be a *Frozen* character in this moment and just . . . *let it go.*

"Or maybe she'll go with her second choice, medicine," Krish's mom interjected, washing dishes behind the counter.

Eh? She must've been delusional, just because Krish was super-doctor material and we'd been joined at the hip since we were in diapers. She must've forgotten where Krish ended and I began.

And with that, we really had Naveen's mom's attention. She said to me, "Medicine is a superb route. My Naveen doesn't like blood and hospitals so much, but he's brilliant with math and engineering. You must've met him? The tall one sweeping? Isn't he helpful?"

I looked over my shoulder and watched him through the windows as he used a scrub brush on the deck after someone else had doused it in soap. He playfully flicked droplets at the guys and then at Neha when she inadvertently strolled in between them. She scrunched up her shoulders and stuck out her tongue. But she behaved and didn't grab the hose to soak him.

I said, "Um, yes. We've all met for dance practice."

"He's a good dancer, no?"

We could definitely agree on that.

Before she dived any deeper into surveying me as potential future wifey material for her baby boy, I smiled and said, "It was nice meeting you! I hope you enjoy your visit. I think this wedding will be something you'll never forget. It's going to be like a big Bollywood production!"

Mummie shook her head but laughed. "These young ones have come up with a movie production! Can you imagine? I don't even understand it, but let them take care of it. We just take care of the important things, like puja and the actual ceremony, huh? They will make the fun, and we make everything official."

Naveen's mom, along with all the aunts and aunties around them, agreed.

"We incorporated some Trinidadian traditions. Tomorrow, we start with the cooking night. It's usually for the bride's side, but you must come. All the ladies must come," Mummie said.

And just like that, Mummie highlighted a few traditions from her homeland as I slipped away to help Neha unfurl new strings of fairy lights for the guys to string over the deck. Ya know? Because we definitely lacked in the fairy light department.

As I passed Naveen, I snickered.

"I told you," he said as he turned on the hose, "we're meant for each other."

"Yeah, yeah. Just hose down the deck, will ya?"

He grinned at me and squinted in the sunlight.

My dad and uncles had stained the wooden deck a few weeks ago. Now that it was all frothy and scrubbed, Naveen blasted it clean with a hose. Then he went on to hose down the back of the house and windows.

The deck ran the length of the house, complete with an outdoor kitchen, four ceiling fans and lights, and three steps leading down to the grass. At some point, the guys had erected two tents with tables and chairs for the mehndi dinner on Friday and pithi lunch on Saturday.

Silly me to have thought the decorating was complete. How could we neglect the backyard? The guy cousins had mowed the grass and trimmed the trees and shrubs. Pranit had brought over a large portable firepit that he set up on one side of the yard, between the deck and the dining tent, which ran the length of the back fence, and across from the catering tent.

I helped him set up the firepit. Then I walked with Pranit and Naveen around to Pranit's car. Our garage door was open, on account of Mummie frying up goodies, to circulate the smoke and smell of oil. She had camp burners set up in the garage on top of cardboard to prevent splatter stains, our living room and dining room furniture off to the side and covered in sheets.

She supposedly didn't want to mess up the patio kitchen or be in our way as we set up, so here she was with an assembly line of women squatting on the garage floor. They were frying everything from crispy mathiya snacks to crunchy sev noodles, from spicy pea-filled kachori to ghughra stuffed with sweet ground nuts spiced with cardamom.

We brought in cases of bottled water; various flavors of soda; heavy-duty disposable bamboo plates, bowls, utensils, and napkins; fixings for s'mores; and a giant stack of fresh banana leaves, because we were about to get Indo-Trinidadian.

By the time we returned to the backyard, the guys had set the patio furniture back in place. Maitri's friends rushed in and sat on the padded turquoise wicker lounge set with boxes and a lattice frame with four poles in front of them. From the boxes, they pulled out plastic vines and silk blooms and twined the pink, red, and white roses and orchids around the wooden phoolan ki chaadar that would create a canopy of flowers for the palki for the bride's grand entrance.

Maitri was extra. She wasn't walking down the aisle like normal people. She was going to be carried in a bridal palanquin like the queen she was.

"I still think if the groom can ride in on a decked-out white horse, then I should be able to ride up on a royally blinged-out elephant," Maitri said. Unfortunately, the city of Atlanta begged to differ.

People came and went, but I had to shower. During the rare ten minutes of solitude, I thought long and hard about finalizing my competition solo. By the time I slathered on lotion, it had clicked. Before, I hadn't been able to commit to the final-level songs because nothing felt right—nothing felt strong enough. But now? Everything was falling into order.

I shuddered, nervous I wouldn't be able to pull this off, but it was all down to going big or going home, right? I had to amp up my game to the furthest reaches of my ability to get noticed by anyone.

My solo would be—ya ready for it?—Beethoven's Sonata No. 9, something I'd played at my last orchestra concert, and I had killed it. It was *not* for amateurs. The piece had a proven complicated and nightmarish technical difficulty and speed. Basically, I had to wow the scouts with one of the hardest classical songs to play on the violin.

Goose bumps skittered down my body as I shivered. Ooh!

All excited over my final decision, I hurried to tidy up my room a bit, now possible because two boxes of dabbas were out of my room and downstairs, ready to be packed with sweets. On top of that, all the extra clothes and accessories that had been stored in front of my bed had been taken by whomever was wearing them.

Finally! More and more carpet magically reappeared as the clutter vanished. I could breathe again. A plan was forming. Things were going to be OK!

I turned on my Fave Songs of All Time playlist.

Music vibrated through the speakers as I observed my outfits. Beneath them was the one pair of sparkly gold shoes that matched them all. On my window seat, a pink-and-gray plaid organizer held all my bangles for the weekend, arranged by event, twelve per arm per outfit. Jewelry sets were stacked on top of that, complete with chiming anklets.

As I floated around the room, picking out my audition dress and shoes and stuffing overnight clothes and toiletries into my suitcase for the hotel, I danced and sang along with the songs. The list was eclectic and ranged from classical to nineties hits to

Bollywood, punk rock, reggae, pop, hip-hop, rap, K-pop, J-pop, and so on.

"Are you ready to go with us to Pranit's?" Urvi asked from the bedroom door. She never opened my door without knocking, but Neha . . . she still had her hand on the doorknob and a smile on her face after opening it herself. Without permission. Yet. Again.

"Can you stop just coming into my room like that, Neha?"

"You know, you used to do the same thing to Maitri and me," Urvi said. Neha stuck out her tongue.

"I can't go with you. I have to practice for the weekend." By which I meant the competition songs. Gah! People, please leave me alone!

Urvi frowned. "You have to. Just come for a little bit and leave early."

"You can hang out with your *boyfriend*," Neha teased.

"Stop spreading rumors," I warned.

"You like each other," she sang, and then made kissy faces.

"Go on. Get ready." Urvi gently pushed her down the hall. "And you, too. Bring a different car. Maitri has to stay here. If you need to leave their place early and anyone gives you a hard time, you can always say Maitri needs help with something, or you have wedding stuff to finish. That's not a lie."

Eh. Sort of. I sucked it up and got dressed.

Seeing that the younger gen, as in Neha and Krish, wore jeans and T-shirts, I opted for the same. Mummie, Papa, Masi, Urvi, and Jijaji #1 piled into the van while Neha and I rode in the sedan. I plopped my violin case into the trunk so that I could leave early and practice.

We met the cousins there, and it was almost like walking into a mirror image of our house.

All the lights were on, including the outdoor and indoor string lights. The AC was cranked to industrial-level high, but it was still too warm with all the bodies. I walked around with my family and politely greeted everyone, all the while ticking off the time in my head until I could make my escape.

CHAPTER NINETEEN
(Wednesday Afternoon: Four Days Until the Wedding)

#TeamUp

Papa clasped his hands behind his back, tilting his chin up, and proudly introduced me to everyone we hadn't yet met with a smile that could light up the world. "My beta Zuri," he said, like I was the best thing since boba tea. "Starting college soon. We're excited to see where life takes her."

Naveen's dad nodded his head in understanding. "My son is starting college soon, too. He's going to be a brilliant engineer, just like my oldest, Neelish. Our job is almost over, huh? Get the kids through college, into nice careers, and settled down with good people."

Ugh. Please don't tell me he was in favor of trying to match me with Naveen, too.

"My job will never be done with my daughters. I'll always think about them," Papa said, shooting a megawatt smile at me as he patted my shoulder. Maybe we were sort of daddy's girls, but I never wanted my dad to stop thinking about us.

He bragged about my violin skills to everyone he talked with—the best in the biz, he kept saying. My cheeks were hurting from grinning so hard.

"Wait until you hear Zuri perform at the reception. Smart and talented. Our next lawyer! So proud of her."

Heat curled over my neck. Ah! Why did he have to mention law! Couldn't I just be the talented violinist?

I slipped out of the conversation with Papa and avoided others.

"Don't look so down. Patels aren't so bad." Naveen spoke from behind me.

I startled and turned around. He smiled, as per usual. He always appeared to be consumed by devious thoughts.

"You've worked on our song?" he asked.

Unlike my packed schedule and endless tasks, he had loads of time on his hands to practice. "Look where we're at. It's one thing or another."

"Come with me." He glanced around the house. "Everyone is paying attention to Pranit and the adults. Come on."

I sort of eyed him like he'd lost his mind. Sneaking off together was not a good look for either of us if we wanted to live past this weekend.

He must've read my very flat expression, because he held a hand to his chest, his cheeks redder than I'd ever seen them, and said, "Not like that. I promise I'm not up to anything. I want to show you something."

I regarded him for a minute, assessing the situation and how much of a risk I wanted to take by disappearing. But I trusted him to some extent, that he wouldn't be another Adam. One, Pranit would end him. Two, Maitri would end him. Three,

Urvi would end him, probably with a fork, and so on and so forth. I was sure he wasn't willing to endure a thousand ends for me.

I carefully followed him, not too close and ever vigilant of anyone watching us. We wove through the throngs and emerged in a near-empty hallway and went upstairs to his room, or at least the guest room where he was staying.

My heart beat a little harder, and I kept checking the hallways and over the banister to the rooms below to make sure no one saw us. "Do you know how much trouble we'd both get into if anyone found us alone up here?"

He closed and locked the door behind him. "Hard to see through walls."

So much trouble, to answer my own question. But there was a certain thrill to this, even if we weren't up to anything scandalous. I'd never been *alone* alone with Naveen, unless you counted the car—but a car was no locked bedroom. It wasn't that my parents would be incredibly furious if I had a boyfriend or anything, but I'd never been there, never liked a boy that much for that long. I was always busy, and with a big family and lots of sisters and cousins all up in my business, there was no alone time with boys. So now, suddenly alone with Naveen in a bedroom felt too real, too forbidden.

I stood rigid in the corner.

The spare room had a nice bedroom set and a whole lot of mess in one corner. Luggage bags and shoes and a dresser piled with hair-care products and colognes and whatever else boys used.

There was double everything, and my guess was that Neelish and Naveen shared the room.

"We're only here one more night. Then we're off to the hotel, *finally*," he said, as if reading my thoughts.

I swallowed, looking anywhere except at him. "My sister insisted on getting hotel rooms, too. We're all gonna need that space to get ready. I can't imagine cramming everyone into the bathroom together. We only have so many mirrors."

"I think Pranit is checking into the hotel Saturday afternoon, between pithi and garba."

I rubbed my arm, focused on the blinds for whatever reason. "Same."

"At least we get some privacy and quiet after today."

"You'll miss mehndi night," I said sweetly, teasingly, dragging my eyes back to him.

"Are we even invited?" He chuckled. "I've never been to mehndi. It's usually just girls, right?"

I smirked, imagining a bunch of girls holding Naveen down and forcing him to get mehndi designs stained on his hands. "I don't think my sister had intended on it, but I heard my mom tell your mom to come."

He frowned, more thoughtful than worried. "So maybe we'll be there?"

I laughed, wondering how he'd even occupy his time other than eating. "If you want to see a bunch of girls in chaniya cholis getting mehndi done. Nothing saying guys can't do mehndi. Guess we need guys to help get us food and drinks."

"At your service, then. But you had me at food."

I knew it! "Actually, our mehndi is also maticoor night, where we welcome the groom and his fam to the wedding weekend, so it'll be sorta like a huge party with a lot of dancing and music."

"That'll be cool!"

I leaned against the wall. "So, why are we up here alone?"

"This." He handed me his tablet, which was set to an image of sheet music with lyrics. "To see if the reception song will work. I don't want to step on your toes, but I seriously want to duet with you. Just try it once, and if you really hate it, I'll back off. We don't have to share."

I shook my head in disbelief. "You did this so quickly."

"Yeah. I hope you like it."

"I couldn't even get Maitri to let me wear the color I wanted, and you got them to change the entertainment? Are you even human?"

"Pranit actually thought it was a really cool idea. It's one of those things that most weddings don't have. You know them—they're competitive and want to do something extra special. This is it," he said proudly.

"I bet you're a robot. A cyborg? A brainwashing android?" I poked his forehead.

He tugged at my curls. "Are you a robot? Maybe you're an alien?"

I pulled away. "Hey! No one touches the hair."

He cleared his throat apologetically, but then said, "So you can touch all over my face, and I can't even tug your hair?"

"Them's the rules. A girl's hair is sacred. Especially a girl with curls." I bounced a hand beneath my spirals.

"So, let's say, if I ran my fingers through your hair—"

"I'd hit you."

He sat on the edge of the bed. "Might be worth it."

"Why would you want to, anyway?"

"Are you kidding me? That hair is . . . sexy." He muttered the last word and pushed his ring around.

"Whatever." I clamped down my smile and ignored the tumbling in my belly. He was so stupid, with stupid words coming out of his stupid face.

I looked through his lyrics, surprised at how accurately he'd remembered my composition. Just another skill to covet. I was baffled, actually, and amazed. Even though he hadn't gotten every note right, it was pretty freaking close. Envy reared its ugly head.

"Jealous?"

"Don't be so full of yourself," I muttered.

He cleared his throat and asked cautiously, as if he were anxious about my response, "What do you think of the lyrics?"

I read over them again, my head filling with soft notes, bringing the lyrics to life, cushioned by the strings. It was one thing to read music, another to hear it, and a completely different plane to feel it. It was almost ethereal, and together, we'd somehow created a path toward that delicate, otherworldly level. But he didn't need to know that.

"Pretty on point," I replied. "Are these your original words? Like, to your original song that you were going to sing?"

"Sort of. I adjusted them to your notes. And I tried to put myself in your shoes, what you're saying with the music, and tried to put that all into words. Did I get it right? Wanna give it a shot? We can change the lyrics if it's not what you envisioned."

I swallowed as I lingered on some of the most romantic rhymes I'd ever seen, singing them gently in my head. The way he touched on romance and feeling the wonders of first love, how it had found the couple so suddenly and strongly when they'd always noticed each other from a distance, made me ask, "Have you ever been in love?"

He hunched over, looking down at his clasped hands. "I don't think so. Definitely crushed on lots of girls, but I don't think it was ever love."

"How can you write a song so expertly on something you've never experienced?"

He slowly swept his gaze up to me. "There's always inspiration."

My skin flared hot. He couldn't be saying what I thought he was saying. No way could he have these kinds of feels for me. We'd just met.

But then the twitch returned to the corner of his lips. "I mean, you told me what you were trying to capture in the song, about how the couple feels about each other."

"Right . . ." I handed him the tablet, imagining my sister going gaga over this if we pulled it off just right. "This is like old-school boy bands. Maitri is going to love this."

He seemed pleased. "Pranit may have given me a list of Maitri's favorite love songs."

"Your inspiration?" I wagged my brows.

"Maybe not the only source, but yeah. Do you think you can play while I sing? It won't be strange? To have someone else adding to your song?"

I scoffed, a tad protective of the gift that I'd worked on with my entire being from the moment Maitri and Pranit got engaged. "What kind of a question is that? I've been working on this for months. Nothing will change what's being poured out of my heart for my sister. The question is, can *you* add to it? Do it justice?"

He nodded and sighed. "I hope so."

"Can you perform it right now?"

"Sing? Sure . . ." He took a moment to breathe. And then he began, stunning me immobile with his fluid, sometimes throaty, sometimes smooth vocals. This song, *my* song, surged to another level in Naveen's hands. He was born to sing. Like, why wasn't he starring in some Disney show by now?

I pushed off the wall and sat beside him on the edge of the bed. I imagined the violin notes in my head and fell into a world where nothing else existed except this music. I almost wanted to cry. We had created something so powerful and beautiful that there was no way either of us could ever be anything other than musicians.

Maybe I got lost in my moment for too long. Maybe I sat there with my eyes closed for too long. Because when I snapped out of my daze and opened my eyes, Naveen, having finished singing, was watching me. And not in his usual playful way, but in a genuine, interested sort of way.

"What?" I asked, my cheeks warm and my throat dry.

"What are you thinking?"

I shook my head as I admitted, "This dream of ours is going to happen, I think."

"You want to share the reception song?"

"Yeah. As much as I hate to admit it, this will be extra amazing. You're amazing," I said without thinking.

"Really?" he croaked.

I cleared my throat and looked down at my feet. I didn't want him to think that I liked him or get a bigger head than he already had, but Naveen was star-level talented, and from one musician to another, I respected his skills. I might never be able to play a song with him again. Besides, put two good artists together, and we were bound to blow everyone's minds.

"Think we can practice?" he asked.

"Yeah. For sure. I don't think anyone would have a problem if we went to the park to practice for the reception."

And I was right. My parents and sisters were OK with letting us go, particularly because they all seemed to know that our musical pairing was going to wow them. It was going to be a special night no one in attendance would ever forget.

We hopped into the car with my violin in the trunk, getting giddy and nervous to spend time together . . . to practice, that is. Yeah, just practicing.

We returned to the same park, the same table where we'd met before.

Naveen held the tablet to sing through the lyrics and follow my music. It was rough at first, lots of stopping and starting. We practiced a few times, taking breaks to align his vocals to my violin. He was getting frustrated with himself, and I was constantly laughing at him, which seemed to make him relax.

"Sorry," he said, his face red with exasperation.

"For what?" I asked, blowing away a few blossoms that had landed on my arm.

He grunted. "I get irritated when I can't get something right. It's like it's there in my head but can't get out."

I totally got that—it was like trying to smooth out bumps or undam a wall, desperate for any sort of creative flow. Like ants marching up and down your brain when all you wanted was for them to settle down.

We tried once more before Naveen synced with the violin. Once that clicked, everything was pure magic. It was hard not to watch him as he crooned, even though he wouldn't look at me. I was practically facing him, but he kept his eyes either closed or focused on the tablet.

When we finished our last run-through, after about eight attempts altogether, I said, "Wow. I hate to admit it, because I didn't want to share this song, but it's even better."

"We go good together, you and me," he sang to the tune of "Sucker."

Oh boy. Singing like Nick Jonas would get us in trouble.

I stared at my shoes. A few seconds passed before I mustered words. "Saturday's contest is going to open a giant door for us. One way or another, something amazing is going to happen."

"Yeah. Speaking of the contest, I was going to do something a cappella."

"Jonas Brothers?" I grinned.

He shook his head.

I looked at him for a brief minute, reading all the underlying thoughts on his face. "Nope. Still not telling you what I'm doing."

"No. No. That's not it. I got to thinking and wondered if you wanted to pair up for the second audition piece? I mean, just for practice. Like, I would do it a cappella for my audition and you'd do the violin, but it would be the same song with our own spin to it."

I searched his face, trying hard to figure out what he was really fishing for by offering this collaboration. It would help me settle on a second piece as well as lend me a listening ear. "You want to do that with me?"

"Would be goals."

"What's your endgame?" I eyed him. What was in it for him?

"Winning," he said simply. "We have an even better shot if we work together and challenge each other. There's no better competitor, and, honestly, no one as competitive."

"How's this for a challenge?" I played a few notes on my violin.

"K-pop?" he guessed. I nodded. Then he began singing lyrics that had goose bumps crawling across my arms.

"A boy band," I mused, before finally placing which one. I shouted the answer triumphantly, then zipped out a melody he'd never guess.

"Rap." He looked impressed, then correctly guessed the musician.

"Ah!" I threw my head back.

We went back and forth, challenging each other until we'd played through our cards and finally entered the competitive-even-for-us zone with increasingly more difficult pieces.

"Come on. Give me something hard," Naveen jested, but we both knew we'd hit our limits, the notes getting trickier, more complicated. There was a delineation between challenge and setting ourselves up for failure. We tiptoed along the line between what we could pull off and what was out of our current skill set.

"All right." I played the climactic end to an oldie, then let the violin swing at my side as I touched my tongue to my lip. "Let's see you get that."

"Rock and roll," he said slowly after a beat.

"Let's see you hit that."

He blew out a breath, and I knew I had him.

I baited, "Unless Aerosmith is too hard for you?"

He narrowed his eyes, pulled up the lyrics on his tablet, and sang the hook from "Dream On," his voice lyrical and magical and low and high and everything in between. He obliterated my goose bumps.

But I wasn't one to be shown up, so I found a big rock near a tree, placed it on the table in front of us, took the tablet from Naveen, and propped it up so I could see the sheet music. I played and he sang, and we kept going until we were both seamlessly hitting the climactic pitch.

Wow. He actually hit the high notes.

He stilled and quieted. I dropped my hand so that my violin tapped my knee.

We stared at one another, unaware if others in the park had heard us, if it had gotten too dark or chilly. We just stood there, in awe of one another as the rest of the world faded away.

"Damn," he finally said. "You played the hell out of that song."

I blinked, my chest tingling with all the feels. But I wasn't quite sure if they were more like crushworthy vibes or appreciation-of-my-gifts vibes.

"What?" he asked.

"I, um, just love the way you told me that I 'played the hell out of that song,'" I said, mimicking his accent and then laughing at how ridiculous I sounded. Heat rushed to my cheeks.

He tilted toward me and said, "Well, I know you love the way I say *water*."

I laughed harder, barely getting out a "wha-tur."

"Keep practicing, smart-ass." He chuckled.

"I think my ahc-cent is spawt-own." I nodded and pointed a finger. "Ah. See? I can sound like that, too."

He poked my side. "I think you're making fun of me."

"All right. All right." I gently slapped his grinning face, then pushed him to the side. "Are we . . . doing rock?"

"I think we have to after that."

I scratched my temple with the end of my violin bow. I'd never done rock well, but just now? That had been different, but

I couldn't tell if I had pulled it off or if Naveen had just sounded so good that my violin had sounded good, too.

"I just hope I'm not following you onstage. Should I make a sacrifice to the music gods? How many jalebi do you think that'll require?" he asked in all seriousness.

I laughed, imagining him summoning the mighty music gods with a platter of orange sweets. But then he took the tablet as we sat beside one another on the table. He leaned over to show me the notes and lyrics to "Dream On," because we'd been far from perfect, pointing here and there and quietly singing. There was something very professional about his focus, but there was something else in how his shoulder pressed against mine, how his skin brushed mine when he moved his hand along the notes.

I leaned in, too. I wanted to think that I did it to see better, hear better. Maybe it was his smell that made my stomach tie into knots. Or maybe it was because I liked being pressed against him, all warm and nice. Something stirred in my belly, like butterflies fluttering all around.

His head was close to mine, too, so when he tilted it toward me to ask, "What do you think? Can we pull it off?" his face was way closer than I'd anticipated.

"Um . . ." Crap, what had he been saying?

Naveen searched my eyes for a second that felt like eons before dropping his gaze to my mouth. And then all I could do was stare at his mouth, too.

Those small butterflies that I was feeling? Well, they mutated into giant things with heavy, fast wings, overstimulating my insides, making me both hyperaware and numb at the same time. He made it worse when he pressed his lips together in deliberation. Like maybe he wanted to kiss me, too.

I almost leaned in. *Almost.*

But then I snapped back to reality. He was still my competition, and there were way too many things to focus on without losing myself in some short-lived, wedding-time rom-com feels.

Also, his cute mouth started to twitch. Which was . . . kinda sweet, actually. If I knew one thing about his mannerisms, it was that twitching equaled nerves, which had me wondering if he'd ever kissed anyone before. I was sure he had with those looks.

He sat back and cleared his throat, rubbing the back of his neck. We sat there on that lone picnic table into the late evening, the ground littered with fallen cherry blossoms, watching the birds on the water and the sky changing into darker colors.

CHAPTER TWENTY
(Thursday Morning: Three Days Until the Wedding)

Wednesday had zipped by in a blur. I'd spent all morning practicing my solo piece for Krish. Then we'd spent *three* grueling hours at Priyanka's garage as she whipped our dances into shape. Then another two hours practicing with Naveen.

Sleep? What was that?

Because Thursday started with one of my longest routines.

Naveen: Do you want to meet up and practice today?
Me: Sorry. Hair wash day.
Naveen: Is that a real excuse girls actually pull?
Me: Curly hair girls do. Especially when you have this much hair. It's a long process.

And by long, well, I meant it. There was detangling and leave-in oils and hair masks that I'd started last night—I'd slept in a protective hair cover. I jumped in the shower to shampoo and deep condition. There was an abhorrent amount of scrunching involved. From there, I swept my hair up in a microfiber towel for a bit, more scrunching, then applied leave-in conditioner and painstakingly dried my hair with a diffuser while scrunching even more to add volume. This took a couple of hours. When you had waist-length spirals, there was no reason to go to the gym. This *was* arm day.

By the time all that was done, my sisters and I piled into the car for our spa morning, where we were greeted with the finest chocolates, coffee, tea, and fruit. Maitri had champagne. Urvi opted for herbal water. Neha and I took caramel lattes, heavy on the whip.

We started with massages. There was nothing weirder than stripping down to nothing and lying on a table beneath a sheet that barely covered the girls and privates, just so a stranger could rub you all over. Yuck. But once the massage therapists started, my sisters got to chattering, and it wasn't so bad.

We then had facials and got our nails done. Since I had several outfits varying in every color imaginable, I opted for a classic French manicure with a sparkling pink base to match.

Selfie time with shimmer filter. And post!

We came home to a house filled with even more people. Mummie's sisters and other cousins had just arrived, a few from across the States and several from Trinidad. They had come just in time for cooking night/bhatwan with a little maticoor mash-up where we tied in a few traditions from my mom's side.

I got reacquainted with all of them. If I'd thought the house was a zoo before, I hadn't seen anything yet. But there was so much melanin and curly hair and accents floating around that I absolutely loved them for it.

The frustration of realizing violin practice opportunities had come to a dead end buzzed up my skull. I shoved down all the anxiety crawling around beneath my skin and picking away at my brain, put on my best smile, and socialized. Naveen probably had plenty of time to practice for his big career break.

Cooking night was . . . well, just what it sounded like. Except back in Trinidad, this would've been cooking for the wedding, done the night before the wedding. So *all* of our family came over to cook and eat. Most of the food was for tomorrow's mehndi dinner. Maitri had wanted everything else catered so we didn't have to fret over cooking.

"You have so much to focus on, and we want this to be as easy on you as possible so you can just enjoy it," she'd tried to explain to our parents when she was going over wedding details.

Mummie had instantly put up her hand. "Cooking is part of the festivities. We sit around and cook and eat, and it brings us closer."

"Fine. Then just for the cooking night."

"That food will go toward the mehndi."

"Fine. But everything else will be catered."

A few of the food items from tonight would roll over to Saturday's garba, like Mummie's baklava rolls with an Indian twist: pistachio filling with vibrant green pistachio sprinkled all over the tops, cut slanted like egg rolls. Masi orchestrated the nutty almond barfi, buttery peda, coconutty chum chum, and gooey orange jalebi (yes!).

I was pleasantly surprised at the bright treat. Masi patted my head and said, "I remembered you loved jalebi as kids. I wanted to make sure you had this."

My heart swelled with joy as she doted on me with something so simple and yet so profound. I guessed that was how I'd describe her love for me.

Despite her age and having been away from us for most of our lives, she seemed to remember a lot of the little things. Food was big in our family. Our lives really did revolve around it. Food was love, and Masi's love for us poured out in her cooking.

A lot of the sweets were remakes of yesterday's dabba stuffers, but there was no way they could've made enough for the tins *and* for garba at the same time. Besides, as Mummie had said, it was better cooking with family. So she'd split the sweets-making into two sessions.

Masi handed me a tray of various treats. I looked at them, filled with the awkwardness of having basically called out her colorism beliefs the other morning. She smiled with that grandmother-love-type warmth. Her eyes creased behind her glasses.

I took a bite.

Jalebi looked like small funnel cakes. They were orange discs of batter fried into thin crisscrossing rings and soaked in saffron syrup. The first bite was a little crunchy, the inside soft, and the entire thing coated in gooey, sugary syrup.

My eyelids fluttered. "This is so good. Just like I remember."

She said, "Everything is about Maitri this week, but since I can't stay too long after the wedding, I wanted to make sure that you got something special, too, beta. Especially with all the hard work you've been putting in."

She hugged me and kissed my head, and my eyes watered.

"I love you," I muttered into her shoulder, overcome with sentiment and missing my grandmother and loving Masi and just, ugh, knowing she wouldn't be here forever.

"Why are you so emotional?" she asked, and rubbed my shoulder, offering another sweet.

She handed sweets out to everyone, absorbed all their praise with humility, and told them the sweets were inspired by me. It was why my sisters called me "sweets." It had all started with Masi.

Since Masi didn't have ties to the Trinidadian wedding traditions but wanted to help, she, as the matriarch, took a role in parching laawa on an open flame in the backyard. Mummie was getting teary-eyed watching her, and I bet she wished her mom was here to do this.

We stood around Masi as she worked. Mummie explained, "People say the more the grain parches, the happier the marriage will be. Later, we'll put the rice into a container for the ceremony." We oohed and ahhed and clapped as the grain transformed.

"Maitri and Pranit will have a long and joyous marriage!" Mummie declared and hugged Maitri. Who, of course, started to cry. And I was posting it all to social.

"That's so awesome! Good to know," a deep, familiar voice said behind me, his hands gently touching my back in a way I hoped no one noticed unless he wanted us to die before the wedding.

"You made it," I said to Naveen and his mother. Neelish and his dad were nowhere to be found. "But . . . why are you here? This is mainly for the women," I teased.

He shrugged but smiled a little, like he didn't mind being here. "Escorting my mom."

All the men, as few as they were, were noticeably inside the house. My mom's side . . . was about to get a bit rowdy. Their noise level rose, chattering, laughing. They sat around Maitri on the deck as some of my visiting cousins read poetry and sang . . . some pretty raunchy lyrics.

Then my aunts pulled out an eggplant. At first, I was like, huh?

But then Naveen's cheeks turned red, and he quickly ducked inside.

I turned back to the married women cackling around the eggplant from my remote spot near the back door. They took the eggplant and, um . . . chimed in to tell Maitri all the things she could do with it and how to handle it. And not like cooking it. So not the conversation I needed to hear. It wasn't like I didn't know what sex was, but dang, I did *not* want to hear my mom and my aunts giving details and advice on how to get freaky in the sheets.

My eyes went wide, and I froze. My jaw dropped—I mean, the hinges barely stayed stuck together. Ew. By the looks of Maitri's bright-red face, she didn't know how to react, either. She sure knew what sex was, but she probably wasn't prepared for this level of graphic description.

This was definitely *not* in the schedule.

Maitri glanced over her shoulder, catching my eye with equal parts horror, humor, and embarrassment on her face. She bit her lip and gave a long blink, trying not to laugh, which in turn made me want to laugh.

This was like health class in ninth grade when the teacher had pulled out a banana to show us how to properly put on a condom. I had never looked at a banana the same way again . . . and I would probably never look at an eggplant the same way after tonight.

"This is how you should hold . . ." my forty-something-year-old Hetal Masi from Trinidad began. She was fresh off the plane and getting fresh with that eggplant.

"And maybe . . ." another chimed in.

"Oh my god," I muttered. Shaking my head and standing, I grumbled, "I can't even right now."

"Oh, ha. You don't need to be here for this!" Mummie chided. "Much too young! Go to your room."

I immediately went inside. Heat crept up my face and arms. At least all the men were focused on a cricket match and didn't notice me stumble in.

The gang of unmarried female cousins grinned when I approached.

"You should've known to get out of there!" Neha said.

My face was all kinds of warm as I fought off the knowledge of how the older women in my family handled their men. "How was I supposed to know? No one warned me!"

They laughed so hard that I thought my dad would tell us to be quiet.

Krish wiped her tears of laughter and said, "Your mom warned us earlier today."

I scratched my neck and let my hand hang there, my gaze wandering off. "She didn't warn me. Now I'm scarred for life."

"Oh, come on!" She nudged me. "Like you don't know what happens."

Ah! How could she even joke like that with Naveen walking toward us?

I grunted. "It's the fact that I now know what all of my aunts do. I might never be able to look my uncles in the eye again. Your parents still do it," I concluded childishly to shut them up.

They cringed as I edited and uploaded some pictures from tonight—minus the eggplant. There were lots of shots of sweets and food and family. Heart emojis galore!

CHAPTER TWENTY-ONE
(Friday Evening: Two Days Until the Wedding)

#MehndiNight

My mom, my sisters, and I sat in a row like an efficient assembly line. The makeup artist lifted a foundation brush to Mummie's face, but she pulled back and said, "That's enough."

"Mummie," Maitri said, "she's not done."

"I don't want to look like a streetwalker."

I giggled, but Maitri rolled her eyes with a sigh. "She only put primer on your face. You don't even have makeup on."

Mummie grumbled but let the artist put on a very light layer of makeup, then left Maitri's room to tend to a million things downstairs.

The artist in front of me worked on my . . . I dunno . . . third layer? . . . of makeup and patted false eyelashes on. They were heavy and encumbered my vision. I kept squinting, hyperaware of their presence.

"First time wearing false lashes?" the lady asked.

"Can you tell?" I reached up for them but stopped before I rubbed my eyes. I wanted to peel these creepy things right off.

"You'll get used to them after a few minutes."

"Do we have to wear all this?" I muttered to Maitri, who sat to my right.

"Yes," she replied as someone else on the makeup/hair team worked on her long, dark hair, pinning little silver stars throughout so she looked like a cosmic goddess. "The professional photography and videography starts today. We need high-def makeup. And what are you complaining about? You'll never have on as much as I do."

True, but Maitri liked makeup. I couldn't care less.

Soon enough, the hair lady came to me, and I balled my hands into fists.

"How would you like your hair?" she asked, but she knew. We all had our hair designs prepared, fully approved by the bride, of course.

"Top bun," I said, trying to keep heat and harsh products off my hair for as long as possible. A top bun just called for a hair tie and bobby pins.

She was done with my hair in no time, pulling out a few ringlets from my bun to frame my face.

"So, you've been spending a lot of time with Naveen?" Maitri asked.

"Kissing?" Neha asked, making smoochy noises.

"Where's my fork?" Urvi teased.

They laughed.

I grunted. "OK. Let's get one thing straight. I am *not* interested in any guy, much less someone who's returning to his home halfway around the world next week. We've got important things to focus on. Remember? So, no. There are no feelings to be had or kisses to be made. Nothing but hard work, and we now have one day left to practice because someone decided they wanted us to do a duet."

There was a brief pause, a moment when I foolishly thought this conversation was over. But then my sisters, all at once, said, "Nah!"

"We see how you look at each other," Urvi commented before taking a sip of water and laying a hand on her belly.

"And how you blush when you're dancing," Maitri added.

"I do not!" I protested.

"And how he flirts with you," Neha said.

My face turned red as I glared straight ahead at my reflection in the mirror, refusing to meet their stares. "No. Just no."

But they didn't relent. Not even when the photographer knocked on the open door to Maitri's room and started taking pictures of this very important wedding moment. We posed and stopped talking for a second here and there, but my sisters kept on with the questions.

"That's it. I'm done with this nonsense. Are you done, too?" I asked the hair and makeup ladies, who nodded and stepped back.

"Thanks." I picked up the skirts of my hot-pink–and–lime-green chaniya choli and went to my room, my bangles tinkling and anklets chiming, leaving the cackling behind.

"Oh! You look so beautiful," Masi said, catching me partway down the hall. "Like a Bollywood actress." She cupped my cheeks in her small, warm hands and invited the attention of my parents, who had just opened the front door to a sea of family below. The women all looked up at me and whistled. And not delicate whistles, but full-on catcalls.

My neck turned hot, especially when Papa *applauded*. He practically waltzed up the stairs in his brand-new metallic orange-and-cream sherwani, took me by the shoulders, and studied me with misty eyes. "My beta, you are perfection." Then he kissed my forehead.

"Are you losing it because Maitri is getting married?" I asked.

He hugged me tight. "I just want you to know."

"Are you worried because Mummie thinks I'm going to mess something up?" I asked, straining my neck so that my made-up face wouldn't smush against his shoulder and stain his outfit.

He laughed, which was his nice way of saying, *Yeah, so don't mess anything up.* Instead, he said, "It's an important time for you, with college letters coming in. I want you to know that I'm so proud of you, no matter what happens. But no worries! I know the best colleges will make offers, and soon you'll be applying to law school and, before you know it, getting ready for your own wedding."

"You really mean it? That you'll be proud of me no matter what?"

He pulled away. "Of course. Why are you worried?"

I shook my head and forced a smile, my heart pulling every which way. Would he really still say this if he knew I was planning on studying music instead of law? "I want to make you proud."

"I have no doubt that you will."

Did he, though?

"I'll see you downstairs soon."

"OK." I watched as he poked his head into Maitri's room and gushed over the bride.

God. He was *so* proud of us. I didn't ever want to let him down. But how much pride would he still have in me if I didn't get into any college, much less law school? What if I made it as a musician? Would he still be this happy? What if I tried my hardest but failed at becoming a professional violinist? Would he care?

One thing was for sure—he couldn't catch me sneaking out tomorrow night for the final audition.

I backed into my room to check my reflection. Well, what do ya know? I only barely looked like a streetwalker. But seriously. Wow.

I turned my face this way and that. Even with lighter makeup, the artist had made me look . . . beautiful. My skin was flawless. There were no irritated red patches or dark spots or freckles or that pimple on the side of my face that I always slept on. My eyes were awake and glowing, and those lashes . . . yep, they made a world of difference. And the lipstick, OMG. Hot pink, of course, to match my shimmering chaniya choli.

My hair was super cute, too. It was in a high bun, not so tight as to be flat, but better done than my normal loose bun that looked like an exploding hairpiece as big as my head.

I twirled, loving how my pink chaniya flowed and the way the stitched green-and-purple floral designs sparkled with metallic zari. The skirt grazed the floor and matched the choli, which had a modest neckline over my nonexistent boobs. Built-in padding for the win! The sleeveless, nearly backless, crop top–style bodice was tied and tight with tassels at the back of my neck. My bangles matched in alternating bands of pink, green, purple, and gold.

We all met downstairs, a rainbow of colors. Seriously. We even posed for pictures from lightest (yellow on Jyoti) to darkest (purple on Krish).

The dhol and tassa players arrived, all women. Bam. The dhol player adjusted the straps on the big barrel hanging from her shoulders and readied her drumsticks. Her movements, her energy, her flow—I couldn't even understand the coordination. Plus, that thing looked heavy hanging from her neck, covering nearly her entire torso and thighs.

The musicians and photographers took their places. When the videographer set up at the bottom of the steps to capture the bride as she entered her mehndi/maticoor night, my heart skipped a beat.

The pros were here now. We were less than forty-eight hours from losing her. As long as she didn't cry . . .

When she waltzed down the stairs in an elegant midnight-blue–and–gold chaniya choli, silver stars sparkling in her hair, we held our collective breath and then clapped. She held a hand to her chest, and, seeing this ocean of loving family swarming around her with hugs and chattering and beaming smiles, she started to tear up. When Mummie hugged her and all our aunts squeezed her, tears trickled down her cheeks.

Papa came over, and everyone parted like the Red Sea.

"My beautiful little girl," he said, embracing her. And then Maitri lost it.

I rushed over to wipe her cheeks. "Don't ruin the makeup. You're not done with pictures."

"Thank you," she mumbled.

"Let's get the puja going." Mummie took it from there, giving thanks and offering blessings over Maitri.

I zoned out with Krish and Neha at my side.

We hung around the outskirts of the ornately decorated living room as my girls munched on nutty sweets. Krish spooned up flavorful bites of warm and spicy potato-stuffed samosa chaat, piled with chutneys and garnished with crunchy fried sev, drizzled with yogurt and a sprinkle of chopped cilantro and tomato.

"Try this," she said, feeding me a spoonful.

Bursts of spice, tartness, and sweetness mingled in my mouth. Yum! We were all about street food tonight. Mini dabeli toasted to buttery perfection. Pani puri stuffed with savory potato and lentils and dripping with mint water.

The puja ended pretty quickly. My parents kept the sacred prayer tray in front of the shrine while the party got underway. Our house basically turned into a club: dancing, karaoke, jokes, poetry readings, and more, um, eggplant enthusiasm, all in a storm of music, laughter, and upbeat conversations.

"Let's get our mehndi done!" I said, pulling Krish up and tugging her along behind me before Neha cut in front of us.

Of course, Maitri had hers done first, so elaborate that she required two mehndi artists to work on her at the same time for more than an hour. Maitri, like the queen she was, sat on a throne draped in glittering gold cloth. One artist worked on each hand/arm and then switched to her feet. We all watched her for the first few minutes and took pictures as the artists deftly created intricate designs of flowers and peacock tails from her pedicured toes halfway up her shins, and from her freshly manicured fingernails halfway up her forearms, front and back, until she was covered in delicately detailed designs made from green paste.

Mehndi was hands-down one of the most exciting things about big festivities. I didn't know how to explain it, but almost every desi girl I knew, whether they were into mehndi or not, was excited to get it done for weddings. The food and clothes were the next best things.

Before Krish and I sat down to get ours done by the other two mehndi artists, we used the restroom first, 'cause there was nothing worse than ruining your mehndi game because you had to pee before the paste dried. We sat on plush pillows on the floor while an artist worked on each of us.

I sat opposite the woman and offered my right hand, palm up.

"How far up?" the artist asked.

Most others just had simple, quick designs on their palms. I was going to be extra and asked, "Can you do front and back partway up to the elbow?"

"That's a lot . . ."

"Oh, sister to the bride." That was a card worth playing all weekend. Eat first, get third helpings of dessert, cut in bathroom lines, get the second-to-most mehndi done.

"Oh, OK."

She rapidly laid cool paste on my skin in designs, both mesmerizing and calming. The earthy, leafy scent filled my nostrils. I took a short video capturing the speed, accuracy, and skill of the artist and one-handedly posted it to the joint social media.

The artist worked quickly on my hand as music played around us, thankfully drowning out rowdy aunties getting wild with once-beloved vegetables.

Behind us, a wild party raged, but around the artists, it was like being in a salon, everyone chattering and gossiping about all the eligible bachelors.

Thank goodness whatever nonsense my sisters and mom were up to hadn't entered the gossip mill. I was happy just to listen to all of them. Even more so, against my instincts, when they mentioned the "überhandsome Patel brothers," as in Neelish and Naveen.

I craned my head back to check out who was raving about Neelish. Priyanka, with her rocker-chick bangs and hot-pink nails to match her hot-pink–and–teal chaniya choli. Hmm. I wondered if she knew he was dating someone.

"My back is killing me," I groaned, and awkwardly shifted on the floor. I couldn't even raise myself to stand. My core muscles sucked.

"You look like a beached whale," Neha said from down the line of plush pillows.

"I got you," Krish said. She'd only gotten partial hands done and was finished. She crawled on her knees to sit behind me. My own personal backrest.

"Thanks, cuz."

"No problem. Are you almost done? I can't wait to eat dabeli," she said.

My mouth watered at the thought of biting into a savory mini-burger filled with a curried mashed potato patty, topped with cilantro, pomegranate seeds, and onions and a spread of both sweet and spicy chutneys.

When the artist finally finished my mehndi, I managed to get to my knees. From there, I eventually made it to my feet.

"All those squats in PE paid off," I said, all proud of my little core muscles that could.

We posed around Maitri on her golden princess throne. She was all smiles and blushing cheeks and absolutely flawless. First, the photographer took pictures with just Maitri and the parents, then we sisters were added, then Urvi's husband, then just the sisters, and of course, one with my arms flung around Maitri's neck, just the two of us.

We partied and helped Maitri eat and drink, and someone (not it) helped her to the bathroom, until our mehndi fully dried after an hour of keeping it moist with sugar-lemon water. If the stain didn't set after all that, then it was hopeless.

"It's time!" Mummie said in a loud voice quivering with excitement. "The groom will be here any minute."

A new thrill wriggled through the air as maticoor began. A more hyped party was definitely about to start.

"The youngest sister to the bride," Mummie called.

I nudged Neha forward. As Mummie handed her the tray, she explained to everyone, "In Trinidad, part of maticoor night is giving blessing to the bride during puja. Then the youngest sister, for her youth, purity, and innocence—"

I snickered. Young? Yes. Neha was a jubilant blob of energy wrapped into a fourteen-year-old body. Pure? Maybe. Who knew? Innocent? Definitely not.

"—she'll carry the aarti tray. All of the ladies, married and single, young and old, follow me."

We followed Mummie outside. She walked with Maitri by her side, Neha and Urvi behind her, and then me. The dhol and tassa players started up a soft beat while flanking us. Mummie carried a garden shovel, and we literally danced our way to the neighbor's house.

Our neighbor and one of Mummie's friends, Sally (who was at the party tonight), led us through the gate into her backyard. She was pretty cool to let us do this. Here, Mummie dug up some rich dirt above an underground pipeline and placed it on the aarti tray. This was supposed to be nutrient-rich dirt from beside a flowing river, but whatever. We were in a suburb of Atlanta, and this was the closest we'd get.

It was all tradition, and I wasn't sure how much of it my sisters believed in. One thing we all knew for certain was that tradition was important, as it brought us closer to our elders and generations past. Mummie's parents had passed away a long time ago, but in this moment, we all felt closer to them. I was sure my mom was remembering how this had been done for her right before she'd married Papa.

Another thing we were certain of was that most every tradition happening this weekend was about seeking or giving blessings, washing away impurities, and preparing the bride and groom for their new life as a married couple.

We headed home as soon as the dirt had been collected. Back in Trinidad, we'd meet the groom and his family at the river, but we met them in our driveway instead.

And you didn't know what a party was until an Indian bride welcomed the groom into the wedding festivities.

The drummers went into full swing, their hands moving super-humanly fast against their taut instruments, the beats challenging us all not to dance to the rhythm. The sun was setting beyond the trees, and the groom emerged from his family crowd, all decked out in a shimmering midnight-blue sherwani to match the bride.

Papa and the men met us in the driveway, the guys to our left in front of the garage, the groom and his family in front of us with the street to their backs. Papa went to Pranit's dad and embraced him. It was the meeting of the dads, a moment that made us all smile and clap and go *aw*!

The drummers shifted into high gear, fast, loud, and club-worthy. *Yes, dhol player, with your obvious greatness!*

Papa hugged Pranit next and pulled him into the center of a growing crowd beneath the outdoor lights and a sky full of stars.

The drummers played faster and faster as Papa and Pranit danced around in a circle, linking feet and hopping, adding some shoulder shrugs. Then Mummie joined in, and my parents took out cash, circling it over Pranit's head for blessing and good fortune and then tucking it into the sides of the dhol and tassa drums.

The videographers and photographers were all in the mix to capture every single moment.

Papa didn't stop there. He joyously pulled in Pranit's parents, who dragged in Pranit's older brother and bhabi. Mummie pulled us sisters into the dance, and there we were, in our driveway, dancing our hearts out.

Maitri joined in, dancing beside Pranit, which set off another roar of applause and cheering.

The music never stopped as the bride and groom danced their way into the house and into the wedding celebrations. Pranit was finally able to step over those little foot stickers as he and Maitri, his family and ours, became one. That one step over the threshold led to another outburst like we'd just scored a winning goal.

The party didn't stop there. We danced in a circle in the living room, which was void of furniture for this very reason. I was not the best at dancing freestyle and kept trying to get out of the circle. Even when Pranit pulled me back in, I tried to dance right on back out.

Of all the people in this gigantic crowd, I somehow ended up bumping into Naveen. He was wearing the heck out of a dark green–and–metallic-silver sherwani that made him look like he'd just stepped off a runway. He scratched the back of his head, his eyes wide and his brows high, his cheeks a little on the red side.

"You look . . ." He swallowed hard, a twitch at the corner of his mouth.

I pulled my head back in a way that probably gave me three chins. "Don't say 'like a streetwalker.' My mom already coined that."

"Absolutely stunning. I mean . . . *wow*, Zuri."

Oh. My heart skipped a beat, and suddenly I was very aware of my skin-baring outfit and all the makeup. His appreciative gaze locked me into place. His reddening cheeks and mouth twitch had me believing I'd never be able to move from this spot. Awkward-liking someone was a real thing, and it was absolutely happening to me right now.

"Get back in here!" Maitri called out to me.

I shook my head, bringing myself back into the moment. I was done with all the intense dancing in front of everyone, especially with this racing heart. It was crowded and getting muggy, and I was nearly flush against this cinnamon-scented boy. My head began to reel.

Until Naveen gently grabbed my wrist, then suddenly, I was stuck. I had no desire to escape dancing with Naveen Patel, especially under the safe guise of dancing with family.

This wasn't gossip-worthy or fodder for our moms' wild matchmaking schemes. It was just a family celebration.

Nothing more.

Right?

CHAPTER TWENTY-TWO
(Friday Evening: Two Days Until the Wedding)
#StrokeOfDeath

There were many, many pictures to take with various combinations of the groom's family members and ours, along with friends. My face hurt from smiling. But I also managed to get lots of pics for social media when I wasn't in the professional pictures.

As the couple moved on to the next thing on the schedule, the party kept raging. The guys hurrahed when Pranit, after several minutes of studying Maitri's dried mehndi, found his name delicately and intricately intertwined in the designs. It was like finding Waldo.

Mummie clapped her hands. "Ah! Pranit found his name in the mehndi! Good fortune! Lots of love!" As was the saying. For sure, Pranit was a good detective. His name was very well hidden. I couldn't even see it until he found it.

My mehndi was dry enough that I could eat again. I took a huge helping of pelau on a banana-leaf plate, a perfect rice dish with curried veggies. I ended up having to sit on the swinging bench on the deck because the tables under the tents were full. I tried to eat fast, mainly because I knew Naveen was looking for a seat and there happened to be one right next to me. But with my mehndi having just dried, I ate daintily and awkwardly, trying to avoid dropping crumbles of dried mehndi paste into my food.

"This is so delicious!" Krish said beside me as she stuffed her mouth and placed an extra dabeli on my plate.

"Good looking out!" My eyelids fluttered at the spicy, tangy, buttery explosion on my taste buds. That extra bite from the pomegranate seeds was everything.

"Pace yourself. We've still got s'mores," I said around a mouthful.

"Nice! I don't know what it is about s'mores, but it just makes everything extra special."

"Truth. You're reading my mind! But how will we avoid the stickiness getting on our mehndi?"

"It'll be set by then. Let the crumbs fall. Don't be afraid to wash your hands."

The more packed the tents got, the more crowded the deck got. More and more guests looked for seats. It was a good thing we'd gotten our mehndi done first; we might not have had any-place left to sit!

In the distance, Papa joked about getting Mummie's name on his hand in mehndi. She playfully slapped his shoulder and laughed, as if Papa having a temporary stain representing his undying love for her was madness. Aw. They were so cute.

I snapped a quick picture and uploaded it with heart-eye emojis.

"Is this seat taken?" Naveen asked, glancing at the space to my right.

"No. Sit!" Neha said from two spots over on the other side of Krish.

"Is that cool with you?" Naveen asked me.

"Yeah. Of course," I replied, and scooched over to give him space, although there wasn't much room to spare.

Naveen's butt had barely hit the swing bench when Neha moved Krish over, pushing her into me so that I was crushed against Naveen. My heart did backflips from the adrenaline rush, but I wasn't sure if it was from the sudden jolt, the brief trauma of almost spilling food onto my new and expensive-AF outfit, or touching Naveen.

"Watch it," Krish chided Neha. "I almost spilled my food."

"Yeah, let's not waste any of this amazingness!" Neha said, somehow grinning while shoveling a spoonful into her mouth.

"Sorry," I muttered to Naveen, practically on his lap. I shot death glares at a giggling Neha. An unmarried duo couldn't be this on top of each other in public in my family, but considering the growing crowd and the celebratory atmosphere, only a handful of aunties gave us nosy looks.

"You should be sorry more often," he whispered, his lips twitching the second he said those words.

There was no witty remark that came to mind. No casual way to play that off. So, I did what came naturally—I stuffed my face and ignored him. Yeah. Seemed like the mature thing to do.

We sat cramped on the backyard swing, meant for three but now holding four. Poor Naveen sat on the end, but better him than me. He had a more muscular body and could better withstand the metal armrest from slicing through his side. Granted, he also had a pillow to cushion him against it. We tried not to be right up on each other, so we kept our hands between his thigh and mine in a joint effort.

Soon enough, we melted into conversations as the music of the dhol player reverberated around us. She had been playing since the groom had arrived and now played in time with a playlist Maitri's friends had put together. It was amazing, really, the way she could sync up with today's biggest hits in hip-hop, pop, rock, and of course Bollywood and bhangra. Right now, she was playing along with Rihanna . . . how did she even do that? The woman was like math—incomprehensible.

"She's really good," I commented to Naveen.

"Yeah, she is."

My eyes could barely keep up with the fast pace of her hands as she beat her drum. God, what sort of sorcery was this? Who had that kind of coordination? While her hands were blurs, her body swayed with the music, her head bobbed, and she kept a smile on her face, watching others instead of her instrument.

He whistled. "Leveled up."

"I'm glad the instrument of my heart is small and easy to carry."

"I'm glad my instrument is built in."

I shoved him with my shoulder before realizing what I was doing. More touching? Shame.

Naveen smiled, hiding the twitch of his lips, and watched her again.

We sank back into silence. Not that awkward, what-do-we-say-now kind of silence, but a comfortable let's-be-quiet-and-enjoy-this-time silence. The dhol player changed her tempo as soon as the next song on the playlist came on. She was playing along to Beyoncé's "Single Ladies" like she'd been on the record herself. Wow. Respect.

Pranit held out a hand and pulled Maitri out of her chair when the next song came on, a sultry, soulful one with some pretty racy lyrics. He placed his hands on her hips, and she delicately laid her mehndi-stained arms around his neck. They giggled over trying to keep their outfits, and her mehndi, clean and intact. Which reminded me of my own mehndi.

I glanced down at Naveen's warm, inviting hand, the back of which was resting against my skin. I glanced away, trying not to smile, and focused on the couples dancing. Urvi and Ji-jaji #1 danced, too, encouraging some of the older ones to join them. Only one uncle and aunt from Pranit's side followed. The rest were younger couples and a few kids, who did their own funky thing. Little girls in sparkling chaniya cholis clanked their tiny bangles together while studying their dried mehndi patterns in bursts of giggles and swaying hips. Little boys in kurta pajamas jumped up and down out of pure joy, probably high on sugar.

The only thing that drew me out of the heartwarming scene was Naveen brushing a finger against mine. It was a subtle, highly evocative gesture. It was . . . flirting. I thought.

He did it again. Another stroke. The stroke of death. Because

Naveen Patel was actually getting to me. A guy could be charming and supportive and all that, but if the barest brush of his skin on my skin incited a jumping jack marathon in my stomach in point-two seconds flat, then I was in trouble. Because now this thing was going from friendly to crushworthy. And the cosmos knew when I started crushing on a guy, all hope was lost. All rationale jumped out the window. All logic flung itself off a cliff. All reasoning hurtled into space.

We couldn't do this. I couldn't feel this way for a boy, especially not Naveen. Not like this. Not when it was crunch time. All my other crushes had happened from afar. Like, celebrity, never-going-to-happen, got-over-it-in-a-week afar. Not up close and personal. Not in the flesh, right beside me, touching me, flirting with me, and flat-out challenging me *not* to like him.

My breath hitched when he stroked my finger a third time. I *felt* that one. All the way to my core. Crap. It was happening, wasn't it? And what was I going to do about it? Retrieve my hand and get up? Yes. That was the logical thing to do.

My finger twitched as our gazes fell to our hands. Then my treacherous little finger stroked his hand back. Ah! *WTF?* Shame!

Well, I'd said crushes made logic fling itself off a cliff, didn't I? My brain was losing this battle, and Naveen knew it. In the corner of my eye, I saw his lips lift into a grin. And curse the cosmic rule of crushes, because I smiled, too.

All might be lost.

We sat there for a few minutes longer, knowing we could get

pulled away at any time. For now, we enjoyed this calm in between storms, when no one seemed to notice our hands barely touching.

The number of people dancing increased. I'd danced when I played violin, when I'd been in ballet, when I was alone in my room with my playlist cranked high and the door locked, in garba, in mandir dances, and for festivities like this weekend. I'd definitely never slow danced with a guy, though. It seemed way too intimate. Putting our hands on each other and being that close. There was something very soul-piercing about that, being exposed, raw, self-conscious.

So when Naveen nudged my shoulder with his and cocked his brows, jerking his chin toward those dancing, I just about puked in my mouth. Talk about ruining a gorgeous moment. My heart palpitated hard.

"No thanks," I said, my head down as heat crept across my chest.

"One dance?" He immediately swiped the back of his neck with his free hand. "We wouldn't be the only ones."

"No. Lord, you really want our moms planning our wedding, don't you?"

He chuckled and looked over at me. "Would it be a big deal? I mean, to dance."

I shook my head. No. Not really, not here. So many people were dancing with friends and family, and no one would likely think too much of me having one dance with a visiting cousin from halfway across the world who was set to depart in another week.

I swallowed. My chest tingled with an ambush of excitement when he asked again and added a decadent "please." OK. There wasn't anything smooth or charming about when his voice cracked, except for the fact that his voice cracked. Also, that accent. How was a girl supposed to say no to that? Not when he was literally shoulder to shoulder with me, holding my hand, his warmth and cinnamon-spice scent all over me.

Gazes fell upon us like snowflakes, subtly and fleetingly, when Naveen leaned into me and whispered in my ear, "OK. Let me know if you change your mind?"

My heart dropped into the pit of my stomach, where hordes of butterflies were already freaking out. I was getting dizzy. Yeah. I knew exactly what was going to happen if he kept touching me, if he kept whispering in my ear.

The only thing that would get me out of my head was to move.

I sighed, shivering. "Fine."

"Is that a yes?" he asked, hopeful and sort of shocked.

"This *one* time." I held up a finger. A crumb of dried mehndi paste tumbled off the crease.

"If I ask again?"

I shook my head in warning. "And you play this game? I might actually throw my drink in your face."

"Good thing you're not holding a drink."

Oh crap. I wasn't? "Not this time."

Naveen stood and offered his hand with a short bow. I'd hoped those fleeting glances from others would move on, but then someone—possibly Neha—whistled, and suddenly a whole bunch of eyes turned toward us and a whole lot of tongues started wagging. But when the guys joined in, it turned into teasing instead of chiding. Embarrassing nonetheless.

I begrudgingly stood, holding my hands up to remind him of my mehndi.

"Can't ruin a girl's mehndi, can I?"

I cleared my throat and muttered, "Nope."

He placed his hand on my lower back, on the bare skin between the top of my chaniya and below the hem of the snug choli.

He immediately retracted his hand, saying, "Sorry," just loud enough for me to hear him.

Naveen followed me, barefoot, to the unofficial dance area out on the grass, hiding behind other dancers. We hadn't bothered putting on our shoes when we came into the backyard, not when we had a nice large clean deck. Now, my soles pressed into cool grass, tickling my toes. There was something soothing about being barefoot in the grass, and there was something very romantic about dancing barefoot in the grass. Wasn't there a song about that?

I found myself facing Naveen and the iridescent red buttons of his otherwise forest-green kurta with shimmering green mandala designs, paisley, and swirls.

We danced back and forth, his hands light on my hips, barely touching, his thumbs gently grazing the skin just above my chaniya. My wrists hung loose around his shoulders, careful to not ruin my mehndi or his clothes. This seemed romantic but was turning awkward. Heat gathered at my neck as I wondered if people were watching us, wondering about us, and if Naveen was trying to get me to lower my guard or if he was just nervous.

At least he was a good dancer and wasn't stepping on my feet the way I kept stubbing my toe against his.

"Ow," he teased, feigning injury.

"Yeah, yeah."

"You really do look amazing," he said.

I glanced up at him and then away. I knew I looked good. I didn't need anyone to tell me that, but coming from Naveen, the compliment felt nice. Instead of a simple thank-you, I replied, "Thank you. It's all because of the pros who worked on my makeup and hair and an outfit that took me four days and fifteen stores to put together because the bride had to approve."

He chuckled. "Weddings are a lot of work when you're immediate family."

"You don't even know the half of it."

We swayed for a bit longer, but dangling my arms from his shoulders without getting mehndi on him was a literal stretch. I scrunched my nose.

"What?" he asked.

"You're too tall for me."

He threw his head back in laughter as he guided us toward the fence so that other dancers blocked us from needling eyes. "I thought girls liked tall guys."

"There has to be a happy medium. I can barely reach around your neck."

"Well, here." He hoisted me onto his feet in a quick, fluid movement. "Is that OK?"

I nodded, ignoring the jitters in my stomach and how warm his hands were, holding on to my waist so that I wouldn't fall. We continued to slow dance into the next song, my feet stuck on top of his as he led our movements.

My arms wiggled farther up his shoulders.

"Better?" he asked.

"Yes. But you're still too tall for me."

He shrugged, the movement shuffling my arms closer to his neck. "Tall guys are good for reaching things on the top shelf, changing lightbulbs, um, dusting . . ."

I giggled at the thought of Naveen not needing to stand on his tiptoes or on a chair as he used a Swiffer to clean the perpetually dusty vents at our house. "OK. OK. Your height isn't the worst thing about you."

"So what is?"

"The worst thing about you, Naveen? Oh, easily your continual cockiness and the way you think I'll catch feelings for you before you leave. Ya know? To your home. In South Africa. Half a world away."

"Whoa. Don't hold back."

The thing about standing on a guy's feet while dancing, other than wondering if I was hurting him, was that there wasn't much room left between us. Our fronts were practically pressed together, no matter how much I struggled to lean back. If I leaned back any farther, I'd for sure topple over.

Still, this wasn't terrible. Especially when the couples, mainly my elder sisters and cousins, all converged into a barrier of slowly moving bodies to shield us from prying stares. I couldn't help but inhale Naveen's scent. Honestly? I'd miss him come next week, and that made my heart fracture a bit. What was this? What a horrid feeling gnawing at my insides. I didn't want to feel this way about anyone because . . . well . . . it was really going to hurt when he left.

His hands were on my back, and I could feel his left thumb push around the ring on his left hand. He twisted his lips in thought, then said, "I'm not really cocky, you know."

"Could've fooled me," I said cautiously.

"It's an act," he confessed.

Anyone could say that, especially if they were just trying to deny a negative trait or throw me off. But the short-lived twitch of his lips spoke volumes—more than words could have, probably. Sure, he could've faked the twitch. Maybe the twitch was a long con. But it was hard to fake blushing, and boy, did he blush.

"You got an Emmy for that acting?" I asked, because what was up with the ring? Did he play with it to concentrate on lies? Or was it a nerves thing?

He swallowed and smiled a small smile.

I asked, "Why the act? You don't know me. We probably won't ever see each other again."

"Defense mechanism, I think."

"You think?" I asked. "Or you know?"

He blew out a breath over my head. "I know."

"What are you covering up?" I probed.

He stretched his neck one way and then another. "Being nervous, or scared, maybe?"

"Of what? Li'l ol' me?" I said with an innocent smile.

He laughed. "Yeah. You make me nervous."

"Why?"

He looked off to the right, at the wall of people, when he replied, "You going to make me say it?"

"Mmm-hmm," I mumbled, expecting him to say something about how I was hot or whatever guys thought girls wanted to hear.

He took a big breath and released it, his gaze coming back to mine. "You're amazing and a little intimidating and brilliant with the violin. And that makes me not know how to act around you, maybe?"

"Oh," I replied, flattered and totally not expecting to be.

He cleared his throat and quickly added, "Not that it's an excuse to mess with you, but it was kind of fun."

"Quit while you're ahead," I said.

"I didn't mean to add stress or fill up your headspace by making you wonder about my intentions. I'm not like that, I promise. Plus, there's too much connected family between us for anyone to let me get away with hurting you. I'd never want to hurt you."

I bit my lip to keep from smiling.

He pushed the ring around more against my back. "And, um, I'm also scared that I won't make it with music, which gets me depressed. Like, I'm afraid my creativity might die."

Oh, yeah. I knew that feeling all too well, and boy, was it numbing and nasty and at the same time volatile and consuming.

"So I guess my brain puts up barriers to make the rejections less painful. Probably makes me look stupid, too?" he half asked, half admitted.

I smirked. "Yeah, it does."

He sucked in a breath and pulled away when the song ended and another began. "You cut me so deep," he joked.

My hands dangled at my sides, and we watched one another while others danced around us. Some continued on from the last song; some walked away and were replaced by others.

Slow songs were few and far between tonight. We'd have more during the reception, but for now, almost all the music was lively.

"Thanks for the one dance," Naveen said, lingering in place.

Oh, what the heck! "Hey," I said when he turned to walk away.

"Yeah?"

"One more dance?"

His grin gradually stretched across his face. "OK."

We kept a short distance between us and danced. Not too fast, not too slow, not too clubbish, not too prudish.

"Don't get too cocky," I warned. "I can still push you into the firepit. It's right behind you. Don't tempt me."

He laughed close to my hair, his breath smelling like mint chutney.

"Did you just sniff my hair?"

His face turned red. "You smell very nice. Have to get my fill of you before I leave."

"That was so cheesy that I'm embarrassed for you."

"Ouch." He pouted.

"You have a few days left," I stated, surprised by how sad that made me.

"You'll miss me?" he asked, hopeful.

I scoffed, brushing off the truth that maybe I would miss him. "You'd be out of my head then."

"So I *am* in your head now?" He pressed his forehead against mine for a brief second.

My gut tied into knots from that simple, unassuming tap. "Now you're wearing makeup, too," I teased.

"What?" He rubbed his forehead.

"So not your color!"

He rubbed even harder, and I laughed. My makeup had been covered with setting powder, and there wasn't anything on his face. But it was fun to watch him rub his forehead red.

For one more song, we danced just like this, in our own little corner of the backyard, beneath the dark shroud of night illuminated by a giant moon and a million stars. Fairy lights twinkled around us, snaking across the fence and up the trees. Behind us, the backyard lights shone faintly over guests enjoying the deck. Open windows displayed another crowd inside the glow of the house.

A photographer and videographer waltzed past us, capturing every moment, but we were only vaguely aware that they'd captured ours, too.

CHAPTER TWENTY-THREE
(Saturday Morning: One Day Until the Wedding)

#PithiHaldi

By seven in the morning, Maitri was dressed, with the pros fixing her hair and makeup. Beside her were Urvi and even Neha, who was usually the last of us to rise. Today, I was the last one to wake up from the dead. Seriously, how was everyone so rested and energetic after last night?

My sisters glanced at me as I dragged myself past Maitri's open bedroom door, mumbling greetings on my way to pee.

"Morning, sleepyhead. Better hurry up," Urvi said, looking perfectly content sitting there with her water bottle and letting someone prep her.

"Notice you went missing again last night. And so did a certain boy," Neha teased.

I groaned and slumped into the bathroom for a quick shower.

With the crowds downstairs last night, it had been easy to sneak off to my room with Naveen again. Better than that, it had been easy to practice. The pounding music had drowned out my violin and Naveen's singing.

While most movies and shows and books suggested that being alone with a boy in your bedroom was prime time for romance, it hadn't been that way with us. While the mehndi party had raged on until one in the morning, we'd worked. Hard.

"It's perfect," he'd finally said last night with a yawn. "Your mehndi didn't get messed up with playing?" He took my hands in his and examined them. Pieces of the dried mehndi had broken off, revealing burnt-orange stains, but most had stayed intact. I'd found some Medfix breathable tape and bandaged my hands and wrists to protect my mehndi from getting ruined while I practiced and, more importantly, to protect my violin from collecting crumbling pieces of dried mehndi paste.

After Naveen had left, I'd kept the tape secure while changing and washing up. It had taken *three* makeup remover wipes to get my face as clean as possible without washing off the mehndi. I was lucky I hadn't woken up with a bunch of pimples.

I washed off the mehndi during my shower, giddy that the stain had darkened to red. Hopefully, it would deepen to full dark maroon or near black by tomorrow, in time for the wedding. It put a smile on my face and zapped some much-needed energy into my sleepy bones.

I hurried through my shower, masterfully keeping my hair dry, changed into a peach-and-gold salwar kameez, and got my hair and makeup done. I went sleeveless again, which might make Masi wince a bit at my risqué choice, but it was flattering. Funny how we wore midriff-baring chaniya cholis and saris but drew the line at sleeveless clothes. Whatever.

The top was snug around my boobs and flowed a little looser all the way to my calves. It was heavy with mirror work and metallic stitching and ornate designs that shimmered with every movement. The leggings were . . . tights. Ugh. Again with this trend? And my dupatta, all gold net, hung over one shoulder.

I slipped on matching bangles, of course, in alternating colors of matte peach and glitzy gold.

The stylist did my hair in a loose, thick braid that swept over my left shoulder with ringlets framing my face again. She was the same woman from yesterday, as was the makeup artist. They were a team and would be meeting us at the hotel to get us ready for garba tonight and the wedding and reception tomorrow.

I smacked my peach-colored lips at my reflection. Dang, I was looking too cute not to take a few selfies in the morning light inside my bedroom. And post them to my own social media, which had been pretty dry since I'd been covering the couple's joint social.

Had I gotten up earlier, I could've eaten breakfast. But it was too late for that, and surely a scolding from Mummie was waiting for me. Besides, the much-needed sleep was worth it, and it wasn't as if I'd starve this weekend. Lunch was on the schedule right after pithi.

Family had already arrived by the time I got downstairs. Pithi started with—ya guessed it—puja and aarti in front of the shrine, with the same Brahman and emblems and gestures that we'd done last Sunday. Pithi was the second-most-important ritual after the wedding itself.

I sat on the outskirts, as per usual, nudging Krish with my shoulder when I found a tight spot beside her. All the women sat around on the floor closest to the shrine, diligently engrossed in the religious stuff, my parents next to Maitri and the Brahman, but the rest of the guys congregated in the other rooms. Snacking, chatting, playing on their phones.

Lucky bastards.

The videographer and photographer did their thing, capturing moments. There weren't nearly as many people here as there had been last night, and this definitely wasn't a loud party. There was only family present, plus some of Maitri's closest friends and bridesmaids in order to help the bride get ready for her big day.

Now the fun stuff—smothering my sister with haldi! The turmeric-milk paste was supposed to soften the skin and give her a glow for the big day. While it did make the skin soft, it also left horrible yellow stains that were impossible to get out, so we were careful not to get it on our clothes. As for the bride? Of course she was going to get it all over her. Her outfit was a one-time wham-bam, thanks-for-the-haldi-ma'am ensemble.

When the puja was over, everyone got up and shuffled over into the family room, where the guys had cleaned up the last of the previous night's party, leaving just Maitri's throne. Her princess-in-another-life vibes were basically calling all weekend. She had three more thrones to sit on.

Maitri was decked out in a red-and-yellow chaniya choli with matching flower bangles and floral jewelry, looking like an ethereal meadow goddess. Her makeup was light and glowing with a tinge of pink blush and light pink lipstick. Her yellow floral earrings dangled partway down her neck. She even wore a wreath of yellow and pink flowers tucked into her waves.

She sat on her throne, posing for pictures solo and with vari-ous groups, including just us four sisters. When that was done—and boy, I knew her face was hurting from all the smiles, because mine hurt from just the few—the videographer set up shop several feet in front of Maitri while the photographer moved around us.

Mummie went first. From the offering tray, she placed a pinch of red sindoor powder on Maitri's forehead at her hairline, then pressed rice grains against it. Then she took one of many cut-up banana leaves, scooped a small amount of sun-yellow haldi onto the tip, and gently rubbed it against Maitri's cheeks. We applauded as Maitri and my mom embraced. The crying hadn't commenced yet. Then went Papa. Then Urvi, then me, and finally Neha.

We were kind about it this time around, because all the women in the family had to get their turns. We'd already smeared her entire face, now bright yellow. Others began smearing haldi across her upper arms and forearms and hands, then others to her shins and feet.

Everyone offered her an envelope of cash when it was their turn, always a denomination that ended with a one—eleven dol-lars, twenty-one, fifty-one, one hundred and one, depending on how much someone loved her. Ha, just kidding. Well, actually . . .

By the time everyone was finished, Maitri had thin smears across her face like eye black on a football field, all over her arms up to her sleeveless top, and on her exposed feet and calves.

But when everyone had had their turn? I got back in line after her friends, forwent the banana leaf, scooped up a big ol' glob of haldi with my fingers, and gave Maitri a menacing look.

"Be careful," she warned.

Then Neha followed suit, raising her brows in that mischievous, fear-for-your-life look. And then we lunged for our sister, trying not to knock her over but launching into an all-out haldi battle for our lives. Intertwining limbs struggled for dominance while Maitri arched back away from us, but here was the thing: She wasn't allowed to get off her throne. She was stuck and at our mercy. She cried out, half laughing along with everyone else, as we smeared inordinate amounts of paste all over her face and neck, up one nostril, in her mouth, and in her hair.

"Agh!" she squealed and spat, her eyes half closed from the weight of paste on her lashes. She swept off some of the haldi from her face and returned the favor by smearing it on us, too.

But we were not doused like she was.

The crowd laughed at us, with us. We cackled, and Papa chuckled, pulling us off and letting the rest of the morning get on its way.

"Wait until we're done," Maitri playfully warned.

Then Mummie's brothers lifted the princess up, throne and all, and carried her to the backyard. How she didn't tip over or ram her head into the door frame was beyond me. More cheering and applause, and more pictures were taken.

We were supposed to gently help her clean off some of the paste before she went upstairs to shower. Some wet washcloths would suffice. But then her friends ambushed her, and we grabbed the hose, and yep . . . literally hosed her down. But just her face. We weren't trying to do a wet choli contest.

Maitri screamed and froze when a splash of water hit her. Her hands were up in the air, her mouth gaping open, her eyes blinking away droplets in absolute shock.

"Stop that before she gets sick," Mummie scolded, although she was smiling, so she couldn't have been too upset.

Papa wrapped Maitri in a towel. "Being so mean to my baby girl," he said with a chuckle.

"You're dead," she mouthed to us, but then she laughed with a shake of her head and hurried upstairs to shower quickly while we feasted on the deck and underneath the tents still set up from last night.

The Brahman and videographer and photographer bounced to Pranit's for his pithi/haldi with his side of the family. Having ours first gave us more time to get ready for tonight.

I didn't hang around for long this time. We'd serve everyone lunch to thank them for coming, and they would eat and go before my family started napping before garba or got errands done.

After scarfing lunch, not bothering to mingle, I ran up to my room, changed into jeans and a T-shirt, and grabbed my already-packed suitcase. I double- and triple-checked that I had everything I needed: my next three wedding outfits with matching shoes, jewelry, and hairpieces; my audition outfit; pajamas and undergarments; toiletries; and my beloved violin.

"Be on your best behavior," Mummie warned as I packed the car.

"Of course!"

My parents, Masi, Urvi, and Jijaji #1 were staying at the house, but my parents were actually letting me stay at the hotel! Granted, I had to share with Neha and my room was next to Maitri's, but still!

Krish: You ready for tonight? Got all your stuff? Ready to do your thing at garba and sneak out?
Me: You know it! I'm getting ready to leave for the hotel.
Krish: Right after our dance, we'll run up to your room. Sethal and Jyoti will stand guard.
Me: You are AWESOME! <3
Krish: I know. I want you to remember this moment when you're living your dreams.

I grinned and left without my sisters. Neha could come later with Maitri. I took off on the fifteen-minute drive north, which placed me closer to the competition venue by eight minutes.

As soon as I arrived at the giant ten-story hotel with its own one-acre parking lot, I went straight to the elevator, looking all around at the massive chandeliers, gold-rimmed paintings, and fancy metallic decor. It felt pretty grown up getting our own room with no parents, getting to wear robes and slippers and drinking juice out of wineglasses.

I quickly unpacked my bags and hung the DO NOT DISTURB sign on the doorknob, where it would remain for the rest of my stay. I shimmied off some of my anxiety by sitting on the bed and practicing soft chords. The hotel was nice but not too fancy, quiet but not dead. It was clean-smelling, with shimmering wallpaper and gold-framed paintings and large rooms. Alone and relaxing.

I played until my fingers ached, until someone knocked on the door. The clock on the bedside stand told me that I'd been playing nonstop for an hour. Wow. Time really had no meaning when my violin and I got things going.

I swung back the door, expecting Neha but coming face-to-face with Naveen.

"Hey," he said.

My stomach did a flip. "Hi. Um. What are you doing here?"

"We're staying at the hotel, too, remember? We're down the hallway around the corner, of course, so the groom doesn't see the bride. Guess the whole wedding party is on the same floor."

I spilled out a breath. "Oh yeah. That's right."

"Can I come in?"

"Uh . . ." I panicked and froze on the spot.

"Maybe we can practice a few times before the finals?" he suggested.

Right. We needed to practice for tonight and tomorrow, and the stupid clock was counting down. I nodded and let him in.

"Neha will be here any minute," I announced a little too loudly.

"Cool. She knows, though, right? About us? Practicing, I mean."

"She thinks we're practicing for the reception. Only some cousins know about the competition. Not that they'll stop attacking me with questions every time we disappear to practice."

He shrugged and stuffed his hands into his jeans pockets. "What kinds of questions? Probably not worse than what I get."

"Who's asking you questions, and why?"

He smiled, melting any flicker of annoyance. "You first."

I rolled my eyes. "My sisters think we like each other."

"Don't we, though?"

"I mean, *like* like."

"Still don't get the confusion."

I gently shoved him into the wall. "Your turn."

"Well, my side definitely knows we like each other."

"No. Because . . . no." Ugh. That was all I could come up with?

"Strong argument."

I shoved him again. This time he kept my hands and held them to his chest. I gasped. There was no place to go, not with the wall behind him and the bed behind me. How did we always end up in a bedroom alone? And where was nosy-body Neha to storm in when she was actually needed?

I stopped myself from biting my lip, from hinting that maybe I wanted him to kiss me.

He leaned toward me, and I could *not* move. Maybe I didn't even want to move.

The pull of Naveen was powerful, ruthless but mesmerizingly intoxicating. His smell, always of cinnamon and wild spices; his warmth, always cozy and inviting; his height, so tall yet perfect; and the way he made me giddy every time his hands landed on my body. Like right now—they gently touched my waist, and I was practically seeing stars.

My breath burned in my chest, and I didn't think I'd ever wanted to be kissed so badly.

My fingers twitched, and my arms almost moved up to wrap around his shoulders, to pull him into me. I almost rose up onto tiptoe to finish initiating this maddeningly evasive kiss. His lip twitched, and his skin flushed.

Then Naveen tilted and lowered his head. To my side. And plucked something off my pant leg.

"Um. You had tape there. It was driving me nuts." He smiled, walked away, and tossed it into the trash. "So, are we going to practice or what?" he asked, his voice cracking.

I pushed out a shivering breath, regained my composure, and turned to him, hoping that I appeared as cool and unaffected as possible. By the way he kept that impish smirk on his stupid face, I'd say that he probably knew how I was really feeling.

I picked up my violin and sat across from him on the bed, my back against the headboard. "Were you about to kiss me?" I blurted.

"No," he blurted back.

"Oh, good. No one wants to kiss you."

He tickled my sock-covered foot, and I yelped. "Lies."

I accidentally kicked him. Naveen grabbed my foot and tick-led some more. I released my violin before I broke it or hit him with it. I kicked and scream-laughed. I thrashed around while he mercilessly tickled until I got to his sides, because lo and behold, guess who else was ticklish?

He roared with laughter, but we kept at it. I guess the com-petitive spirit ran deep, even when we were wheezing and my arms were sore, even when our hands were gridlocked and we couldn't move. Except I could. Ballet meant I was pretty flexible.

"You gotta give sometime," he said, as if me relenting made him a winner.

"You give up. You tickled me first."

He shook his head. So I pulled my legs into me, between our bodies, and said, "I can leg-press more than your body weight. I will crush you."

He laughed and, in a maneuver so deft and impossibly fast, released my hands and snatched my ankles to assault my feet. But I moved fast, too. I meant to roll onto my side and hop off the bed, but only one foot escaped his grasp. So here we were. Alone in a hotel room. On a bed. Naveen practically on top of me. With one of my feet in his hand beside his left knee and the other on his right side.

We froze, both realizing our very scandalous position. Be-cause if he leaned into me even two inches, we were done for. And if I moved in any direction even two inches, we were done for.

He gulped. I knew he was flirting, but I didn't think he'd meant for us to end up like this. And worse? I wanted him to lean down. I wanted his mouth against mine. I wanted to feel the weight of his body pressing me into the bed.

For a few wonderfully long seconds, we simply stared at each other. This was one of those situations where one kiss wouldn't be enough. And I think we both knew that.

But then, for some weird reason, maticoor night came roaring back into my thoughts.

"Eggplants!" I yelped, absolutely wrecking the moment.

"What?" he asked, confused.

I jumped at the sound of a furious knock on the door. Swallowing and swerving off the bed as Naveen scrambled upright, I ran to the door and swung it open. "Hey, Neha. Just in time."

She lugged her bag into the room and eyed Naveen, who was sitting on the edge of the bed. "What were you two doing?" she asked in a singsong, jokester voice.

"See the violin there?"

"Mmm-hmm . . ." She clucked her tongue, telling us she didn't believe me one bit. She glanced around the large room and smiled gleefully. "Whoa! This place is so fancy!"

"All right, parents said to behave. Whatever you're doing, just be quiet. We seriously have to practice." I returned to the headboard and kept myself away from Naveen.

"I want to hear!" Neha said, sitting on the edge of the bed with us.

"All right. Just don't tell anyone." I looked at Naveen and said, just to be super clear, "The reception slow dance."

He nodded.

I placed my chin on my violin and got into position. Closing my eyes, I chased off all the feels Naveen had sent fluttering through me and all the uncertainty of college and all the stress of the finals. The bow sang against the strings, and moments later, Naveen's baritone voice lit up the room.

Admittedly, these were some seriously lovey-dovey romantic lyrics, seeing as we'd tried to capture what we thought Maitri and Pranit were feeling. I made the mistake of glancing at Naveen. His face was beautiful and poetic when he sang—the way his expressions changed, the narrowing of his brows, the way his lips formed sexy words or turned soft when he hummed.

It was when his gaze landed on mine that it seemed as if all those romantic words and hidden meanings were meant for me and only me. My body temp skyrocketed by a hundred degrees as he sang about falling into her eyes and dreaming of her touch and living every second just to see her again. I had to remember that these words he was crooning represented the love between the couple, not between us. He wasn't singing this to me. He hadn't written this for me. But it sure felt like it when he sang about how hard his heart beat when she walked into the room and how her scent lingered long after she was gone.

Naveen Patel was . . . inescapable. More than that, Naveen was absolutely talented. He knew his worth. He knew he didn't belong at some tech company. He knew what he was meant for, and he wasn't going to stop trying to get it at any cost.

Naveen was actually a pretty good guy with an amazing

talent. It sucked really hard that one or both of us might not win tonight. I just didn't know if I could take another blow after Juilliard's rejection.

Neha clapped when we finished and jumped on the bed. "OMG! That was the best thing ever! Dude, you can sing. And sis! *Damn!*"

"Neha! Watch your mouth!" I told her.

She shrugged unapologetically. "You guys can be all lovey-dovey at the reception now." She swung around and unpacked, leaving Naveen and me sitting on the bed, watching each other without saying another word.

CHAPTER TWENTY-FOUR
(Saturday Evening: One Day Until the Wedding)

#Garba

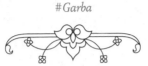

A gush of excitement burned through my veins as I dressed. Yeah, it was almost garba time, time to dance and twirl and tap dandiyas. But also, finals were only a few hours away! Ah!

I pulled up my chaniya and tightened the drawstring around my waist. The large sparkling orbs at the ends of the drawstring flew up and around and clanged against each other and then against me as I tied it. Why orbs, though? I'd never been so confused when tying two strings into a bow.

The heavy, thick skirt, with its ornate stitching and gems, weighed down my hips. Maybe my hip muscles would be rock solid by the time the weekend was over. Sheesh.

The choli was so much lighter, seeing that it had very little fabric in comparison, but it was still heavy enough that I never forgot it was there. The crop top–style blouse ended just below my boobs. It was a little low cut, but since there was no cleavage to be had, it didn't matter. The sleeveless choli showed my back in a wide circle of skin, closed with three clips at the bottom, and stayed in place with a string tied at the back of my neck with two glimmering orbs hitting where my bra strap would've been . . . if I needed a bra. Stitched-in padding for the win!

Chaniya cholis were known for their bright, festive colors, and this one did *not* disappoint: It was vibrant fuchsia with hot-pink, gold, and dark blue stitching throughout in bold geometric and peacock designs. I felt like live-action Princess Jasmine . . . or, ya know, any desi girl during a wedding.

We went to Maitri's suite, her counter cluttered with a million brushes, makeup in all sorts of colors, hair sprays and gels, curling irons, and flat irons.

Maitri was all made up, looking more beautiful than humanly possible as she put on jewelry. Ornate twists of her hair were braided over one shoulder, bedazzled with silver spangles. She was dressed in an elaborately embroidered chaniya choli with shimmering golden threads. Her skirt was super heavy, pista embellished with pink designs, her choli pink with pista designs.

The photographer took a hundred pictures of her getting ready while I snapped a few for the joint social media account.

Our mom and Pranit's mom were here as well, getting all done up along with my sisters and me. The hairstylist worked on my hair, half down and half loosely pulled back with a clip and fresh roses, while the makeup artist worked on my face. Masi was here, too, along with Maitri's best friends, aka the bridesmaids. Masi lovingly doted on us, exclaiming how beautiful all the girls looked.

"Very fine actresses," she said as she touched all our cheeks and smiled warmly. "Actresses" meant Bollywood starlets, which meant unearthly beauties. But she kept glancing at the clutter of makeup.

"This is nice color," Masi kept suggesting to the makeup artists, pointing to the lighter shades of foundation and blush. "Why is that so dark?" she asked us in Gujarati, pointing at something.

"It's bronzer," I tried to explain in Gujarati. "For cheeks, usually."

"It's too dark," she complained. "Maitri has the perfect glow. She should have light pink."

"Well, Americans like tan skin and this thing called contouring." But she couldn't comprehend the concept, and her eyes flitted back to the lighter colors.

Mummie gave me a warning look, but I wasn't going to say anything. All I could do was politely explain, and if I couldn't do that without raging about colorism, then it was best to let it go for now.

"We wouldn't want to look too dark in photos, huh?" Masi said in that innocent way of hers. Right, we wanted a complimentary look, not a fake one. We could all agree on that, but beauty standards had changed considerably and also crossed continents and generations. No one was about white powder anymore.

Urvi politely said, "It's fine, Masi. Maitri will look her best, and this style of makeup is meant for her to look great in photos. It's the perfect match for her skin and outfit. Come, relax, sit with me and feel this baby kicking."

And just like that, Masi was overcome with joy and immediately sat beside Urvi to touch her belly while others *ooh*ed and *ahh*ed over her, turning the conversation toward the baby.

When we were all done, Masi adjusted my gold dupatta. She tucked in one corner at my left hip, drew it over my chest, draping it over my right shoulder, and then tucked the other end in near my left hip at the back. I shimmied a little, my matching bangles chiming, and she smiled. Masi adjusting my clothes and touching my head had me feeling complete, as if my grandparents were here with us.

"You're going to enjoy this, Masi," I told her. "Just like being in the movies."

"Oh?" she replied, not believing me, probably. But just you wait.

"Are we ready to dance or what?" Neha asked as Masi helped her tie and clip and tuck with the help of a million safety pins.

"Look at this—beautiful Damani women. My girls!" Papa said from the doorway. He was decked out in a blue-and-gold sherwani with matching blue-and-gold mojri, which looked way more comfortable than my high heels. They had curls over the toes and made Papa look like royalty.

He kissed us all on the head and then came over to Mummie and said, "Hello, darling. Have you seen my wife?"

"Oh! Stop that! I look like a streetwalker," she muttered, her cheeks a lit furnace.

"You look like the day we got married," he said, and looked deep into her eyes.

Ah. They looked so in love. Insert heart-eye emojis! I grabbed my phone and took a picture, capturing Papa holding Mummie's hands up like he might kiss the backs, but instead he kept gazing into her eyes.

And snap, caption, post!

We all cheesed. Mummie tried to wave off Papa's comment, since she claimed she didn't like being this made up, but he was practically all over her. Streetwalker level: expert.

In a large group, we made our way downstairs to the hotel ballroom, where there were a couple of Indian street food vendor–style carts set up in the atrium. One had a welcome sign for the garba, complete with the couple's best engagement pictures on display beneath strings of wooden parrots and peacocks. The other had playful signs like TEAM BRIDE and I'M HERE FOR THE CAKE and masks and other props for photo ops in front of a bright curtain in every color that read HONK OK PLEASE behind a bicycle-led rickshaw reminiscent of India. Where had they even found a rickshaw? Definitely gotta get pictures in that thing later, but for now, we were herded into the ballroom for a photo shoot.

All the guys were already here: Pranit with his parents and brother and bhabi, his closest uncles and cousins, and all the groomsmen, which meant Naveen was also here. He was doing stupid poses with his posse in front of a wall made from a hundred bright and glimmering ornamental umbrellas from India, heavy with tiny round mirrors that flashed in the ballroom lights like diamonds. He was decked out in a rich burgundy sherwani with gold leggings, a pair of gold mojri on his feet. He looked like a prince.

When the mass of women walked in, all eyes fell on us, like maybe this was the part in a Bollywood movie where we burst into song and dance. We met the guys in the wide and spacious center that doubled as a dance floor between rows of chairs to the left and right. Beyond the chairs were six food carts: five featuring foods from around the world, and one called Patel Ice Cream. I wanted dessert first. In a waffle bowl with every topping, preferably.

We all posed for pictures. There were so many, especially around the ornate bench swing with ribbons curling up the wooden sides in front of the wall of decorative mini umbrellas. Of course, we had to get Boomerangs of us twirling in our skirts. Blowing kisses at the bride. Sweet family poses. Memorable sister poses. Sassy cousin poses. Diva single poses.

Before we parted to get ready for the big entrance, Maitri hugged me tight and said, "I just want to tell you that I appreciate all your hard work and patience."

"It's nothing!" I mumbled into her hair. "You're going to ruin my makeup."

"Oh!" She pulled away and let her hand slip down my arm to take my hand, swinging it gently. "I know everything has been wild lately, and my wedding might be taking away from your college excitement, but I deeply appreciate this. And once it's over, we can sit down and talk all about school and your future, OK?"

"Oh, sure," I pushed out.

"I knew that I could count on you to make this weekend perfect. Thank you."

Eh? A tinge of remorse sparked in the back of my thoughts. Hopefully I could keep the perfect facade up and she'd never find out about me slipping away. More than that, I prayed that my absence didn't unravel anything.

She glanced behind her at Priyanka and said, "I have to go. Almost time to get started."

The couple slipped away through a side door before the main doors opened to let in guests.

"You look very pretty, Zuri," Naveen said as he walked toward me. Our moms gabbed several feet away and cast knowing glances at us with the utmost approval. Then there was Papa, who gave a warning nod of the head. What? We weren't doing anything.

"I know," I said with a shrug.

He laughed. "I'm glad you know, then."

"Don't you get tired of complimenting me on my obvious awesomeness?" I asked nonchalantly, like I didn't care what he thought.

"With you? Nah. Never."

"I guess you look all right, too."

He clutched the front of his sherwani as if it were a jacket. "I know I look good. Don't even play."

I laughed and brushed past him as Krish skipped toward me in her brilliant peacock blue–and–green outfit.

"Are you ready?" she asked me, ignoring Naveen completely. Which didn't go unnoticed by him.

"Yes. So excited, so nervous. I'm going to enjoy garba for as long as I can."

"Good. It's going to be so fun! OK, but after our dances, right when they start playing the shoe game, that's our cue," she said in a lowered voice. "You hurry upstairs, change, and meet me at the back entrance. The front and side entrances will be too packed with people from garba, 'cause those are the closest doors to the ballroom."

"Gotcha! I know how to get there."

She cocked her chin. "You got this!"

"Yeah. As long as I get there in time." I shook my hands like I was shaking off water. Maitri's words stuck with me and I tamped down the nugget of remorse. She was proud of me for nothing more than behaving and not running off during her weekend. Ahead, Papa grinned his big, proud grin as he greeted everyone he could. "Tight timing, though. And hopefully I don't get caught."

"There are four entrances, one on each side of the hotel. No one is ever at the south entrance in the back. It's like a ghost town over there." She glanced past me at Naveen. "How are you getting there?"

"Was going to Uber, I guess."

"No," I told him. "We can go together."

"What?" Krish asked, displeased.

"Listen," I told her. "I know him, and that calms my nerves, and I need as little stress as possible. Better than trying to find the place by myself and getting lost."

She relented with a grunt.

I gently shook her wrists, adding with confidence, "I know how good I am, and I don't need to take out anyone. My talent speaks for itself."

"You're a better person than me." She cackled. "I'm already plotting how to annihilate the competition when I apply to med school."

Oh lord. I bet she was.

The last of the guests trickled in, filling the ballroom with nearly two hundred people dressed in their finest garba outfits. I tapped my toes, waiting and waiting, until finally, one of Pranit's friends grabbed the mic beside the DJ table and asked everyone to take a seat. The main doors closed. A hush spread across everyone in giddy anticipation.

Our family had never had this sort of extravagant wedding garba, so most wouldn't be expecting what was coming.

"During the shoe game, back entrance," I whispered to Naveen as we passed one another on our way to our seats. The groom's people were on one side, the bride's across the dance floor on the other side.

The last people hurried to their seats as a side door opened and the dhol player came in, playing like she was leading a marching band. Everyone started cheering when Pranit rode in on a bicycle, pulling Maitri in the rickshaw from the hallway photo op display. He was decked out in a shiny pistachio-green sherwani to match the bride, and he shrug-danced while pedaling. Maitri sat back and waved like the princess she was. They did one round around the large, empty dance floor in the middle. Lots of people got up to look closer and clap and take pictures. The videographer and photographers followed the couple. Music reverberated through the room, shaking the floors.

During their next circuit, the parents joined them, dancing around the vehicle and pulling us siblings along with them. I had *not* been told about this, but I went with it anyway in my very awkward sorta dance.

The couple dismounted and sat on the swing bench as the show started. We had the girls-only dance numbers, the all-Damani-girls performance, the all-guy dance numbers, mixed dancing, and the little kids rocking their own adorable routines.

It was all a blur, and how I kept my performances straight was beyond me. I was out of breath, shaking from the physical push *and* the adrenaline rush. My skin was hot and sweaty, but it was *so* exhilarating. Especially when the couple clapped and whistled and the crowds of spectators roared with applause.

As pro level as our dances were, the most memorable were definitely the numbers where the bride and groom outdanced us all. I guessed that was the way it was supposed to be. They added so much love and enthusiasm and stole the spotlight.

Everything was full of splendor and glitter. And the wedding hadn't even begun.

The crowd got more vibrant, chattier, as people moved around, socialized, ate. The music seemed to blare even louder.

I couldn't wait to get out of here, though. The massive ball-room seemed to shrink, getting too warm and too loud. I just needed to breathe, to get to the audition, to get it over with before anyone caught me. I needed to know what would happen to me after tonight, if I was good enough for any of those music schools or if I had to put away childish things and start adulting toward law school.

Three of Pranit's friends set up for the shoe game, bringing two chairs together back-to-back for the couple to sit on. The host would ask questions, and the bride and groom would hold up their own shoe or the other, depending on who they thought the question pertained to. That was our cue. I walked out of the room, but as soon as I pushed open the doors, Papa appeared at my side.

"Where are you off to, beta?" he asked, his cheeks red from laughter and happiness.

"Magnificent garba, Akash bhai!" someone said to him in passing, slapping him on the shoulder.

Papa waved at them and looked back to me.

I stuttered, "I need—need some fresh air. It's so hot and loud in here. Bathroom break, too."

"Garba with me when we start?" he said, hopeful and exuber-ant. Papa wasn't typically the dancing type, but the atmosphere had swept him up and turned him into a dancing, soon-to-be dandiya-wielding machine.

I bit my lower lip. *Crap.* Garba would start after another few games, and Papa would be looking for me. It wasn't an intimate dance. You wouldn't necessarily notice someone missing because it was done in a big group. But of course my family would be looking for me!

My heart raced, exploding with the adrenaline coursing through my veins. My body was telling me to turn into a pillar and freeze on the spot or get back inside; my thoughts screamed how wrong this was, that I was selfish and disappointing.

I managed to smile and pushed out, "OK, Papa! I might not make it for the first rounds, but definitely a little later?"

"Why not?" He frowned, worried.

"It's been a super long day. Maybe I'll lie down for a minute?"

He touched my forehead. "You're not getting sick, are you?"

"No. Just so much going on, and I need a break to keep my energy going."

"Eat something. You'll feel better." He clucked his tongue as he gently urged me out the doors. "Go, beta. Get some rest, but come back down soon, huh? We can't miss this. Challo."

"OK." I swallowed hard, my throat suddenly parched.

I held my breath until the doors to the ballroom closed behind me, shutting me off from the party and hiding my deviousness from Papa. Ugh. Why did it hurt so bad? I hadn't technically lied to him. But between him and Maitri, that nugget of remorse grew.

I hadn't lied. Right?

Everything was cool. So why was my lunch trying to hurl itself up?

I stepped out of the elevator into a deserted hallway. Krish, and then Naveen, appeared around the corner near my room.

My feet turned heavy, and my body went numb.

"What's wrong?" Krish asked.

"Is it wrong for me to skip out during my sister's wedding weekend for this?" I gnawed on my lip, Maitri's loving words haunting my thoughts and Papa's look of pride in me crushing my soul.

"You have to do what you have to do," she said quietly. "But no one can force you."

"It'll be OK," Naveen promised. "Some risks are worth it."

I swallowed and nodded. I had to do this. The reward was too great, too career-defining, too future-forging for me to miss out. I would only be gone for an hour or so.

"Meet you at the back," Krish said.

"Yeah."

My stomach turned queasy when Naveen looked at me and asked, "Are you ready for tonight?"

No. No, I was *not* ready for tonight. I was not ready to know in definite terms if my dreams were about to die or if I would single-handedly bring sorrow to my family by leaving like this.

CHAPTER TWENTY-FIVE
(Saturday Evening: One Day Until the Wedding)

#BigGame

I quickly changed out of my garba clothes, tossing them onto the bed, and shimmied into a pink-and-yellow dress. No one said classical had to be boring or that Aerosmith had to be brooding.

Naveen had changed into slacks and a dark gray button-down shirt and met me at my room.

"Ready?" he asked.

"Yes. Oh, wait."

"What?"

I set down my violin case and adjusted his collar and middle button, which kept flipping half down. Maybe it hadn't been sewn on right. Realizing how close we stood to one another, I took a deep breath and rested my palms against his chest, shuddering when he tilted his face down toward me, a centimeter at a time.

I . . . almost lifted my chin. Almost rose up onto my tiptoes. But I caught myself and broke the moment that could've been *the* moment. Because we did *not* have time.

"We should go," I said softly.

He cleared his throat with a twitch at the corner of his lips and nodded.

I gathered my stuff and peered down the hall, practically a ghost town since everyone was downstairs having the time of their lives. Guilt fluttered in my chest, but this was worth it, right?

"Coast is clear," I said, and out we went.

We took the other set of elevators to avoid running into anyone, placing us at the south entrance of the hotel. We met Krish outside. She left the keys in the ignition and ushered me into the driver's seat.

"Wait, you're not coming?" I asked.

"No," she replied.

My heart sank, like I needed her to hold my hand to keep the anxiety away.

"I'll keep an eye on things here and try to divert the family if they start looking for you."

I nodded. Yeah, that made sense. "Thanks."

"Knock 'em dead!" she said, her hands on my shoulders. She looked me in the eye and went on, "You've got this. You are Zurika Damani, born to be a musician, born for Juilliard, born for great things."

I cracked a small smile. "You are so corny. But I love it."

"Don't worry about anyone or anything here. People are going to be so preoccupied with the fun that they won't notice you're gone," she said with a reassuring grin.

I gulped. Right. Because this was a time to have fun and celebrate. I could just imagine Papa passing out dandiyas for garba and looking around for me, waiting for me to join our circle for the family dance, everyone else in place as the photographers and videographers swarmed around us to capture the moment. Was he wondering about me already? Worrying about me? Was Maitri looking for me? Thinking about where I'd gotten off to instead of being carefree?

Krish cut through my thoughts, "Now, go! Before you're late and disqualified."

Right. I drove while Naveen navigated.

The ride over was fraught with simmering nerves and excitement, drowned out by Naveen moving between conversation and practicing his vocals. My grip on the steering wheel tightened as I blew out a harsh breath.

"Are you all right?" he asked.

I nodded, not wanting him to know how anxious I was that he had the upper hand.

We drove around the parking lot twice looking for a spot, finding one just before panic hit. Disqualified because we missed sign-in time due to parking issues? I think not.

"Let's go!" Naveen said, hopping out of the car and grabbing my violin case as I locked the doors and hurried after him.

He ran ahead and found the sign-in table. Everyone else was already in line and watching us as we breathlessly asked, "Are we too late?"

"No," the man behind the table said with warmth in his

tone. "But you're cutting it close. Less than five minutes left for sign-in. Auditions have begun."

"Oh my god," I grumbled as we signed in and took our spots at the end of the short line of top-twenty finalists, minus the ones who'd already performed.

I breathed in and out, trying to find gratitude that we'd managed to get this far in the competition, that we'd managed to practice our songs enough, that we'd sneaked out of garba without getting caught, that we'd signed in just in the nick of time.

Now I had to push the nerves and negativity and doubts out of my head. I closed my eyes, concentrated on all the passion I had for the violin, and tried not to think about how everything hinged on this contest. My life would *not* spiral into a black hole filled with law textbooks.

My stomach tied itself into wrathful knots, and all the food from last night, this afternoon, and this evening started to climb up my throat.

Oh lord, please don't hurl. Just hold it in, guts, until after I get back to the hotel.

The clock ticked down to the moments that would change my life forever, be it for better or worse. I tried not to bite my nails as my gaze flitted back and forth between the stage and the clock on the far wall.

Naveen had stopped talking altogether, his eyes glued to the stage as he pushed his ring around. He was nervous, too. Possibly even scared. I took his hand and squeezed. His gaze fluttered down to mine, and I expected a cocky smile. Instead, he wore a vacant look. *Terrified* might've been an understatement. You and me, both, dude.

In the near distance, performers sang and played onstage and filled the building with beautiful music, spurring applause.

The big event would happen on a stage in the center of a room with three levels of balconies from which the audience would watch. When people performed, everyone above could see everything below. We were surrounded. But the unique structure of the room allowed the music to bellow up and outward and vibrate off the walls.

It was way cool. Who knew if I'd ever get the chance to perform here again, but the way the auditions were set up to feel like a normal concert somehow took the life-changing, make-or-break edge off. Maybe it was easier to ignore the blur of faces in an audience filled with regular people than it was in a quiet auditorium with only a handful of important judges staring at me.

I could do this. I had this. I'd done so many shows before, played my heart out, and this would be no different.

"You've got this," Naveen said in my ear, snapping out of his stupor and squeezing my sweaty hand.

But as much as I tried to treat tonight like any other show, it wasn't. I couldn't even appreciate all the talent ahead of me as my nerves started to unravel.

On the wall behind us was a clock, shaving off minute after minute of garba, ticking off second after second where my dad was anticipating me, waiting for me so that we could dance together as one big family in a moment of a lifetime. How many important pictures were being taken without me?

Just breathe. In and out.

Before I knew it, I was at the edge of the stage.

"Up next, Zurika Damani, performing on the violin," the woman at the front announced, waving me toward the stage.

I clambered up the steps.

I searched the front row of judges, finding Ms. Ronald watching me sternly, waiting for me to blow her mind, though her look said I probably wouldn't even get close. She held all the cards, was the absolute decider of my fate. She was sitting beside Mr. Merchant. His expression was almost as fixed but slightly softer.

I positioned the instrument against my shoulder and neck and faced Ms. Ronald. I was playing for her, for Juilliard.

I had thought this would be easier, playing for a bunch of blurred faces as opposed to a few. It wasn't. So I played for one person instead.

My arms trembled under the weight of this moment. It was do or die, electrify or fizzle. It was redemption or failure. It was following my dreams or having to pursue something like *law school*.

I breathed in and out for a few long, excruciatingly silent seconds. The audience had quieted, stilled, waited. My breaths buzzed like voracious growls in my chest. My pulse raged in my ears. Sweat trickled down my temples.

I sucked in a long breath, closed my eyes, and started.

Beethoven's Sonata No. 9 was a "do well or do not" type of piece. There was hardly ever an in-between. It was ambitious and theatrical, technical and roaring with speed. You were either skilled enough to pull it off or you weren't. I would either amaze the judges or embarrass myself.

My entry was *not* a smooth one. My arms were actually trembling. My bow shifted slightly, causing a slight screech that had me flinching, throwing me further off the path of concentration.

But I persevered and played. I wasn't going to stumble down a rabbit hole. It was just a glitch, right? Move past, play on. It was a classical melody, one that allowed for only slight sways, but even then, my body remained stiff and unyielding.

My piece was over after an eternity of hyperawareness of every mistake and unimpressed sigh.

The crowd applauded still, bless their kind hearts. Ms. Ronald nodded once, pushed up her glasses, and made notes on her tablet. But I wasn't done yet. Or maybe I was done, in her eyes.

I walked offstage with the best smile I could manage, with the most confident poise my shoulders could muster. *Just get offstage and then go cry in a corner, and it will all be over.*

The announcer called Naveen next, and whatever nerves we'd shared backstage seem to melt away for him. He looked unstoppable when he jogged up on that stage and gave a short wave, lighting up the room with energy.

He cast a killer smile at the audience. The girls practically combusted with squeals and screams. The scouts all sat up with a newfound expectation. He had them eating out of his hand, the one constantly pushing that ring around.

Maybe it was a nervous thing he did, and maybe that idle movement helped him to concentrate and get over those nerves. Maybe he wasn't like Adam at all.

Naveen Patel sang. He crooned, and the entire audience seemed to roll into the lyrics with him. Some were even singing along, and I could see him headlining a concert one day.

Music had always been my everything, but in this moment, I felt like an outsider looking into a place where I no longer belonged.

CHAPTER TWENTY-SIX
(Saturday Night: One Day Until the Wedding)

#MicDrop

A s I stood behind the curtain against the wall on the other side of the stage, alongside the other contestants, I closed my eyes and breathed, shaking.

My eyes stung as reality settled down around me, as Naveen walked offstage.

He was the last to perform, and now we waited to see who would move on to the final round.

Everyone congratulated him. I couldn't even remember if anyone had said anything to me. The last few minutes had been surreal, a daze. Where even was I?

Naveen was trembling, his smile gone and his face a bit pale. He looked like he could barf, too. He instantly turned his laser focus on me and frowned as he approached.

He placed a hand on my waist and stared at me with those hypnotizing eyes, and all I wanted to do was lean into his chest and hug him. "Are you OK?" he whispered.

I meant to nod, but it turned into a half nod, then a shake of the head.

"You did well," he said.

I swallowed. Pity words. My ears rang from the sudden silence as everyone quieted for the announcer's next words.

"You did amazing," I told him, and tilted my forehead against his chest.

"*You* were amazing, Zuri. You always are. Don't let anything get in your head, OK? You've got this."

I wanted to believe him, but what an epic fail.

"Take a deep breath. We have a little time before the next round. Gather yourself and get ready for the next chance." His pity went even deeper? God. Had I done that badly?

He wrapped his arms around my back and fully hugged me, pecking my temple.

We pulled away from one another when the announcer instructed, "For round two, we will go through the contestants one last time in no particular order. First up, we have . . ."

Not me.

I glanced at the clock and went to bite my nail, stopping myself halfway. "How long before we can leave? I have to get back," I mumbled.

The grinning, happy faces of my family flashed across my thoughts. Papa and Maitri, so proud of me for being there for her this weekend. Not a single scold from Urvi. Not a single rebuke from Mummie. They were all together, celebrating my sister's huge transition as she began her marriage.

And where was I? Secretly chasing dreams they'd never

approve of because I was too scared to be real with them? Maybe I should have just come clean. I may have missed the competition, but at least I wouldn't be missing some of the biggest moments of Maitri's life, of my life.

I checked my phone for messages. Nothing. But a little red number appeared over my email icon. Without thinking, I opened it. My breath caught in my throat as my eyes skimmed down the message.

Not just any message. But an acceptance letter. Finally. Oh, I knew I had no chance in Hotlanta of getting into Emory and coasting through college alongside Krish. But I had decent enough grades to get into at least one college: Georgia State.

This was good news. Kids would kill for this college admission. Yet . . . all signs seemed to be pointing away from music college for me.

"What is it?" Naveen asked.

I closed my email and put the phone away. "Oh. Nothing important. Let's go see how long this is going to take."

Naveen walked with me to a staff member with an earbud in and a tablet in his hand. He looked up at us and smiled as he asked, "How can I help you?"

"Was wondering where we were on the list," I said.

"Sure thing. Names?"

"Um, Zurika Damani and Naveen Patel."

A cello player ended his performance behind us and the next contestant was called. Also not me.

"Random selection. Naveen is number three, and Zurika is eighteen."

My heart faltered. "Oh. That's like, almost another hour?"

"Yep."

"Is there any way I can move up in line? I have a wedding event I'm supposed to be at."

He shook his head. "I'm sorry. I'm just the help."

"Is there anyone else we can ask, then?" I pushed out, clenching my free hand, the other tightening around my violin case handle as panic slashed through me.

"I'm sorry. The selection is random and can't be altered. It wouldn't be fair to the others."

"What if she just switches with me?" Naveen offered. "I'd agree to that."

He shook his head again. "I'm sorry, folks. It's part of the rules. First set was done in order of signing in, second set by random number generator."

"Oh, OK. Thanks," I muttered, and turned back to the stage, now definitely nipping at my fingernail.

"It's fine, right?" Naveen asked. "You'll just get back late."

"I'll miss the entire garba."

A heaviness crushed my lungs. Remorse sprang from the nugget in the back of my thoughts and evolved into full-on regret. My breathing came out shallow and burning. Was this worth it? Was missing my beloved sister's wedding festivities worth this? A shot, and probably not a great one, all riding on some wild contest.

As I peered around the curtain to watch how the judges reacted to the current performer—grins and nodding and furious notes—I knew they hadn't adored me nearly that much.

Urvi had told me to woman up. It was time to be an adult. Adults had to make hard choices. They had to be logical and accept outcomes and move on.

So Juilliard had rejected me. Fine. This wasn't the end-all. It couldn't be. I was still young and ambitious and talented AF. Juilliard's rejection and this one night weren't going to define me. I wouldn't let them.

I narrowed my eyes and glanced down at my violin case, at the mehndi pattern now blooming deep red on the hand gripping the handle.

I had to decide. Not forever, but at least for tonight. I could find another way into music school. I could take a detour, wait another semester or two. I couldn't, however, dance another garba with my family in honor of Maitri's wedding.

I took a few breaths as Naveen watched me, pushing around his ring.

"Why do you do that?" I finally asked.

"Huh?"

"Your ring. You play with it a lot."

"Oh." His face flushed as he explained, "It's a thing I do when I'm really nervous. My therapist suggested doing something to take my mind off what's making me anxious, a combination of physical and mental. I push the ring around and recite a lyric that calms me down."

"You go to therapy?" I asked, impressed.

"Yeah," he muttered. "Being our age isn't easy. I have to find a way to deal, and, as someone pointed out, getting critical of others ain't it."

So he definitely wasn't an Adam after all. A nervous habit, yes, but not because he was lying or manipulating someone.

I ran a finger across the mehndi on the back of my hand, my grip slackening just a little on the handle of my case.

I smiled at Naveen, the weight of a thousand suns crumbling off my shoulders as my decision became clear, and I said, "Knock 'em dead! You're up next!"

He huffed out a breath. "Wait. Are you leaving?"

I nodded. "I can't miss another moment of my sister's garba. You might have to call an Uber like you were planning to."

"Are you sure?" He glanced behind him at the stage as the current performance ended. They were going to introduce him next.

"Yeah. My family is everything, and I should be celebrating with them."

". . . Naveen Patel!" the announcer called.

I gave him a quick hug and a gentle push. "See you back at the party."

I kissed his cheek and hurried out.

I didn't look back, couldn't look back. I was doing the right thing. No regrets.

As I pushed open the doors to the parking lot, Naveen's mesmerizing vocals pierced the air, and there he went singing

Aerosmith, the song we'd practiced together. He hadn't lied about that, wasn't planning on throwing me off my game by singing something completely different.

I hurried to the car and tried not to speed back to the hotel, no matter how much I wanted to. It wasn't too far, but I had to remember that getting into an accident would make things worse. My heart beat faster and faster as the minutes ticked by.

Were they still doing garba? Were people still dancing and eating? Were people starting to leave, calling it a night?

I parked the car somewhere in the south parking lot and sneaked inside through the back entrance. I was giddy again, this time with an eagerness to rejoin my family and be in the moment.

I made it all the way to the elevator and slumped against the wall, my shoulders slouching. Almost there. The elevator stopped on an empty floor. I walked toward my room and pulled my key card out when I caught sight of a figure out of the corner of my eye.

My breath hitched as I looked up and saw Papa walking down the hall.

"Oh crap," I muttered, petrified and stuck to the spot like a statue. I blinked a dozen times just to make sure I wasn't seeing things.

Nope.

He was walking down the hall toward me, *me* in this not-garba outfit with my violin hanging from my hand.

Papa did *not* look happy. Oh boy. How pissed was he? How *disappointed* in me was he?

I managed to move my legs and forced myself to turn toward him.

"Pa-Papa," I stammered. "What are you doing up here?"

His voice was low, calm. "Looking for you. We've been looking for you for the past thirty minutes. The better question is: What are *you* doing? Huh? Why are you dressed like this? Where did you go? What is so much more important than your sister's wedding weekend, than garba with your family?"

I swallowed hard, my throat dry and raw. Words got stuck in my throat like those annoying little burrs in summer grass.

"Was it a contest? Another show?" He scowled. "You did this during Urvi's wedding. We asked you not to repeat that mistake. I even told your mummie that my Zuri wouldn't mess up a thing this weekend."

Tears stung my eyes, and words came up cutting my throat like daggers. "Um, it was a music audition—a contest for college scouts."

He blew out a breath and looked skyward for a second. "Ah. This music business again. You went to the Atlanta musical competition?"

"Y-yeah," I stammered. "How did you know?"

My fear grew even more profound. Did someone tell him? Was the nosy uncle network working its magic? Did everyone know?

"Your papa has many contacts," he replied in a deep, unnerving voice.

"Are you mad at me?" I asked in a small voice.

He wore an impassive, flat expression, one that I could never quite read. Sometimes he sported it when he was meditating on something. Sometimes it was when he wasn't amused but didn't want to express it, or when he was just dead exhausted, or when he was upset but trying to stay calm.

I suspected it was the last one.

"You could've ruined your sister's wedding weekend," he stated.

My throat went dry.

"You're young and brash right now. You're thinking of yourself. You have no idea how important every one of these traditions is to us. To you, perhaps they are tedious or boring or pointless or too numerous. You don't understand the significance of them.

"Your elder sisters don't know or appreciate all of our traditions, either. But they're mature and respectful enough to take them seriously, because they know it's important. Otherwise, do you think they would go through the headache of trying to uphold everything? Do you think they do all this just for fun? Or that they wouldn't think it's easier to have a simple ceremony and sign papers and be done? There are such things as bad karma, consequences, to having an incomplete wedding. Things that could affect your sister and our families, not just you."

"I'm sorry," I said, biting the inside of my cheek to keep from crying. I'd had this intense desire to make my dreams come true, no matter the cost. I had wanted to do everything right, but I also couldn't let my chance drift away because of atrocious timing. Did that make me a bad sister? Selfish?

Blood drained from my face, and I could do nothing but stand there, immobile. I fought back tears, my lips quivering. I wanted to explain to him that all I wanted was to get a scholarship so he could see that I was meant for music.

Papa released a deep breath, as if he were mad but wanted to sympathize, too.

"Did you perform well? Did you win?" he finally asked.

My heart circled the drain, and tears prickled my eyes again. I blinked them away and offered a shaky smile, my lips trembling.

Keep it together. Naveen might get his pick of music college offers after tonight, but there was still a chance for me. Right? Right . . .

There were still scouts who might give me a second thought when my college applications came across their desks.

"I . . . I didn't do well," I mumbled.

Papa took in a long, deep, calming breath. "It's not good to be upset during this weekend. We will not have bad fortune mar your sister's wedding because of negativity."

"Yes, Papa," I said, pushing aside my misery.

"You will rinse off the negativity, change back into garba clothes, and we will go back to the party. We will embrace the happiness of this weekend and prepare for tomorrow."

I nodded. "Of course."

He looked around at the still-empty hallway and said, "I know how incredible you truly are, beta. I know you are good at music and that you love it. We will discuss this another time, huh?"

My heart dropped into the pit of my stomach. I nodded in a

very surreal "oh crap" moment. It would definitely be worse next week, when all the guests had left and the last of the wedding traditions had ended. Basically, when the time came to tell Mummie.

"Go. Get dressed before someone sees you. The entire family is expecting you downstairs. Return with a smile and happiness and enjoy tonight. It only happens once."

"I know. I'm sorry."

He hummed and held his hands behind his back before walking away toward the elevator. He didn't look back at me as I hurried into my room to change.

CHAPTER TWENTY-SEVEN
(Saturday Night: One Day Until the Wedding)

#GoodNightKisses

After changing back into my garba outfit, I dabbed beneath my eyes and checked my makeup to make sure crying hadn't turned me into a hideous clown.

I let Krish know that I was back, and she was at my door in a matter of minutes.

The second she saw my face, she pouted, her eyes glistening, and hugged me. "Did it not go well?"

I shook my head.

"Did Naveen screw you over?" She pulled back and put her hands on her hips. "I swear I'll end him."

"No. You've got to stop with that," I said, harsher than I meant to.

Disbelief crossed her features. "Why? Because he said he was a good guy and you believed him? Where is he now? Taking his shot after you left?"

"I left because it was wrong of me to ditch garba for a far-fetched idea like it's the only thing that can save my future. It's not. I've accepted that, and I'll work harder before I apply to music schools again for the spring semester. But Naveen isn't Adam."

She crossed her arms. "How are you so sure?"

"I've spent time with him. How are you so sure that he is?"

"The way he acts, like he's all that, that nervous thing with his ring, the mouth twitch . . . Adam did all that."

My voice rose higher. "He's not Adam! Some guys are—not every guy. Not Naveen. It's a nervous thing he does when he's stressed out. And he didn't do anything except help me with the contest."

Her shoulders deflated. "I'm sorry. I'm just trying to protect you," she said quietly.

I sighed. "I know. But I left because Maitri is more important, not because of him. I left because I can make music school happen a different way. But then my dad caught me." My lips quivered, my gaze darting to the floor.

She hugged me tight and whispered, "It's OK, Zuri. He won't be mad for too long. You can apply to Juilliard again next year. Like you said, it isn't over."

I pulled back and nodded, forcing my sadness to dissipate. "We'll talk about it after the weekend?"

She twisted her lips and nodded.

"Come on. I hear there's a big ol' family wanting me to join in," I said, smiling. I shuddered and dramatically shook off the negative feels. "I stand by my decision. I'm going to enjoy this night for what it is—a celebration!"

Krish linked arms with me, and we rushed back to the ballroom downstairs, back to the party that still raged on.

"Where have you been?" Mummie asked as she walked

toward me just inside the double doors to the ballroom, armed with dandiya sticks wrapped in shimmering ribbon.

"I just came down from my room," I said.

"Are you OK?" She touched the back of her hand to my forehead. "You feel a little warm."

"It's nothing," I assured her.

She clucked her tongue. "It's because you don't eat enough."

"Oh my god . . ."

She handed me a pair of dandiya. "Dancing will make you feel better."

I smiled. "You're right. It will."

So we got into formation in the garba line, armed with dandiya, as I put on my best smile. Despite my shattering heart. Despite the anguish in my gut. Despite the awkwardness of having Papa nearby. He didn't let on that anything was amiss, but he also barely made eye contact with me. And my heart broke a little more.

Thank goodness for Krish, who hip-bumped me and made cross-eyed faces to crack me up. Krish, who swiped the giant centerpiece laddoo from the sweets booth, pulled me into a corner, and let me devour it, all while laughing and shooing away any prying eyes.

"Food truly does cure all," she said, stuffing her own face.

Krish, who let loose on the dance floor, taking my hands and spinning, spinning, spinning until we fell, dizzy and cackling.

Thank the lord for cousins and sisters for making me take a million photos, silly photo booth snaps and poses on the rickshaw.

Maitri and Pranit retired around midnight. By then, all the

adults and little kids had headed off, and just a few of us younger ones were left. The couple's crew of besties tore down the decorations with the staff, and the rest of us finally went to bed.

I ran into Neha in the elevator. She slumped against the wall, coming down from her sugar high after one too many waffle bowls of ice cream. She barely made it to our room, kicked off her shoes near the door, and plopped onto her bed with an exhausted groan.

I yanked her toward me by the ankles, dragging her down the bed. "Nope. You need to change and wash all that makeup off."

"I don't wanna," she mumbled into the pillow.

"Ew. Gross. You're going to get makeup all over the pillows and sheets and have giant pimples in the morning. Do you want big zits in all of tomorrow's pictures that Maitri will have hanging in her house till the end of time? Or to give four hundred people something to stare at when you walk down the aisle?"

That got her going, albeit sluggishly. She dragged her feet as she changed and washed her face beside me in the bathroom. I was dead tired, too, so I felt her pain. I just wanted to collapse.

I'd just slipped into my ultra-comfy pajama shorts and T-shirt when Naveen knocked on the door. He looked cozy and überadorable in a pair of red basketball shorts and a fitted gray T-shirt.

"How did it go? When did you get back?" I asked anxiously.

"It went good. I just got back and showered. How are you doing?" he asked, his brows furrowed a bit and his cheeks flushed.

I glanced over my shoulder to make sure Neha was still in the bathroom before slipping into shoes and stepping out. "I'm OK."

We slowly paced the hall between the bride's side of the floor and the groom's.

"Is that your brother?" I asked when Naveen stilled beside me.

He immediately took my wrist, pulling me back, and sank into the shadows behind an ornamental plant. Neelish opened the door to his room, leaving it propped. A moment later, a woman strolled out of the elevator and into . . . his room. Her grinning face flashed at us for a brief second when she checked to see if the coast was clear, her rocker-chick bangs brushing her brows. She slid into Neelish's room as easily as sliding into someone's DMs, her hot-pink nails flashing in the light.

My mouth dropped. "Dang."

Naveen scratched the back of his head as his face burned red. "Um, you know that girl my brother's been seeing?"

"That's my cousin Priyanka. Hehe. I've got *so* much dirt on her now." And suddenly, it all made sense: her leaving kankotri right away, her giggling with Neelish in her garage during practices, her swooning over him during mehndi.

What was it with Damani girls falling for these Patel guys?

We pivoted, turning back around to take a walk in the opposite direction around the massive rectangular floor.

"So? What happened?" I asked.

"I performed, and it went really well. I think."

"Did you win?" I bit my lip.

He nodded in the glow of the hallway sconces, but his smile didn't reach his eyes when he said, "Yeah. I won."

I gasped and slapped his arm. "Dude! Why didn't you lead with that? Congrats! Why aren't you happier?"

"Well, first of all, my only real competition left, so it wasn't really fair."

I clucked my tongue. "True. But you got what you wanted, what you worked so hard for. You have a strong case for your parents now."

He nudged my shoulder with his. "Are you OK? I know it was hard for you to leave. I explained to the judges why you had to go. Sometimes they contact other contestants they liked, you know? Just because you didn't win doesn't mean they won't reach out to you."

I shook my head. "I can't think about that right now, not until Monday. I don't want to be sad." But even as those words came out, my lips quivered, and I blinked away tears.

"Hey. It's OK," he said softly.

Easy for him to say, having just won a music scholarship.

He reached over and wiped a tear from my cheek. I hadn't even realized that it had fallen. I stilled, and it was all that I could do to keep from crying in front of him. "One performance doesn't define you. One competition doesn't, either. So what if you can't start music school in the fall? Maybe spring? Or summer? Or the next fall? This isn't the end. You're meant for music, that's all I know."

"Thank you," I said.

"It's the truth."

I cleared my throat. "How do you feel? Being the winner?"

"Happy for sure. Sad that you're hurting. Freaked out about telling my parents."

"You have a huge card to play. Don't waste it." I poked his hand with each word.

"I won't."

"Congrats again. You really do deserve it," I said, in all honesty.

"Thanks."

I let out a breath. It was all over, and the winner deserved the win. "What are you going to do tonight, with your room occupied?"

"Maybe crash with someone else or hang out with the guys until Neelish texts me. Why? You calling it a night?" he asked, disappointment dripping from his voice.

"Yeah. I gotta get some sleep. Good night."

"Night."

I leaned into him and kissed his cheek. "Thanks for tonight, though."

"Anytime," he whispered.

CHAPTER TWENTY-EIGHT
(Sunday Morning: Wedding Day)

#GlowUp

Neha slept through my phone alarm. I hit snooze at least three times before groaning from sleep deprivation. At this point, I'd rather just sleep through the wedding.

It was almost six thirty, and there would be bridesmaids zombie-walking through the halls to get their makeup and hair done in Maitri's room right next door, and I had to join them. *OK. Suck it up. Final day.*

I dragged Neha out of bed, thankful she didn't kick me in the face. "God. Are you acting like dead weight, or are you just this heavy?"

She'd finally made it to the bathroom when Naveen knocked on the door.

"Are you stalking me?" I asked him.

He rubbed his neck. "Good morning, beautiful."

If beautiful meant greasy face from all the makeup yesterday, under-eye bags from lack of sleep, and wild hair? Yeah, I was gorgeous AF this morning.

He held up a white paper bag. "We went to this really good

bagel place down the street. Thought maybe you'd like some if you didn't have time for breakfast."

"Oh. Thank you . . ." I took the bag and peered inside. Bagel sandwiches, smelling of gooey cheese and avocado. Yum! "Talk about a good morning!"

"Hey, look." He took my free hand and studied the front and back.

"What are you doing, weirdo?"

"Your designs came out nice," he replied.

"My mehndi game is *strong*."

He stroked a thumb across my palm, and my breath hitched. "It's almost black."

"Really?" I looked it over for the first time this morning. What do ya know? The stain had darkened to deep maroon, almost black. "It hardly ever turns out that dark."

"You know what they say."

"What?"

With the most serious expression I'd ever seen on his face, he declared, "The darker the mehndi, the more you're loved. Guess someone must be loving you pretty hard right now. Better let you get ready. Enjoy the bagels."

Then he walked off, leaving me speechless. I hugged my hands to my chest and smiled uncontrollably.

"Did, uh . . . he just say he loved you?" Neha asked from the bathroom. Her gaze dropped to the bag in my hands as her nostrils flared, inhaling the scent of freshly baked bread. "Is that food?"

I groaned and let her have a sandwich. "Better leave me some!"

I showered fast, seeing as I didn't need to shave or wash my hair, and dressed in a glimmering dark green–and–maroon georgette-and-silk chaniya choli, the heaviest I'd ever worn in my life. God, the thing weighed like twenty pounds!

I scarfed down half a bagel sandwich in between shoving my wrists into a dozen matching bangles.

Neha was barely dressed in her own beaded chaniya choli when we hurried to Maitri's room.

I picked up my heavy skirt, the mirror work and glittery threads catching the light like a hundred diamonds, and my shoes. The carpeted hallway was gross, but I didn't want to wear these torture devices for longer than necessary.

Priyanka swung open Maitri's door the moment I knocked. I froze, and we sort of stared at one another. How did I act, knowing that she'd been knocking some foreign mojris last night? Her cheeks flushed at about the same time I *felt* flushed. I did what I had to do—walked right on through.

I squealed the second the bridesmaids parted enough to reveal Maitri in her snow-colored lehenga with dark red stitching and mirror patchwork in tiny, intricate designs. Her skin glowed, her makeup sparkled, her lips were red and sultry, her outfit shimmered in crimson and gold, and her hair was in an elegant bun decorated with a red rose and dotted with Indian jasmines, wavy tendrils framing her face. The photographer and videographer recorded her while Mummie pinned her dupatta to her bun, and we all clapped. They took pictures of her slowly putting on her shoes and bangles and jewelry. It was a real process that would make for some artistic pictures.

"Drop. Dead. Gorgeous. Desi. Bride," I said.

"You look beautiful," she said to me, her hands clasped at her mouth.

The bridesmaids put on their finishing touches. Mummie and Pranit's mom were all done up. Urvi, Neha, and I sat together while the team did our makeup and hair. The room had been turned into a salon full of frenzied women. All the high chattering and conversations and laughter. All the older women helping the younger ones pin their saris and tuck in ends.

People came in and out of the room, adding jibber-jabber to the already-rising noise level.

"Maitri, you use lovely shades of makeup. Is this ivory?" A foi held a bottle up to me and said, "Ha, yes. Try this out. You will look fine."

I rested my chin on my fist, my elbow on the couch armrest, and blankly stared at her. "You think Maitri uses bone-white makeup?"

"Must be what gives her such a light coloring—refreshing."

"That's not even coloring. That's translucent setting powder. It's clear, not white. There is no off-shading going on here."

"All the pretty girls use lighter colors."

"*These* pretty girls like foundation that matches the skin. The point of foundation is to make skin look flawless and natural, not to change the color."

"Just try this."

"No. I don't look at anything lighter than deep bronze and medium brown and Fenty Number 360."

"But your skin will be whiter," she insisted.

"We'll look like ghosts. People will see the wedding pictures and wonder why there are wraiths in them."

Neha snickered. Foi frowned, not understanding. Urvi stifled a giggle, plucked the container from her hand, and set it down on the dresser beside a huge array of cosmetics. "Thank you. We'll probably all use the translucent powder to set our makeup."

I gave our aunt some serious side-eye but stopped myself from saying anything else. There were too many witnesses, anyway.

The hairdresser pretty much left my spirals alone, so the hair session didn't take long. I wore it down with full curls on display, shiny and frizz-free. She wove strings of Indian jasmine blooms through my hair. But the makeup took considerably longer and was much more layered and detailed, seeing as this was *the* big event. Those fake eyelashes came back at the very end.

I happened to glance at Neha, who grinned and said, "Think some caterpillars died on your face."

Maitri and the bridesmaids left for the wedding party pictures. We were up next for family photos.

I opened the door when someone knocked a few minutes later, expecting a bridesmaid returning for something. But it was Papa. Whatever excitement I felt for my sister's fast-approaching wedding dwindled at the sight of his face, as I remembered all too vividly the frown lines of deep disappointment.

"Hi, Papa," I said quietly.

He cocked his head toward the hallway. I slipped out and met him around the corner, where he could see our doors in one direction and the elevators in the other to make sure no one heard us.

I gulped, preparing for a displeased lecture.

His expression was impassive, which was the last thing I wanted to see on a day he should've been grinning ear to ear. Then he let out a long breath and embraced me. I almost lost it, almost cried as he kissed my head and muttered, "This is a good day. We must be happy, huh?"

"Yeah," I mumbled against his chest, against the thick fabric of his sherwani.

"Forget about last night. I know you're upset. For today, we will forget, huh?"

I dabbed at the edge of my eye, careful to not disturb the caterpillar lashes, as he pulled back and smiled. "My beautiful beta. Challo. Let's celebrate."

I grinned. He was totally right. I had so much time to feel sad and bad and frustrated and hopeless, but not today. Today, we had great things happening.

Papa went downstairs to meet Mummie while I returned to Maitri's room. By now, all the cousins were crammed in there, ready to go. They formed a sea of heavy fabrics and glitter bombs and flashy mirror work and gold.

"Are you good?" Krish asked when I returned.

I smiled at her and said, "Yeah. I'm good."

"Now, don't forget the wedding games!" Urvi said, gulping her water between sentences. "I can't partake in any." She rubbed her belly. "But I want you girls to make the Damani side proud. First off, the guys will need to make sure they carry Maitri high enough for the garland exchange. Then you girls need to get the groom's shoes and protect them with your *life*. And then sit on his car until he gives you money."

"Yes!" I added. "We did not come to play. We came to get paid."

The girls laughed. But seriously, this was the only time we could extort money from Pranit. He had to pay us several times, and I meant to get some serious cash today.

We all shuffled downstairs for pictures.

Today, the ballroom had turned classic and elegant, filled with white-draped chairs with large red bows on the backs and pamphlets explaining the components and meaning of each step of the ceremony, with little goody bags on each seat. Yep, the ones I'd painstakingly helped to fill and tie ribbons around, threaded with little heart-shaped notecards.

The main aisle down the middle was made of cream-colored fabric and designs made from white and red rose petals. The aisle was cut off by pillars with huge vases of red and white roses, connected by flowing drapes to keep people off the middle aisle and at a distance from the wedding party as they walked in. At the end was a giant mandap on an elevated stage, covered by a canopy of pink, red, and white roses with flower garlands draped all around. Two golden thrones faced one another with four chairs beyond them.

Wow. *Stunning.* Straight out of a Bollywood romance. We proceeded to take family pictures.

The groomsmen were here, too, and there was no denying the way Naveen kept his eyes on me. He was dressed to kill in a regal-looking sherwani, a heavy coat in red and cream with dashes of blue. A cream dupatta was thrown over one shoulder and wrapped loosely around his neck. He wore matching leggings and cream-and-gold mojri.

He hopped onto the stage and stood beside me, since we had been assigned to walk down the aisle together. Standing side by side, Naveen looked like an actual prince, and I definitely looked the part of a princess.

He clasped his hands in front of him, taking direction from the photographers, and pushed around his ring. "You look stunningly perfect, Zurika Damani."

I grinned. "I know. But you do, too, Naveen Patel."

After a long photo shoot, we returned to the hallway to meet the rest of the bride's side, including all her family and friends, as well as the non-Indians from both sides (they maybe didn't know about the baraat). And food. I'd forgotten there was a full-on breakfast down here. There was a decadent donut wall, fruit, toast, coffee, tea, and juice. Neha, Krish, and I nibbled, chugging back caffeine because we seriously needed it.

"The baraat has started," an uncle told Maitri, and excitement flurried through us. The groom's official procession was underway.

"Ugh, I really want to see the baraat," I whispered to Krish.

While we patiently waited, twiddling our thumbs and downing caffeine, the groom and his side were having the party of their lives.

"Then let's go." Krish took my hand and pulled me away, around the corner and to the front doors, where the baraat had started. Neha and some of the younger girl cousins followed, of course. There was no party without us.

We legit walked into a club, to be honest. They only had to walk from the main entrance of the hotel to the side entrance, just one long corner, and they were taking an hour to do it.

More than a hundred people danced in the wedding procession in beautiful, bright clothes, all dressed to the nines. The open trunk of an SUV held speakers, and a DJ played some heavy Indian beats along with the dhol player. The music roared through the air as everyone cheered and applauded and danced for an hour straight. There was no letup. There was a pause in the very slow progression when the SUV stopped, but then the car slowly inched forward again like a tease, pulling the dancing crowd closer and closer to the entrance.

All the guys related to the groom wore identical head garments—simple red paaghs with streaks of yellow and orange. They danced the hardest, closest to the music. Sweat was literally pouring off them. A few even wore right through their mojri. I mean, were that guy's feet bleeding?

Women danced less hard but still vibrantly behind the guys. Two bearers lifted smoke cannons so that red color infiltrated the air. And behind them? The groom, of course, decked out in his finest red-and-cream–colored sherwani with a shawl, a glimmering red-and-pearl paagh atop his head, and shades for a laugh. He rode an ornately decorated horse, looking as extra as extra could be. Pranit shrugged his shoulders up and down in a bhangra-style dance as his horse slowly walked along with the crowd.

"*Awesome!*" Neha said as she hurried to join his family.

"This is like . . . whoa!" Krish added, gently shaking my shoulders until she had me laughing.

Urvi's wedding hadn't been this extravagant. She'd opted for something more low-key and reserved, as was her style. And while I'd known Pranit was coming in on a white horse for an actual baraat, I wasn't prepared for all this intensity and energy.

A few people did double takes, but no one told us to go back inside. Instead, they welcomed us. Pranit's friends raised their hands and called us over to the dead center. The girls went. I did not, despite Krish tugging at my wrist.

"You go!" I said.

"You sure?"

I nodded and stayed back, moving in jubilant step without actually dancing. I was in heels, after all. No need to break an ankle.

But then a plain red paagh popped up on a six-foot-plus South African boy. He waved me over. I shook my head and tried to hide behind the horse. But Naveen cut through the crowds, dancing all the while, and rolled up right next to me. And believe me, his mom was watching with gleeful eyes.

"You know, this the *groom's* procession, for his side only," he teased.

"So why are you waving me over?"

"Well, now you gotta dance," he said.

"No, no."

"We're almost at the doors. Won't be long. Come on!"

I protested again, but he took my hand. Not even by the wrist, but with interlocking fingers. How scandalous! His mom sure was staring hard now, and with a smile! Oh god. I'd never hear the end of this . . .

I was still protesting when he dragged me into the middle of the entire thing! But then he grinned and did this hand thing that made me feel like we were playing patty-cake. Not to mention that the gold threads on our outfits kept getting stuck to one another. So we were constantly nearly touching, trying to separate our entangled threads.

I laughed, and darn it, everyone around me urged me to dance, and I had to. My feet were gonna kill me!

The great thing about Indian weddings, aside from the love and splendor and energy, was that there was no time to be sad. Not today.

CHAPTER TWENTY-NINE
(Sunday Morning: Wedding Day)

#TeamBride

Making it to the entrance didn't mean the party stopped. The SUV stopped moving, but no one else did. The groom was even off the horse, but now we continued to dance in a circle for another twenty minutes. Baraat never ended on time, and we were most definitely running on IST! Finally, the groom started dancing toward the double doors, but not before we cheered and yelled and looked up at the drones above for an epic aerial shot for the videographers.

Before Pranit entered the hotel, his guy cousins—namely Naveen and Neelish, because they were the tallest and looked the strongest—lifted him onto their shoulders. The bride came out, also on our guy cousins' shoulders, and the couple tried to exchange garlands.

Pranit was easily able to place his string of flowers around Maitri's neck, even though she playfully tried to move away, but Pranit gave her a hard time as the guys raised him up and out of her reach. Worse than that, he started climbing up to kneel, making himself way taller! Totally not fair! First of all, Maitri was shorter than these guys to begin with. And sorry to all the cousins on our side, but they were not South African–cousin tall.

Maitri struggled to reach, and her lips moved in a pleading pout. Finally, Pranit relented and let her put the garland around his neck, inciting all sorts of cheers from an amused crowd.

While they were doing this adorable thing, we girls sneaked back inside as Mummie teasingly rebuked us for having joined the baraat.

So many people tried to squeeze into the small area between the outer double doors and the inner double doors, where they did a little puja ceremony led by Mummie as she officially welcomed Pranit into the wedding. Then she played a game of trying to snatch Pranit's nose while his dad and brother and all the guys tried to protect him. I wasn't sure what this was all about, but it was *hilarious*.

It gave us time to get in formation. Everyone on the bride's side lined up in two rows facing one another and held our hands high up, creating a steeple-shaped tunnel that the videographer taped Pranit running through like some quarterback breaking through a banner and running into the big game.

Now that *that* was done, everyone quickly found their seats inside, and the ballroom doors closed. First, my parents walked down the aisle with Pranit, escorting him to the stage, where he would take a throne and my parents would sit with him. The girls and I gave each other *the look* and got into place near the aisle, right by the steps up to the mandap.

It was time for the shoes. For the sake of our house's honor (or at least bragging rights) and some serious cash.

The guys on the groom's side were thinking the same thing and crouched beside the steps on their side of the aisle. Naveen and I glared at each other, and he nodded once, narrowing his eyes like a defensive lineman about to tackle. The shoe game was serious business.

We leaned forward and rocked on the balls of our feet, barefoot, having tucked our shoes beneath our seats. We had to run, and we weren't messing around. The groom seemed blissfully unaware and focused on walking and smiling for the cameras. But just before Pranit removed his shoes to walk onto the stage after my parents, Naveen muttered his name, and realization dawned on him. He lifted his *right* foot first! The foot closest to the guys. Cheater!

Naveen ducked down as we dived, bombarding the groom and nearly knocking him over. But his guys were on his side, having gotten the right shoe and now positioned to get the left one the second Pranit lifted his foot.

And that's when the girls crossed the rose petal aisle. All bets were off. It didn't matter if someone hissed at us for messing up the petals scattered across the white linen meant for the bridal party to walk on. It didn't matter if the older generation chided us for making fools of ourselves. Or if the audience giggled and snapped pictures. It didn't matter if the non-Indians near the back scratched their heads, wondering what on earth we were doing, and, for the love of god, why we had interrupted the beautiful procession!

The best we could hope for was not knocking down the groom and giving him a concussion.

Naveen had grabbed the shoes and tucked them beneath his arm, against his chest, like a freaking football, and ran. Ran! Right across the empty space in front of the first row, along the far wall, and right out the back door!

I was the only girl who backtracked to the wall on our side.

The girls, fools that they were, went after him. Of course, there were bound to be other Team Groom dudes ready to pounce into the narrow aisle to block Team Bride.

I hiked up my skirt and ran along the wall behind me, where no one waited to stop us. I pushed through the back doors while Neha and my female cousins were blocked on the groom's side of the room.

Amateurs.

I emerged into the hallway and ran after this guy who thought he was so sly, so slick. I rounded the corner after Naveen in hot pursuit, and I ran right into him, shoving him against the wall and into a nook behind the bathrooms. He laughed and kept me in his grasp.

I tried to snatch the mojri from him, but he ducked my every move and raised his hands so high that I couldn't reach them. "You straight up did a football play out there. It was impressive," I grunted as my wriggling arms tried to snake over and through him to get the shoes.

"Don't you mean rugby? It was a rugby move." He brushed a curl out of my face.

Oh god, that accent. *No, woman! Concentrate!* "I'm not leaving until you give those to me."

"You'll miss the entire wedding."

"I don't care."

"You have to walk down the aisle." He didn't seem to care that the stitching on our clothes kept sticking together again, as I was the only one trying to carefully unhook the threads.

"With you."

"Oh yeah. Guess we're at an impasse."

I sighed and planted my hands on my hips. "What do you want for them?"

"Hmm." He regarded me with a devilish smirk. "How about . . . a kiss?" The instant he said that, his face flushed bright red. No way could he handle a kiss from me.

Flustered, my insides tying themselves into knots because lord, I really wanted to, I said, "Fine. I need to win the shoe game for the honor of my house."

He laughed. "What is this? *Game of Thrones?*"

"For all of Team Bride out there."

"So, a kiss?"

I rolled my eyes, puckered my lips, and gave him a come-hither wag of my finger. He lowered his hands to his sides, and just before our lips touched, I grabbed the mojri and took off.

Naveen was a fast runner, but he couldn't take on me *and* all of Team Bride. They were in the halls looking for him and triumphantly grinned when I ran toward them, shoes in hand.

Naveen skidded to a stop and eyed us. But then some of the guys from the groom's side emerged from the ballroom into the hallway behind us. I gave one shoe to Neha right as Krish appeared to my left, crossing her arms.

"There is no way this will end well for you guys," I said pointedly.

It was a shoedown. Were these guys really going to fight a bunch of girls for a pair of mojri? Were a bunch of primped girls going to fight to protect a pair of shoes? When there was tradition (and money) at stake, yep.

But then Pranit's parents walked out, along with the rest of the wedding party.

"You're witnesses! We got the shoes! We win!" I said, and stuck my tongue out at Naveen.

"Nice job, Damani girls!" Urvi said.

"You have to be able to keep them until the wedding is over, though," Naveen reminded us.

Urvi held out her hands, and we gave the shoes to her. "Who's going to come at me?"

"Uh . . ."

"That's right. No one is going to go after the pregnant woman."

"Ha!" I said to Naveen, and turned to my victorious team.

While Pranit was onstage with my parents and the Brahman doing ceremonial things, the rest of the wedding party assembled in the hallway to prepare the way for Maitri's big entrance. Naveen popped up beside me and whispered, "Hello, beautiful."

"Hey, handsome," I replied, my chest fluttering with butterflies.

"That was a slick move."

"You brought it upon yourself. Never negotiate when you have the shoes."

"And your pregnant sister?"

"That was just good timing."

"You're going to pay for this later, you know that, right?"

I snickered. "Bring it."

"Just wait. When you least expect it."

"Promises, promises. Are you ready for this?"

"If you mean, am I ready to walk down the aisle with you? I was born ready." He extended his elbow. I looped my arm with his and waited for our cue.

The doors opened. It was our turn to walk down the rose petal–strewn aisle toward the mandap in front of four hundred people. We walked at a slow pace, grinning for all the cameras, and parted when we passed the first row of seats, just before the steps up to the mandap, ladies on one side and men on the other, and waited patiently.

After all the immediate family and bridesmaids and grooms-men made their entrances, the moment we'd all been waiting for arrived. The double doors opened. Mummie's four brothers carried a palki, in which the bride sat tall and straight, her legs tucked beneath her on one side in all her royal and glimmering splendor. Above her shimmered the phoolan ki chaadar that her friends had worked so hard on: a canopy of silk roses. She was the epitome of beauty, and tears welled up in my eyes.

God. Hold it together.

As our uncles carried her down the aisle in her exquisite palanquin, she passed all the impressed and adoring guests, turning to them and their cameras with a smile as bright as the sun. Then she saw all our happy faces in the front row, and her smile quivered until tears streamed down her face. She gently wiped them away, but more came.

I wiped my tears quickly before I full-on bawled.

At the steps to the mandap, my uncles lowered the palki and helped Maitri out gracefully. They gave her away, each hugging her, and darn if they didn't have tears streaming down their faces, too.

My beautiful sister slipped out of her glittering shoes before stepping up onto the stage and taking a seat on her throne. Then they lowered the anterpat, the cloth partition that Urvi had stitched, to reveal the bride to her groom. We applauded. Pranit made a silly face, which made Maitri stop crying and had her laughing instead.

The Brahman conducting the wedding spoke through a microphone connected to his earpiece and explained in English what everything was while directing the parents in Gujarati. He even made jokes. Boy, he was good, because I didn't get bored once.

But still, a Hindu wedding took some time. Good thing we had snacks in our goody bags. I'd spent so long putting them together that I was absolutely going to savor every crumb. And at some point, the staff handed out mango ice cream. What a nice treat! After that shoe game and trying not to cry seeing my sister so happy, I was feeling pretty warm.

Thank goodness the morning had been hectic and full of life and partying to get my mind off last night. But now, as I sat here through the tedious parts of the ceremony, like tying the ganth bhandan and holding emblems, Pranit placing a mangalsutra around Maitri's neck, and the couple exchanging wedding rings, posing for photos along the way, I had time to dwell on what had gone wrong.

I must've really been brooding over it, because when I glanced toward the back, I swore I saw Mr. Merchant, one of the judges from the competition. Weird.

But soon enough, all of the immediate family was called up to the stage to toss colorful rose petals at the couple as they walked around the sacred fire.

Then it was time for another traditional game: Whoever sat back down on their throne first would rule the marriage. So when the couple made their last loop around the fire, we lunged and tugged and pulled to keep Pranit from sitting first. Mind you, he and Maitri were still bound together with the ganth bhandan, so we had to be careful. We *almost* knocked over Maitri, and Neha nearly hit her face on the stage, because of course she was up front and being the most aggressive. In the end, Pranit's butt hit his seat first, but only by half a second.

We groaned but laughed as Krish gave a thumbs-down, pouting. It was just a silly saying, anyway. We all knew Maitri would rule the marriage.

Shortly after, the couple was finally, officially, and eternally pronounced husband and wife. Forever and ever.

Still, it didn't feel quite real to me. Not when they clasped their hands together and bowed to the guests out of respect, not as they posed for pictures with family and friends, not even when everyone else left the ballroom to eat from the lunch buffet across the hall.

Naveen and the guys had their arms crossed, all butt-hurt about losing the shoe game, while Neha and I each twiddled a mojri in one hand and extended the other, palm side up.

"You guys couldn't protect my shoes?" Pranit asked them when he walked offstage, shaking his head.

"Pay up," I said.

Pranit jokingly, begrudgingly handed Neha and me each an envelope. But even though we were the only ones holding shoes, he had to pay all the girls on the bride's side who had taken part in stealing his shoes.

"Nice!" I whirled around, and off we went to scarf down a quick lunch. We were still on a schedule, but we were also starving. Just one more event to go.

After we ate mounds of fried puri and three kinds of shaak with a sweet gulab jamun to top it off, I returned to the ballroom to find the bride surrounded by our family, bawling. I couldn't handle all the ugly crying. *Everyone* was crying. My parents, my aunts and uncles. Then Maitri saw Neha and me, and we all hugged, but I kept it together.

It was time to say goodbye, as least in the traditional sense.

"Be good," she muttered to us.

I rolled my eyes. "You're only going to live ten minutes away."

"But that's so far compared to being down the hall!"

I brushed the tears off her face as my parents got ready to walk her out the door.

We girls walked out first and found the getaway car for the vidai: a souped-up, high-end, brand-new Porsche Pranit's brother would drive the couple home in. To us girls on Team Bride, it was just another way to get money.

Maitri and Pranit had been bound together with cloth and thread and couldn't be separated until they arrived at their home. My parents walked them out as people gathered around the car, upon which we girls sat. It was tradition that we try to prevent the groom from leaving with our sister until he paid us.

Pranit gamely played along and offered us a dollar, which we negotiated up to twenty. He handed each of us another envelope, after which, one by one, the girls jumped off the car so he could take his bride to her new home.

He handed me an envelope last, a pretty red one. But as soon as it touched my fingers, Naveen swooped in and snatched it, inciting laughter from all who saw.

"Hey! That's mine! Thief!" I cried, and ran after him, back into the hotel and through the hallways as the bride and groom drove off, first to the mandir to offer prayer and then to Pranit's house for more puja before they could be untied. Sheesh! There were a lot of prayers involved with Indian weddings!

I carried my skirt in my hands but could only run slowly in these stupid heels. Naveen, several feet ahead, teased and acted like he was waiting for me for catch up, all the while keeping pace so that I never got within snatching distance.

He backed into an elevator, and I followed. I glared at the closing doors and held out my hand, which he took and kissed.

"I meant my money," I said, hiding the glorious stomach-tumbling things a hand kiss did to me.

He held up the envelope. "Oh, this? Is it the same amount that you got for the shoes?"

"Not like you guys get money for taking the shoes."

"True."

"You failed to protect them."

He laughed and walked me to my room. Naveen leaned against my door, still holding my envelope.

My breath hitched, and my heart fluttered when unexpected words came out of my mouth. "Want to come in?"

He nodded. After checking the halls, he walked in after me, and we sat on the bed. He finally handed over my money.

CHAPTER THIRTY
(Sunday Afternoon: Wedding Day)

#TurntUp

The last thing I remembered was turning on the TV. The next thing I knew, I jolted awake with my head on Naveen's shoulder and two girls staring at us. Naveen also startled awake to Neha grinning ear to ear and Krish wagging her brows.

"Oh my god. We fell asleep watching TV," I muttered, crawling out of bed. "What time is it?"

"Four," Krish replied.

"Four! Ugh. I need to change and get my hair and makeup done for the reception."

"Me, too." Naveen yawned. "I mean, get dressed. My makeup and hair are on point." He patted Neha's head on the way out, and she playfully shoved his hand away.

"Have you guys been kissing?" Neha asked as she changed. She made kissy noises and giggled.

"Ugh. Could you not?"

I scrubbed off my makeup and changed into a dark blue gown with a butterfly chiffon outer layer and matching jewelry—lots of bangles, of course. It was the same thing over and over.

We went to Maitri's room, where she stunned in a lavender, pink, and gold gown.

I slumped down into my chair. All right. This was all beautiful and lovely, etc. etc., but man, was I exhausted. How was Maitri not tired? How was no one else tired?

This time, my makeup was a little lighter, and I had to put my foot down about those caterpillar false lashes. I just could not deal with them again. For the first time in a long time, since I hated putting heat on my hair, the hairdresser gently straightened my curls, adding at least a foot in length. Everyone *ooh*ed and *ahh*ed as Mummie and the older women agreed that straight hair was prettier. Oh, heck no.

Then the lady added loose curls and waves for texture. She pulled back some hair on the left side, above my ear, and kept it in place with a glittery comb and baby's breath blooms.

Maybe I was wiped out because the wedding weekend in itself was exhausting, or because I'd had a nap and was still drowsy, or because there had been too much adrenaline and pain last night, or because everything was up in the air and my life was falling apart in front of my eyes . . . but I dragged my feet back to the dimly lit ballroom, now completely redone with elegant table settings and draped chairs around a hardwood dance floor and a royal couch on the stage beside the cake, all matching Maitri's gown and Pranit's pocket square.

Beside each table setting were the goody boxes we'd constructed and filled; if I didn't see another goody bag or box ever again, it would be too soon. I slumped down into a seat behind a floral and twig centerpiece just as the couple arrived, and then off we went to do more photos, this time just with the immediate family. When we were finished and the guests had filed in, we prepared our last intro into the festivities.

We waited in line outside the closed doors. I put on my best smile as the MCs introduced us one by one.

Neha and I walked in first, smiling and waving and doing a little dance to soft music, as we were instructed to do. We turned around at the stage and waited for everyone else. Urvi and Jijaji #1 were next, followed by our parents, then Pranit's brother and bhabi, then his parents. Finally, the MC gave a big ol' welcome.

"Now, welcome, everyyyyooooone!" he boomed into the microphone. "Get on your feet and put your hands *up*!"

Everyone stood and waved their lavender-and-gold napkins in the air, whistling and cheering as the doors opened and a song worth dancing to roared to life.

"The newly married, beautiful bride and groom, Mr. and Mrs. Patel!"

The crowd went wild as the couple danced their way in and the song played louder. They danced all the way to the center of the room. Then we got pulled in to dance with them.

After a few quick pictures, teary-eyed speeches from the parents, and vibrant dance routines, we did our big finale that told the story of the bride and groom. Toward the end of the flashy choreographed dance, Pranit jumped up and danced like it was spontaneous, wowing the bride and the crowd. Then he pulled Maitri up, spun her, and we finished off the routine with a big group dance.

After all that came the special song for the bride and groom's first dance. After that epic fail last night, I had to pick up my violin and play, knowing that I might never do this professionally.

"You got this," Naveen said to me near the side of the dance floor as I staved off audition flashbacks.

Except I knew these people, and there was no one judging me or making gigantic future-altering decisions about my life.

"Yeah." I smiled and took position with my trusty violin.

No matter what, I still loved playing. I always would.

The vibration thrummed through my fingers and up my hand, engaging my wrist and sprawling up my arm. I felt it in my shoulders and back, through my thoughts and my soul, becoming one with my instrument so that it hummed with every heartbeat.

So what if I had bombed last night? I knew I could perform well and that my music was remarkable. My life wouldn't be defined by one nervous, disastrous night.

I closed my eyes now and then, keeping my focus on the bride and groom as they danced. Fog from a machine created an ethereal setting, glowing in the lavender lighting, prowling, growing, swishing as the couple danced through it.

Naveen held the mic to his mouth and crooned in that irresistible voice of his that made my heart and, well, just about every other girl in this room's heart melt. As we performed, confetti flitted down onto the couple like glitter rain, catching in my hair and falling on Naveen, creating a perfectly romantic moment that I wished would never end.

We glanced at the dancing couple as Pranit dipped Maitri and held her there, looking deep into her eyes so that even I could feel their love. My heart burst, overflowing with so much happiness for Maitri. Invisible notes fluttered down around them like dewy petals. My sister. Living her best life with the love of her life.

The song ended softly as Pranit drew Maitri back up and twirled her into his arms. Perfect timing.

Applause shattered around us.

Pranit and a teary-eyed Maitri embraced us as Maitri said, "Absolutely perfect. Thank you *so* much. I can't believe I'm related to someone with this kind of talent, Zuri. Sometimes I forget how incredible you are."

She kissed my forehead, and I hugged her tight. She had no idea how much I needed to hear that.

Krish nearly toppled me and did a little happy dance. "God, how are you so freaking talented?"

I laughed, and we left the dance floor, which had opened up to the entire crowd. I tucked my violin back into its case at my chair. I couldn't help but notice many people watching me in the dim lighting. Sometimes candlelight made people look teary-eyed . . . but no. Were they *actually* crying? Even the guys?

"So moving," an uncle said as he patted my shoulder in passing.

"Thank you," I replied.

"Exquisite," another said.

"Delightful," an auntie commented as she dabbed her eye.

"Exemplary."

"Beautiful."

"Powerful."

"Such talent."

I beamed from so many heartfelt, sincere compliments, especially when they made a point to tell my parents how amazing my performance had been. My parents grinned, elated to hear the praise. I hadn't expected anyone to say much other than "good job not getting nervous." I definitely hadn't expected anyone to be moved to tears. Maybe to them, their words were short and sweet, but right now, they were the halo of light eclipsing last night's awful ending.

There was no time to thank them all or bask in their awe. I had to get back to the party of the decade.

The reception went on. Maitri danced with Papa, and Pranit danced with his mom. Then they invited others to slow dance. The cake was cut. Massive numbers of pictures were taken. The buffet was unveiled. And the reception raged into the night.

Before the music started back up and the dance floor opened, Maitri and Pranit came over to me. Naveen had just brought me another slice of cake, because I didn't want to look greedy getting my own thirds.

"What's up?" I asked around a bite.

"Hey, so you know how we can all hear you practicing your violin in the house?" Maitri said.

I nodded, giving Naveen a look—he'd stabbed a fork into my cake when he had his own.

"I heard you playing something really . . . rocky?"

"Rocky?" I guffawed. "Oh! You mean Aerosmith. Yeah, Naveen and I got competitive and carried away with a song I didn't know I could play so well. Why?"

She pointed a thumb behind her at the empty dance floor, which was waiting for some bodies to get grooving on it. "Do you guys want to start off the dancing with that song?"

"What?" My jaw dropped, and probably crumbs of cake, too.

"I know! It's last-minute, but all the scheduled things are done! Now we just party and get out of here by one in the morning, when our time's up. I just thought it would be a fun way to segue into the music."

"It's not a reception song, though. Nothing romantic about it."

"Please? Just to get everyone going?"

Naveen looked to me with raised brows and a smear of frosting on the corner of his lips. I burst into laughter. I didn't know if it was me or the happiness it would bring to Maitri or the cake talking, but I said, "Just the second verse through the end?"

"Sounds good to me," Naveen said.

"Yeah, sure! Why not!"

Naveen shrugged. "All right, then!"

Maitri clapped her hands and squealed while Pranit went to the DJ to tell him what we were about to do.

"Hey, since it's not really a reception song, do you wanna do a follow-up with some improv?" I asked Naveen, feeling confident and on a sugar high. It was definitely the cake talking.

"Like what?"

"You know the words to 'Youngblood'? Maybe just the hook?"

He laughed. "I got you. Hook only. Are you nervous? 'Cause I am."

"Nah," I said around my last bite of cake. "I'm so good no one will notice if you mess up. Ha!"

He rolled his eyes. "Har. Har."

He clucked his tongue and cocked his chin toward the dance floor as Pranit introduced us to get the dancing going.

With the high that usually came with performing, I grabbed my violin and shook my shoulders like I was getting ready to go to bat. Pranit handed Naveen the microphone, and the crowds started to hush their conversations and clanking silverware.

Naveen glanced over his shoulder at me and raised his eyebrows. I let go of every fear and tried to enjoy the moment—a chance to perform with this amazing singer who was obviously going places. I tried to pretend this was just us, alone at the park, like we'd done so often.

I positioned my violin, and off we went, adding actual hard rock violin to an Aerosmith song. It was definitely one of the wildest things I'd ever done. And it felt so good, so freeing.

I think the crowd was expecting another slow song, something more classical, more romantic. Not something that got their feet moving.

The music thrummed through my veins and burst out of me like fire engulfing the audience. We had them stomping their feet and cheering and clapping and bobbing their heads. We started off slow, brooding, lyrical. With each reverberating slash of my bow against the strings, music fluttered off my violin like a flurry of tiny notes dancing through the air.

Anticipation rose as the music dipped low, along with Naveen's voice. We all knew the climactic ending was coming, flowing in as we rose higher and higher on this musical wave. I played faster and faster as the music revved up.

Wow. Was *this* how it felt to be on tour, when people paid just to see you? Was this how our favorite singers and violinists and performers felt when they had a captive audience, had an entire crowd going?

I could really get used to this. I had to get to this point. In this one song, with this enthusiastic reaction from everyone, my drive for music returned full force. I wasn't going to stop until I made it.

Naveen sang his heart out, bending a knee and really getting into it on those long, high notes during the explosive ending. Perspiration trickled down his temples. I thought a blood vessel might pop in his forehead or that my arms might snap off from how swiftly I played.

The crowd roared and whistled and applauded, adding to the excitement that already pulsated through us and through the music. When we finished, the violin held loose at my side, we heaved from the afterglow of musical passion raging through us. My heart hammered in a glorious, accomplished way.

And then I immediately changed the tempo and dove into 5 Seconds of Summer, laughing as Naveen basically sang "Youngblood" to me while others danced around us.

My sisters screamed like groupies. Neha and Krish and a bunch of cousins rushed us with hugs as the DJ segued straight into the music and my violin faded into the background.

"You rocked the hell outta those songs. *Damn!*" Naveen roared over the music.

I laughed in between trying to catch my breath. I had no words, just joy.

"Zuri!" Neha practically screamed over the music.

As quickly as she had ambushed me with delight, she and the others commenced jumping up and down and getting hyped on clubworthy music.

Naveen cocked his head toward others around us.

I shook my head. "I'm going to get something to drink," I said over the music, but I wasn't sure if he could actually hear me or had read my lips.

He grinned and gave a thumbs-up.

I maneuvered through the ever-growing crowd of shimmering dresses and jacketless suits with my violin until I found my seat, stopped by countless people telling me how amazing and unexpected our performance was, how talented I was; all the positive reinforcement my battered ego needed.

I picked up my case from our assigned table and placed it on my seat to put away my violin. With the top closed and the last clasp snapped into place, I carried it through the double doors, stopped by even more people. My face hurt from smiling, but I didn't mind it one bit. It was good to know that people loved my music and that I wasn't a talentless nobody.

In the hallway, two long buffet tables held plenty of food, still crowded with guests getting seconds. Small clusters of people chatted here and there. Larger groups lined up for the photo booths. Some family, mainly friends.

I'd pressed the button for the elevator when Papa called out, "Zuri!"

"Huh?" I turned and found him walking toward me.

He was full of smiles, and his eyes glistened. He hugged me, and I *oomph*ed into his shoulder. Thank goodness for setting spray, because my makeup didn't smear onto his gray suit jacket.

"Wha dis fo?" I asked, my words garbled as my face smushed against him.

He pulled back and chuckled heartily. "That was brilliant."

My heart swelled at his words, bursting at the seams.

"I knew you were amazing, but beta, what was that? You can play anything and make it sound better!"

"Thank you, Papa! That means so much to me!" *Ah! Don't cry! Suck it up.*

He went on, "I know how much music is a part of you. I just didn't realize it was so much of you that you'd sneak around trying to get into a music college instead of talking to me."

I swallowed hard. "Papa. You said we'd talk about this later."

"Ha. I did. You wondered how I knew about the contest."

I furrowed my brows, looking around until I spotted a familiar but out-of-place face by the buffet table, talking to Mummie.

"I . . . I don't understand."

Papa explained. "His name is Mihir Merchant. We have a few mutual friends. I found out he was going to be in town, so naturally, I invited him to the wedding."

Oh. The "Mihir from New York" that Papa had wanted to invite last-minute was *this* Mihir? So I hadn't imagined him in the crowd? What the freaking heck were the odds?

He went on, "Mihir wanted to accept, but you see, he had this important competition he was in town for. I kept insisting. He said he would call me if he had time. He phoned Friday night to say that he would be able to make it to the wedding and reception after all. He said he saw someone auditioning with the same last name as me. Zurika Damani. He asked if I knew her. I said, it could not be my Zuri. My Zuri had important obligations on this very important weekend. My Zuri would never audition and not tell me. But it was you."

I blinked at him as he continued with his story, in awe of the uncle network and how my dad really was tied into everything and there was no way I could hide a single thing from my parents.

"I noticed you'd been acting strange and a little distant all week. You were at your sister's most important events, but you were not completely there."

Of course he'd known. He was Papa. He was freaking all-knowing. Mummie was in your face with what she knew.

Papa was quietly perceptive, keeping all his cards close to his chest until he had enough information to swoop in with a bust. And man, what a bust this had been.

"It's true," was all I could say.

He hummed, his hands clasped behind him as he looked off into the distance. "Mihir is very impressed. He said you left before your final performance last night?"

"Yeah. I couldn't stay any longer. I had already been gone too long."

"You damaged your chance of winning?" He quirked an eyebrow, looking down at me.

I nodded. "I didn't choose family at first, but I did eventually."

He hummed again. "Do you want to speak with him?"

My cheeks burned, my eyes widened, and I vigorously shook my head. "Oh lord, no." I was way too embarrassed to meet him. Failing at my first piece and then just running out before my second one? Peak unprofessionalism.

"OK," he said simply. "Go put your violin away and return soon?"

"There's nowhere I'd rather be."

He gave a soft smile as I stepped into the elevator.

A queasiness hit my stomach. I couldn't speak to a judge after last night. It was time to relax and dance and eat more cake and indulge in the chocolate fountain and not think about what a mess my life was.

The older generations and little kids left by ten, but the rest of us partied on. And that was when the DJ really turned up the reception. It was like a memo had gone out that all the kids and aunties and uncles had left, and we were suddenly transported into a club with ceiling lights turned down and strobe lights turned on.

We partied until one in the morning, our hearts full of joy and thrills and our spirits high, knowing we had so much goodness to look forward to in our futures. Whatever they may be.

CHAPTER THIRTY-ONE
(Monday: One Day After the Wedding)

#Fam

I woke up feeling hungover—ya know, if I'd actually ever had a hangover and knew what that felt like. It was all the sugar, noise, partying, adrenaline, being on, and late nights. I might've had a fever at some point.

Sleeping in had never felt so wonderful and decadent.

I stretched out across the bed.

Neha was still snoring the morning away by the time I'd showered and Naveen knocked on our door. He wore a sheepish grin, tousled hair, and a slightly wrinkled T-shirt with shorts.

"Come in," I said, and pulled open the door. "I was just about to order breakfast. Do you want something?"

"Sure." He perused the menu, ordered on the phone, and had both of our meals billed to his room.

With Neha still sound asleep behind us, we ate on the bench-style couch against the window, my feet tucked beneath me with a pillow on my lap.

"You survived the wedding," he said, taking a bite of oatmeal.

I sipped my fancy glass of juice and asked, "How's it feel to have scouts after you after the latest turn of events?"

Naveen twisted his lips as if he felt actual pain. "It's good. But I feel bad that I'm happy, I guess. I feel bad that you—"

"Don't," I cut him off, unintentionally swinging my fork at him. "Don't ever feel bad. I'm not one to be pitied, first off. It's not like you cheated or tried to mess me up. Well, this last time, anyway. You performed exceptionally well, and you deserve all the attention. And I'm happy for you. Do your parents know?"

"No. I'll tell them later today, maybe. I'm not ready for that conversation. It's stressing me out."

I glanced at the ring he pushed around. "You have an upper hand, at least."

"Yeah." He tapped his spoon against the bowl. "I mean, I could soften the blow by saying *we* might have something . . ." He wagged his brows teasingly.

"In your dreams."

"Speaking of dreams."

I groaned. My shoulders deflated in defeat. I didn't need the follow-your-dreams talk. It was still too soon. "Don't. I can't right now."

"It's never too late. It's never over, Zuri. You can reapply next year."

I croaked, "And say what? 'Hey, Mummie and Papa, you know all that money you paid for my first year of prelaw? It's going down the drain because I'm applying to major in music.' It's going to be so much harder to convince them the deeper I get into college. And my dad is mad that I snuck out to the audition. He hasn't told my mom yet. Once she finds out, that's the end."

Having finished his oatmeal, he then drizzled syrup onto a butter-smothered waffle. "We're both stressing out. I swore I saw one of the judges at the reception."

"The Manhattan scout, right? Mihir Merchant? Yeah, he was here. My dad apparently knows him." I chewed on a piece of honeydew melon.

"Wow! Really? Is your dad that connected?"

"Uncle network game is strong."

"Ah . . ." He took a bite and mumbled, "He saw you perform, then?"

I nodded.

His eyes lit up as he swallowed his bite. "Mmm! He saw you perform a bunch of songs at your full potential without the anxiety of competition. He knows how you blew away the crowd. Maybe he'll—"

"Don't even," I interjected, already seeing where he was going with this whole thing. My heart couldn't take another futile hope, only to have it dashed to smoldering fragments. "Don't start saying that maybe he was impressed after all, enough to make a difference. That stuff happens in movies—ooh, watch things turn around for the main characters right before the ending. Never fails. My life isn't a movie. I just . . . need to take a break from all of this."

He pressed his lips together and nodded.

We quietly enjoyed what little time we had left. Naveen would be leaving in just a couple of very short days. And I was already missing him, even as he made faces at his food. I giggled at him and it smoothed away the edges of my anxiety.

We finished breakfast, and I walked him to the door while Neha snored away.

"You're gonna miss me so hard, Zurika Damani," he stated with his back to the door.

We stood facing one another, within hugging distance. With the bathroom to my right creating a brief hallway to the beds, and Neha in the first bed closest to the bathroom, we had a small but private area to say our goodbye.

"I know," I jested. "I'd miss me, too."

He grinned. "I'll be back Stateside soon."

A warmth seeped through my bones. Naveen would be back, and who knew if we'd ever meet again or if our moms would seriously think about trying to match us up when the time came, but a soft happiness blossomed between us. "You're going to music school," I whispered and beamed. "I'm so ecstatic for you. I really am."

He scratched the back of his neck. "Thank you, and thanks for your help. If it weren't for you, I might've missed the first audition, and I wouldn't have had a killer final performance."

"Remember who you owe it all to when your big career kicks off," I teased.

"I will always remember you, Zuri," he said, brushing my cheek with the back of a finger.

Goose bumps ran down my arms, and my stomach dropped. This was probably the last time we'd ever be alone together, me and the boy from halfway around the world who had made this week even more memorable. The guy who had believed in me from the beginning and had never once dismissed my talent, even when he was pretending to be cocky.

His gaze dropped to my mouth, and mine to his. He swallowed and tilted down toward me.

"Can I—" he started. But forget that.

I was here for it. I immediately grabbed the front of his shirt and tugged him into me, raised myself onto my tiptoes, and kissed him.

My lips found his, a little abrupt at first, a bit clumsy. I might've accidentally bumped my forehead against his chin on the way up to his lips. But then I got the feel for his mouth, and the world slowed down for that rom-com movie kiss. The type where everything around us fell away. The whole world—fears and anxieties and the snoring sister behind me—drifted into nothing, and there was just us, here in the moment, but also in a forever moment.

His arms were around me, pressing me into him. I swore I could've kissed him all day.

I slowly pulled away as he sighed against my forehead and I went back to staring at his eye-level throat. My body was trembling in his embrace. My knees were weak. Ah! The songs were right!

He tilted his head to the side, the corner of his lips curling upward. "Does this mean that you *like* like me now, Zurika Damani?"

"Closer." I still couldn't bring myself to look into his eyes, just at his mouth.

"Just a few more days."

I groaned. "Until you leave? Don't ruin the moment."

He placed my mehndi-stained hand flat against his chest and said, "Just a few more days for now. I'll be back. Music school is calling, and I won't be too far then."

I smiled up at him until the bedsheets rustled and Neha woke up. We said our goodbyes, and he left.

Even though he was out of sight, his memory stayed on my lips. I knew I'd be smiling for a while.

When Neha was ready, we packed our stuff, checked out, returned home, and got ready for school tomorrow.

Spring break had come and gone way too fast, but at least we got one extra day to decompress.

While Naveen tried to find the courage to talk to his parents, I had to face mine. Papa called me into the backyard.

Maitri was spending the day at the hotel with Pranit. She'd come home later today for the official farewell, the final tradition in a long slew of traditions.

Urvi, Jijaji #1, Neha, and Masi were in the house, probably plastered to the back door, listening to this big discussion my parents had sat me down for.

I wrung the hem of my shirt in my lap, staring at the deck, waiting for my parents to speak. I could practically hear Mummie's shrill disappointment in me, cushioned by Papa's more quiet discontent. I braced for the pain of having let them down, of deceiving them, of not having the courage to tell them what I wanted.

"Your papa told me you went to a music audition," Mummie began, her voice tight but wildly angry.

"Yeah," I said sadly.

"Your heart is broken," Mummie said. Wow, could she really see that? Was my misery so evident? She added sadly, as if she'd failed to protect me from the world, "This is what happens when you chase dreams."

I squeezed my eyes shut. She was right.

"I'm not happy that you pulled that stunt," she went on. "During such an important time. Even after we told you not to do such a thing."

"I'm sorry."

"No. You're not. If given another chance, you'd do the same thing, because that's what one does when they're trying to succeed at something. They don't stop. They don't let anything hold them back." She paused, glaring. "We want you to go to law school."

"I know," I mumbled.

"Law is respectable, pays well, and can give you a secure future. What will music bring?"

Happiness.

"You have to think about prosperity. We want you to be successful."

"I know . . ."

She sighed. "This is hard to understand now, but I want you to attend a regular college for prelaw. Music is not a reasonable choice for a career. Yes, you are very talented, but it's a *hobby*."

I pressed my lips together. What could I say? *Give me an-*

other chance? Let me waste a year and try again to get into a music college?

She took my hand in hers. Mummie wasn't mad. Her expression was softer than I expected . . . understanding, empathetic, even.

"I spoke with Mihir," Papa said. "He spoke very highly of your talent, especially the reception pieces. He was amazed. I was spellbound. We were all . . . speechless in that moment. I've always been proud of you, but I've never felt prouder than I was last night."

I cleared my throat, trying my hardest not to cry. "I'm, um, sorry for what I did. I should've talked to you. But I didn't do well enough to impress the judges. And I didn't get into the music college that I wanted." My last words came out haggard, shaky.

"Your talent is always going to shine. You're Zurika Damani. Don't you know that?" Papa smiled gently, and I couldn't stop myself. Boy, we'd all thought Maitri was the crybaby, but here I was bawling.

"Beta . . ." Papa whispered, and pulled me into him. He held me as I cried uncontrollably, his cheek against my forehead while Mummie rubbed my back.

"I'm sorry," I hiccuped. I was sorry that I'd deceived them and that I'd failed.

When I sniffled and pulled away, Mummie dabbed away tears and Papa rubbed his misty eyes. I didn't want them to cry or to be sad or to feel bad for me, but I knew then that they felt my pain.

"It's going to be fine, huh?" Papa said as he wiped my cheeks. "Damani girls always come through, no matter what."

"Challo, beta," Mummie added. "Let's get cleaned up and start on dinner."

I nodded and walked into the house, intending to avoid my sisters, when Masi called out, "Beta?"

"Ha, Masi?" I said, turning toward her.

She smiled warmly. "Your music is beautiful."

I blinked away more tears. Dang it. Why? Why did she have to say that?

"Can you play something for me?" she implored, hopeful. And not in a throwing-a-dog-a-bone-out-of-pity sort of way, but in a genuine way.

"Um . . ." My mind went blank as I retrieved my violin. It hurt to hold it, but I had to persevere and push back against the pain. It couldn't control me. It couldn't lessen any of my passion.

My family gathered in the living room. Urvi placed a hand on top of her belly and leaned against Jijaji #1. Neha pulled her knees to her chest and rested her chin on top of them. Masi leaned forward. My parents stood by the kitchen counter. They listened as I played something old-school Bollywood.

Masi clapped her hands to her mouth as soon as she recognized the tune and looked past me at my parents. God, now Mummie was really crying. I'd barely made it halfway through when I stopped and asked, "Mummie, what's wrong?"

Masi answered, "This is your mother's favorite song."

"I know," I said. It was the first Bollywood song I'd thought of, figuring Masi might appreciate something more familiar to her.

"This is the song your papa's parents played for your mummie during their wedding. It was a surprise, and the band played it perfectly. But you play it even better."

I looked over my shoulder at Mummie, who added, "Just reminds me of my wedding day, of leaving my home to be with Papa, of how kind his parents were, rest their souls. But why did you stop?"

I smiled and played the song from beginning to end. Although my family had appreciated my skills before, they'd never so quietly, thoughtfully, intently taken it all in. I'd never felt so much love from them as I did in this moment.

CHAPTER THIRTY-TWO
(Monday Afternoon: One Day After the Wedding)

#NewChances

Neha knocked on my door—like, an actual knock. She even waited for me to invite her in.

"You finally learning manners and boundaries?" I asked.

She smacked her lips, sat on my bed, and asked, "Are you OK?"

I shrugged. "I will be, I guess."

"Do you want to talk about it?"

I stared at her. "Is this a ruse?"

"Not sure what a ruse is, but I'm on the real. I just want to make sure that you're OK . . ." she ended quietly, and drew a line across the bedsheets to focus on instead of me.

"Thanks, Neha."

"What happened? Why were the parents so mad?"

"I'd like to know, too," Urvi said from the door, her water bottle hanging from her hand.

"Same," Maitri added from behind her.

"Oh! When did you get home?" I jumped to my feet and hugged her. Hard.

She laughed. "I'm not gone yet! I just got home a few minutes ago. So, what's the deal? Why is everyone acting weird? What did I miss?"

I stepped back and bit my lip. "Promise you won't hate me?"

"I'd never hate you. But what did you do?"

In the privacy of my room, with the door closed, I told them about Juilliard and the auditions and Saturday night.

"Total respect," Neha said, but she flinched when Maitri and Urvi scowled.

Maitri gently tugged on the ends of my hair. "Pulling that off during my weekend, huh?"

I bit my lip and lowered my head. "I'm sorry."

She rubbed my back. "But you chose me?"

"Yeah."

"You could've just told me."

Urvi cackled. "Yeah, right. You were one step away from losing it if things weren't perfect. And anyway, no, she couldn't have, because everything was a monumental event. We don't always understand the traditions, no matter how fun or how boring or how endless they seem. But we do them because it's important to our parents, so it becomes important to us. And it became important to you," she said to me.

"It's not like we never snuck out," Urvi went on, cocking an eyebrow and leaning back. "College parties and dates, and you were into clubs for a while there."

Maitri waved off her comment. "We covered for each other. It's what sisters do. You were chasing your dream, Zuri, not some drink or dance or boy. You were going after your future. Unlike someone I know, who tried to climb out the window every Saturday night in high school."

Urvi laughed. And then they busted out with all the times they'd pulled a stunt on our parents. All the times they'd failed or gotten caught. All the times they'd thought their dreams were slipping away.

Neha and I listened in awe, seeing a side of our sisters we had never known existed.

Huh. So my elder sisters weren't as perfect as I'd always thought they were. They didn't have easy, straight paths to success that my parents talked about. They were . . . human.

Urvi grinned at us. "You might not see it yet, but you and Neha are getting that way, becoming close."

Neha and I glanced at one another, but she didn't have a smart-butt comeback. Huh. I guessed I could see it, the way she was so concerned for me right now.

The conversation gradually changed topic. When they started talking about . . . um . . . wedding night–related stuff, Neha and I groaned and turned to our phones, trying our hardest to block out that unnecessary info.

I responded to Krish's texts about how things had gone down with my parents, then responded to Naveen.

Naveen: Can we hang out?
Me: I have family stuff tonight and school tomorrow. Can we meet up after school and you can tell me the epicness of what's happening?

Naveen: Of course. ☺ See you in a bit?

Me: You're coming here?

Naveen: Picking up the bride. And ofc, wanna see you as much as possible before I leave.

I frowned, my chest tingling. I knew he was leaving, but I hadn't expected to feel this much.

A red number three popped up over my email icon. I tapped on it.

One: an overdue assignment in bio. *Whomp-whomp.*

Two: an email thanking me for auditioning. Ugh. Why didn't they just stab me in the soul while they were at it?

Three: a huge sale at my favorite store.

But there was a fourth email hiding in the spam folder. Of course. Then I saw the sender.

It was from M. Merchant.

I held my breath and silently prayed that it was decent news, at least a message that verified I had *some* talent. But maybe he was just telling me that he'd appreciated my efforts and enjoyed being at Maitri's wedding.

Dear Zurika Damani,

Thank you for competing. I know it wasn't easy, and sometimes nerves get the best of performers. Although I really wanted to speak with you in person after your audition, I understand why you had to leave. I regret that we couldn't chat at the reception, but we were short on time. I did, however, chat about your musical future with your father. I was honored to attend your sister's wedding and delighted to watch you perform at the reception. You were simply moving.

I noticed that you have not applied to the Manhattan School of Music. If it's all right with you, I'd like to speak with admissions. I'm convinced that you would make an excellent addition to our school. I'm attaching an application. If you're interested, please fill this out and email it back to me, and I will send it directly to admissions so they can move your application to the top. I hope to hear from you soon. Excellent performances!

Sincerely,

Mihir T. Merchant

I flailed and screamed into my pillow, startling all my sisters.

"What!" they asked in unison.

"Oh my god! The contest actually worked out. A scout from a top music college wants *me*!" I exclaimed, and then paused. Would they even support this? Did they still think a career in music was dumb?

Shock crossed their features before they erupted into cheers and bombarded me with hugs. Neha jumped on my bed on her knees and almost knocked me over. Hers was the most aggressive embrace.

"What about our parents?" I asked, catching my breath. "They're never going to go for it."

"Is this something that you really want? That you will dedicate yourself to succeeding in?" Maitri asked.

"Is this something that you can honestly make a career out of?" Urvi added.

I nodded. "I've been wanting this since I was a kid and have been working toward this since freshman year."

My elder sisters gave a collective sigh as Urvi said, "Then let us talk to our parents."

"Really?" I squeaked. "You'd go to bat for me?"

"Yes," Urvi replied.

"Besides," Maitri added, "you're just going to keep trying with or without us. We might as well support you."

"It's what sisters do," Urvi said.

"It's what dem Damani girls do," Maitri added.

I grinned ear to ear as my sisters left the room to talk to our parents. Of course, Neha and I were right on their heels. I eagerly, quietly took a seat in the living room and texted Krish a play-by-play while my older sisters helped Mummie cook. They talked to her and were met with obstinance while Papa silently contemplated.

When the food was ready, Neha and I helped set the table. Papa took me aside and said, "Mihir told me last night that he wanted you to join their program."

I nodded. My heart was beating so fast that my chest hurt. Excitement, pain. Which would win?

"I know he's a college scout. I told him he should come to

the reception to listen to you before I found out that you were participating in the contest."

"Really?" I asked, my heart ballooning. He had that much pride in me?

"Ha. A parent only wants their child to be happy, to have the easiest life possible. I never thought of you majoring in music. Always law. But recent events have opened my eyes. People who are not happy in their programs will not finish, and it's wasted money and time. College is not cheap. People who live for others are not happy, will resent them. I never want you to be unhappy. Your mummie and I want you to be a lawyer first and foremost. That is our first choice. But I want you to follow your passion even more."

"What are you saying?" I bit my lip, waiting for the words I'd wanted to hear for so long.

"I think you should go to music school if you are truly dedicated, but you have to see it through. You must be strong and ambitious, study hard, practice hard. This is not easy or cheap."

I swallowed, my heart jumping for joy. "What about Mummie?"

He glanced over his shoulder at Mummie, who was scowling while my sisters tried to work her over. "I'll talk to her. She needs time. But I know she's like me. She wouldn't want you to hate us."

I swung my arms around his neck. "I could never hate either of you, Papa."

CHAPTER THIRTY-THREE
(Tuesday Evening: Two Days After the Wedding)

#Goodbyes

N aveen and I hadn't had much time last night when he'd come by to pick up Maitri with Pranit and a few others. We had eaten dinner with them and sent them on their way with my sister. Mummie had cried, of course.

Today, I met Naveen at the park after school. It had sorta become our thing, sitting on the picnic table and watching the water. He'd gotten interest from three of the college scouts earlier today, but he had yet to tell his parents about any of it.

"I'm glad your family approves of you going to music school. I'm proud of you," he said.

"Thanks. We'll see how it goes. Mummie sort of runs the show, ya know?"

He chuckled.

"I can't believe you're leaving tomorrow," I muttered, my excitement battling the unexpected sadness of Naveen returning home.

"You sound kinda sad. Don't worry."

"You're going to be half a world away. Your parents might not let you go to school in the States."

He shrugged. "Neelish is really into Priyanka, and I think she's serious about him."

"Wow. Really?"

"Yeah. Like, they might want to commit, which means my parents will be more likely to let me come here if he's here."

"Plus, the Yale thing, if nothing else." I waved my hand in the air, lest we forget that.

"We won't be that far apart for long. I'll be back for sure, one way or another. When I tell my parents." He sucked his teeth.

Ugh. I knew the anxiety of that conversation all too well.

I bit my lower lip, my heart heavy with a different type of sadness.

He drew his arm around me as a soft breeze pushed around the warm air. "Yeah. I did it, didn't I?"

"Did what?"

"Made you like me in one week."

"No," I muttered against his chest, wrapping my arms around his waist and just holding him for a long time. We both knew that was a lie. I did indeed like Naveen. A lot. Which was stupid, because he was leaving tomorrow for at least a few months.

"I'm not gonna lie and say I don't like you," he said.

I pulled back and looked up at him, finding his gaze intense.

"When it's someone like you, how can I not?" He pulled back and tucked my hair behind my ear. Then he gave me a soft kiss while the last of the cherry blossoms scattered over us.

"See you in five months," he whispered against my lips.

Acknowledgments

Strap in and grab a snack, because I have a lot to say and a lot of people to thank.

First off, I hope this story was vibrant, energetic, and full of love, which is exactly everything my brother and sister-in-law's wedding was. They had the biggest, most elaborate wedding my family—or maybe even all of Austin—has ever seen.

My brother married the woman of his dreams, who is nothing less than a blessing to our family. We went halfway across the world to shop for five major events for a three-day wedding weekend. If you're wondering how intense that was . . . well . . . let's just say that I still have shopping nightmares.

They had an incredible dream team of friends who helped pull off this wedding in a larger-than-life way, teams of hair and makeup stylists and videographers and photographers. A year of planning and months of practicing dance routines. Cinematic, my friends, is an understatement.

There was an exceptional amount of delicious food and bling and bright colors. Not to mention the very impressive (female) dhol player. Amid all this joy and awe, what stood out the most was the love and bonding that occurred. My sister-in-law introduced us to the "London girls": a pack of cousins closer than sisters. Thank you, ladies, for inspiring the characters of Zuri and her sisters and cousins.

Thank you to all the moms in my life (I legit have four official moms who take care of me!), but especially to my most beloved Mummie (I just want to hug you forever) and to my sister-in-law's mother (who always makes me laugh) for being the inspiration for Zuri's mom.

Thank you to all the dads who inspired Zuri's dad, especially Papa and my sister-in-law's father, who are so kind that it breaks my heart in the best way.

No one in attendance will forget that wedding. I certainly won't. But can you see how all of this inspired a story? I am thankful for that time, which I'll always treasure, and grateful that it inspired this book.

When I first brought this idea to my agent, Katelyn, I believe her words were: "I am HERE for this!" I can't believe that I get to work with such an amazing person who continues to guide and support me and who absolutely understands me. I vow to bring "K-energy" to every project I work on. I am eternally grateful for you. Katelyn is also quite the bada$$. We went on submission to editors right as 2020 warped into a bizarre, terrifying game-changer. I was certain my little book would never sell in such an unstable and scary climate, but Katelyn dove hopes-and-dreams-first into a freaking pandemic and said, "Nah, we got this!" Two weeks later, we had an offer, and *My Sister's Big Fat Indian Wedding* sold in a four-house auction. And here we are with an amazing team, a polished story, and a freaking fantastic cover. Yeah. I still can't believe it.

I will never forget the day that an offer came in from Abrams—literally minutes from the deadline, mind you—when I thought they surely weren't interested. I happened to be on a call with my "WhatsApp Wifey," Jesse Sutanto, when the email came in, and we both commenced squealing. Thanks for sharing that moment and all the moments that came after. All the donuts!

Thank you, Shaila Patel, for reading an early draft and being real. Thank you, Lish McBride, for reminding me that I have friends; Marissa Meyer, for getting on Zoom happy hour; and Kendare Blake, for the unicorn love.

I'm so fortunate to have teamed up with the legendary Anne Heltzel, my champion of an editor. She brought a great amount of insight and skill to help me shape this book into the best story it can be. And Jessica Gotz, with her sparkling energy and keen eyes. The entire team at Abrams has been amazing.

I also want to thank my husband, who continues to support me and believes in my writing even when I doubt myself. He also brings me ALL the ice cream and unicorn cupcakes because "they match my book covers."

Shout-out to my parents, who do that little half smile like they don't want to full-on smile but then start grinning when they hold my books for the first time and then proceed to WhatsApp everyone from here to India. It's OK to be proud of me! Just let it happen.

Thank you, Meet and Rohan, who may just make an appearance in every book because your awesomeness deserves to be shared with the world. Thank you, Ankita, for completing our little family and for all the love and hard work you put into everything. I wish I had a tenth of your energy.

And of course, thank you, Parth. You've grown into an incredible man who always looks out for me and constantly putting the happiness of your loved ones first. You're one of the most dedicated, hard-working, funny, compassionate, and optimistic people in the world. It's no wonder that you're a favorite in our family and within the community, bringing light and joy to everyone who meets you. You're simply the best brother and one of the biggest blessings in my life. Really, you're a blessing to anyone who's fortunate enough to have you in their life. You get all the Parle-G forever and ever. And yes, I still cry when watching your wedding video.

Many abundant thanks to all the readers out there. I love seeing your enthusiasm for stories. I appreciate your kindness and excitement from the bottom of my heart. I try to respond to as many messages as I can, but you still may never know how much your words inspire me and raise me up and fill my days with happiness. Publishing is a difficult business, to put your soul out there, hoping that someone will enjoy your stories as much as you do. But your love, positivity, and humor make my day. Every. Single. Time.

Thank you for reading, for giving me a chance. I hope you've enjoyed this book! And I hope to see you again soon. Meet ya in the next story!